WHAT PEOPLE ARE SAYING ABOUT

EDDIE THE KID

Eddie the Kid is Leo Zeilig's gripping, vibrant and affecting story of political struggle and psychological

a series of flashbacks and time shifts, *the Kid* follows a family of political ac from 1960s Chicago to the London pr 2003 Iraq war. With brute honesty and tender compassion, Zeilig reveals a cast of compelling characters as damaged and flawed as the world they have set out to change. Charting relationships, resistance, domestic violence, inner conflict, repression, rigged courts, police brutality, street battles.... this is a humane and political novel for our times.

Nicola Field, author of *Over the Rainbow*

This is a powerful and unusual story of a revolutionary activist written with authenticity by someone who knows whereof he speaks. Relentlessly Zeilig reveals and confronts his eponymous hero's dark side—this book is at once disturbing and strangely inspiring.

John Molyneux, author of *Will the Revolution Be Televised?*

I don't know how Leo Zeilig did it. He created a wavering revolutionary, beset with juvenile tendencies and petty bourgeois emotion, and turned him into a wildly, implausibly, universal character. Eddie's struggles with his conscience, the law, his family and his libido are hilarious and moving. He's an Adrian Mole for the age of Occupy.

Raj Patel, author of *The Value of Nothing*

Eddie the Kid

A brutally honest, often humorous and sometimes harsh look at the personal life of an anti-capitalist living under capitalism. This novel captures two generations of anti-war activists in their personal and political turmoil. Warts and all, Eddie is an appealing character and sharp narrator.
Colin Fancy, author of *A Wheelie Bin Ate My Sister!*

Eddie the Kid

Eddie the Kid

Leo Zeilig

Winchester, UK
Washington, USA

First published by Zero Books, 2013
Zero Books is an imprint of John Hunt Publishing Ltd., Laurel House, Station Approach,
Alresford, Hants, SO24 9JH, UK
office1@jhpbooks.net
www.johnhuntpublishing.com
www.zero-books.net

For distributor details and how to order please visit the 'Ordering' section on our website.

ISBN: 978 1 78099 367 6

A CIP catalogue record for this book is available from the British Library.

Design: Stuart Davies

The cover image was taken by Ben Joseph: www.benjosephphotography.com

Printed and bound by CPI Group (UK) Ltd, Croydon, CR0 4YY

To Gillian, Hannah and Maurice

About the Author

Leo Zeilig was, like Eddie, arrested at a demonstration on the eve of the Iraq war in 2002, but unlike Eddie, he is a researcher and has written widely on African politics and history. His books include a biography of Patrice Lumumba, *Africa's Lost Leader* (Haus Books, 2008), and a history of social movements on the continent, *Revolt and Protest* (I. B. Tauris, 2012). His most recent book is *African Struggles Today: Social Movements Since Independence*, written with Peter Dwyer. *Eddie the Kid* is his first novel. He is currently writing his second, *When I Was a Man*. Leo lives in London with his partner and works at the University of London.

27 October 1968
Ad Hoc Committee
Briefing to all demonstrators
'Street Power'

We want no arrests.

Whatever happens, individual adventurist actions never improve the situation. Responsible collective action can only be taken by the mass of demonstrators as a physical whole. We minimize the chance of arrests when we make it impossible for the police to single out any individual. Self-declared martyrs, please note that the Committee has no lawyers and no money to get any!

Chapter One

Demonstrations

Halloween 2002

In the autumn I had my own flat, lined with half-read books. A suit jacket with torn elbows hung on my desk chair and posters in glass clip frames marked my activism. 'South Africa: One solution, revolution.' 'BNP = British Nazi Party.' 'Bush: #1 terrorist.' I spent my days working in the library, my evenings in meetings. The first of two wars had just happened. Afghanistan was flattened, then liberated. Women came out of their burkas and unfurled their hair to the world. We demonstrated, put up posters, got arrested. The triumph of their first war heralded the second. Lies filled the air. The war before the war was a war against us.

I met Rebecca at the Halloween protests outside Parliament.

There were few nights like that one. We gathered in the still-warm streets on our way to Parliament Square. After an hour the square was almost full. It was a fancy dress party, with Halloween masks of Tony Blair and George Bush, plastic monsters and placards declaring a night of horror. A masked samba band drummed in front of Parliament. We were confident. Half-monster, half human.

'We'll scare them out of calling the war,' shouted Mark over the beat of the drums. The square vibrated to the music. The crowd danced.

Unlike me, Mark Ridgeway was elegant, dressed from work in a suit with his white shirt unbuttoned at the top. I scrambled around him like an adoring fan, barely reaching his shoulders. My long, thin hair and round head a contrast to his thick, square jaw and shaved head. My eyes shrunken behind glasses, his wide and alert. 'There are ten thousand,' he shouted. We held the two sides of the Tooting Stop the War banner, holding our poles high. The wind caught the banner like a sail as the samba band moved toward Whitehall.

Mark and I slowly began to follow the circus-crowd to Whitehall. A mohicaned, masked Blair leapt onto the statue of Churchill, took off his mask and strung it around the stone's fat jowls. He swung around the statue's head and sprayed Churchill's hair green. In the twilight it felt as if we had taken over the city. The earth had released us, expelled its forgotten fantasies. We painted our fluorescent midnight on the hard concrete. The band leader visible twenty metres ahead of me commanded our slow progress towards Downing Street. He wore a mask, and on his chest, strap-on plastic breasts. I followed Mark's lead and gyrated along the street. The crowd slowed down; a few hundred people sat on the ground. A chant started: 'Whose streets?' The answer came: 'Our streets!' Now more than a thousand of us were sitting down. The police were quickly erecting a barrier outside Downing Street: two metal fences and a line of police with shields and batons. They stood humourless and still.

A police camera crew filmed us.

An unmasked protestor pointed at them and shouted, 'Do you do functions as well? Can you do my mate's wedding next week?'

'Drumming won't get us through,' Mark said. We rolled up the banner. Mark was a lawyer, a clandestine professional who didn't look like us with our hoodies, jeans and backpacks. I liked that he didn't resemble an activist—that he cared about getting his clothes dirty. He provided equipment for the movement: megaphones, money for posters and glue. From his shoulder bag he pulled out a small loud-hailer.

We could measure presidents and prime ministers by their dead, I thought. I looked back to Parliament Square; it was still full, as white police vehicles trying to herd the protest onto the pavement. Was this the number of those who had already died in

Afghanistan? When I turned back I saw more sitting on the ground, thousands now. In our sequins and glitter we looked like fallen stars, our protest a discordant cry for life. How many bodies would these politicians collect? When they were done, would the war's total equal the number who had protested?

Mark faced the sitting protestors, his tall back to the police lines. He was trying to speak.

'When can we bring these people to justice?' Mark jabbed his finger in the air. 'When will they stand trial for their wars? Will Blair walk free? Tonight we have a chance to stop him. To stop a war. After years of their sanctions, is Iraq a threat? Rubbish. The war they want to fight is for oil. The three-letter curse.'

About thirty people stood listening.

'The men who are doing this wear suits, not beards and turbans. The terrorists, elected and democratic, live here.' Mark thrust his thumb towards Downing Street.

I left the banner and rushed over to him. It wasn't enough to make speeches. I was already bored of our speeches. Our words wouldn't do anything. I was high on action. I wanted to throw our bodies against the machine, stop the cogs turning even if we were crushed. I was cocky and self-righteous that night. Mark was just making another speech.

'The question is, what can we do?' Mark's voice shrieked into the megaphone.

People began to stand up and move toward the barriers. I reached Mark, beckoned urgently for the loud-hailer.

'What we want,' I shouted, 'is a citizens' arrest of the prime minister.' Mark bent down and indicated that I should climb onto his shoulders. He stood.

'This is where he is. The murderer. We can stop him tonight.' I waved my hands, telling the crowd to come to the barrier. The police bunched up to reinforce the fence, shoving the protestors who approached them. I swayed on Mark's shoulders.

'If we coordinate ourselves we can get over the barriers. Come forward. Hold on. After three, push.' People laughed at me, ridiculous and eight feet tall. A policeman pointed his camera at us. Mark lowered me to the ground.

'One, two, three!' I shouted, standing level with the crowd.

Hundreds of hands pushed the barriers. There was a collective rattle as the fencing lifted a few inches from the ground. Batons hammered on riot shields. Police vans drove behind the barrier.

'They've called in reinforcements,' I shouted, indicating the vehicles, 'but we are thousands tonight.' I was being squeezed by the crowd as more people came up to the barrier. A woman smiled at me, her hair tied back, a red and white chequered scarf tied around her neck. 'If you're going to do it, just do it,' she said. 'Go on.'

I lifted the megaphone again and continued, 'If the police don't allow us to exercise our legal right to a citizens' arrest, we will have to force them.'

A policeman lurched towards me and tried to grab the megaphone. I pulled back.

'I hear that the police are very ticklish,' I shouted. There was a howl of laughter. 'So—we must tickle the police.' The megaphone threw my voice across the street. 'After three, tickle the police,' I repeated.

Now no one was sitting. People reached for the barrier and pushed forward. The police did the same thing—as though we were trying to embrace each other.

I counted down: 'One, two, three!' Protestors lunged towards the police and shook the fence. A few tried to climb over. The police hit protestors with their batons, pushed them back, clubbed and bludgeoned. A thunder of blows came down. One segment of the barrier was wrenched away. A small crowd rushed in, but more police arrived. Trapped, the group were surrounded by the police.

We had numbers and humour, but the police had fences, metal and armour. Did I think we could get through? Defeat the

Metropolitan Police by a simple act of will and a loud-hailer? I saw our crowd, with a line of orderly banners, pushing past the police at my call. Mark and me leading the petitioners to Downing Street, besieging the citadel, placing Tony Blair under people's custody—who the fuck did I think I was? Wat Tyler? My father?

We retreated, dishevelled, and the march continued along Whitehall to Trafalgar Square.

Mark dragged me away, stuffing the loud-hailer back into his bag. 'We need to get away from here. They'll want you. The police hate to be humiliated.' Mark was more practical and he knew the police. I had surfed a wave of euphoria but almost caused a riot. We had to get away.

We walked quickly toward the tall stone pillar in the distance. Then two things happened at once. There was yelling behind us and the crowd parted. A group of policeman ran up the road. Their yellow tunics, heavy boots and batons made their charge lethargic: ten of them running in slow motion. I obediently moved away, but they ran toward us, fell on me, two holding each arm and another on my legs. I tried to struggle. A policeman grabbed my hair, yanking my head back until I was still. My arms twisted behind me and I felt handcuffs shut tightly around my wrists. One shouted, 'We've caught him red-handed!' All I could think was, *They still use those clichés?* Mark tried to pull them off, shouting that he was a solicitor. He was picked up and dropped on the pavement.

The women in the scarf ran up to me. 'You were great,' she said.

'Get away from him, miss,' ordered a policeman as they led me up the road, pretending to lead a condemned man to the gallows.

She ignored him, her face pale-white, eyes wide and black. I was hurried on. She shouted as I was dragged further up the road, 'You were the loud-hailer of our Halloween.'

'Iraq Protest Causes Chaos,' 1 November 2002

Traffic came to a standstill in central London last night as 10,000 protesters marched on Parliament against a war on Iraq.

They paralysed a large area around Trafalgar Square during the rush hour by sitting in front of traffic.

The group had marched from Parliament Square to Trafalgar Square last night before congregating outside Downing Street, where they stopped the traffic for almost an hour. One protester carried a banner saying 'Nightmare on Downing Street' and had fake blood smeared on his shirt sleeves.

Although most of the protest was peaceful, some skirmishes did break out and police arrested at least eight people, including one protestor who tried to break through police lines outside Downing Street.

The march and road blocks were part of a national day of action organised by the Stop the War Coalition.

A large police presence monitored the protesters as they moved towards Downing Street, followed by officers on horseback.

In Whitehall, police removed CND demonstrators staging a sit-down protest, including two elderly women who were carried away.

Omar Waraich, 20, a student who helped to organise the protest, said: "We have been apologising to the thousands of drivers caught up in the traffic jams. But we want them to know that the build-up to war against Iraq can be stopped by what we are doing and it is not being carried out in our name."

Addressing the crowd, Labour MP Jeremy Corbyn demanded a Commons-vote on whether to declare war, while writer and broadcaster Tariq Ali urged British soldiers to remember the example of Israeli reservists who had refused to serve in the Occupied Territories.

At the London School of Economics, students debated the threat of war with Iraq, echoing the Vietnam protests of their parents.

The Stop the War Coalition says the campaign against military action is gaining momentum, citing an opinion poll which says 40 per cent of people oppose the war, while only 35 per cent back Tony Blair's approach. Andrew Murray, chair of the coalition, said: "We represent a clear majority."

* * *

Stewart and Jessica, 1966

They made love for the first time after the Grosvenor Square anti-war demonstration. The crowd of neatly dressed students was cornered. Mounted police moved slowly toward the protestors. The effect was beautiful, Jessica thought, the sun behind the horses, the animals' hot breath visible in the cold air. When they were a few metres away, Stewart disappeared. He looked like everyone else: the same greys and blacks and sideburns. The crowd tried to move forward, but they were broken up by the horses. When Jessica found Stewart, he was distributing handfuls of marbles to a small group of men around him, digging deep in his pockets as though he was handing out sweets.

Jessica tried to call that she knew a way around the police. She heard his hushed voice giving instructions. The group turned towards the crowd being pushed back by the line of horses. The animals that had seemed so picturesque now towered over the crowd.

'Go, go, go.... Now!' Stewart shouted.

The group rushed past her and into the crowd. She could see Stewart insert himself at the front of the fracturing protest, his hand holding the glass beads. Then chaos. Hundreds of marbles released under the horses. The animals emitted sharp cries. Some slid, most panicked and retreated. The police, tossed around, held onto their saddles. One horse fell. A policeman was on the ground. A protester rushed to him and kicked him in the chest. Jessica looked on like a pedestrian watching an accident. She wanted to tidy up the street, stop the chaos. The crowd broke up.

Jessica saw Stewart waving at the dispersing crowd shouting futilely.

'Charge, charge, comrades... don't retreat.'

Who does he think he is? Moses?, she thought. *Those wonderful, transparent balls with their suspended, twisted colours, wasted.*

* * *

'Anti-Vietnam Demonstration Ends in Chaos,' *British Pathé*, 3 July 1966

It started as a peaceful anti–Vietnam War demonstration in Trafalgar Square. About 4,000 gathered. Most of them were sincere; they wanted peace. Their motives seemed honourable. They came from most walks of life. Vanessa Redgrave was, as usual, in the vanguard of the would-be peacemakers. But there were also troublemakers, people not content to just voice their disapproval of the war in Vietnam—a hard core with the intention of dragging the majority of well-intentioned demonstrators down to their sickening level. And so they marched through the streets of London to Grosvenor Square and the American Embassy, inciting a riot. At Grosvenor Square, police were waiting, warned to expect trouble—their intention to keep the peace. But at the head and in the midst of the advancing column, the hate-makers were at work. This is how they turned a demonstration for peace into a bloody riot, such as Britain has never before witnessed. One hundred seventeen police officers were injured while defending themselves and doing their duty. Only forty-five demonstrators were hurt. The police have earned the highest possible praise for their self-control against overwhelming brute force on a day when a demonstration for peace ended as a war in the heart of London.

When they found each other again Stewart was dishevelled. They walked together across the river. Other couples passed them. Light from the buildings on each bank stretched over the water. The city had so many ways of forgetting.

'We'll have the revolution north of the river and the south will never know,' Stewart said.

'I want to tell you, Stewart, that I didn't like what you did. I don't think it helped. What was the point?'

'We were being crushed by the police. They needed to have their confidence broken. That happened. It was successful,' Stewart answered.

'From where I was standing I thought it was a disaster. Your bloody marbles.'

'Marbles?' Stewart shouted. 'What the hell are marbles? They were ball bearings. Small metal balls that you find in machines.'

That seemed better. What did it matter if those things were lost?

Stewart led them past the Royal Festival Hall. *This is how we'll build in the future,* he thought. Practical and beautiful: the prerequisites for his socialism. It stood mocking the Victorian grandeur and pomposity of this old city. They passed Westminster Bridge.

'Next time we protest it will be harder for us because of your games,' Jessica said.

Stewart had forgotten their disagreement. 'I don't care. We're on the losing side, Jessie, for Christ's sake. Everything we do is organised for their world. When we protest against the war and your government's complicity in it, we're beaten by the police. Sometimes we need to take the initiative. Humiliate the police. Challenge the state.'

People stared at them.

'You sound like an anarchist, not someone who wants to build a movement.'

They climbed the steps to the station; people hurried past them. A siren sounded behind them.

'For fuck's sake, Jessie. You tell me how to build a movement. Ask the bishops and the lords of the damn manor to join us?' He breathed in deeply. 'Jessie, we'll be on the news now. The politicians won't sleep as well. The US will hear. Next time our protest will be bigger. More people, better arguments. We can't always wait.'

Jessica wanted to disagree, but she was tired. Why did he always have to speak so loudly? 'You hate to be contradicted, Stewart. Like most men I know.'

They stood in front of the flickering timetable in the station.

'You know the reason why you didn't like what I did? Because you took the side of the damn horses. What is it about the English upper class that they think every horse is sacred?'

'Oh, fuck off, Stewart. What is it about every American that they think they understand the English class system?'

She wanted to go home without him. She didn't want to hear his voice again, his hard, silly opinions. He was patronising her. They went back to her flat and finished half a bottle of sour wine. They made love. She liked him because he fumbled and was uncomfortable. After he came, for the first time since she had met him, he had nothing to say.

They married a year later. They had an argument the night before the wedding, and Jessica decided to leave him. She was relieved that they had rowed; now they would be saved from spending their lives together. In the morning he was curled around her holding on so tightly she thought, *It could work. He loves me.* They did everything like this, lurching from argument to decision as though they needed to hate each other for a moment to love again.

* * *

1 November 2002, early morning

Individual policemen can be intelligent, even question their orders, but collectively they struggle over the most basic forms, ask the same question a hundred times. I was held until the morning. 'Is that a B in Bereskin, as in Bravo?' I emptied my bag in front of the arresting sergeant. The room was lined with benches, a vending machine and behind the desk a public advice poster, 'Your Rights to Legal Advice: Our Ten-Point Commitment to the Public.' We were a strange bunch: demonstrators, still excited by the festivities of the evening. Recognising each other. Confident.

I saw someone I knew. 'Helen, what are you in for? Did you see what we did outside Downing Street?' I said.

'Yeah. Great turnout,' she answered, and leant forward, whispering, 'But you were acting like a bloody anarchist.'

There were other arrestees, regulars. Some bleeding from brawls, one speaking on the payphone, 'Of course I love you, babe. Nah, I can't make it over tonight, I'm seeing me mates.'

My bag was confiscated. Three library books were removed in front of me. The sergeant was three times my size. He could have crushed me in his hands. He held one of the books up to the light as if trying to decipher a code. He read the title slowly, enunciating each syllable: 'Vik Tor Ser Gee, The Mem Ores of a Revo Lu Shun Ry.' He repeated the title loudly for his colleagues. "Oh, look what we have here! *Memoirs of a Revolutionary*." He looked at me knowingly, nodded his head. I had been rumbled. He gripped his pen in his fist and wrote the title down. After an interminable agony of writing, he muttered a single word, 'Subversive.' What was this meant to mean? I was a 'subversive.' Was my library book, due back this morning, 'subversive' or had he just ticked a box on the form for 'subversives'?

'What are we doing him for?' he asked the officer who had brought me in.

'Take your pick,' answered a young, clean-shaven man. 'Affray. Public disorder. I would do him for public disorder. Inciting a riot. Anyway, he's a goner, we've got it all on video.'

'Empty your pockets please, sir,' the sergeant ordered.

I imagined, at my execution, being asked, 'Sir, do you want the bullet between your eyes or straight through the heart?' Sir, always sir, right to the end.

The incriminating evidence was two eggs cradled in a paper towel in my jacket pocket. I had brought them under the assumption that in a democracy I could legitimately throw an egg in protest at an illegal war as long as it was not hard-boiled. I removed the two eggs, unwrapping them slowly. In front of me a man the size of a cow, and between us two eggs. The room fell silent. The queue craned forward, trying to look. The sergeant was lost. This went on for what felt like a minute: stretching and peering at the egg in silence. Finally the sergeant stammered nervously, 'What are those?'

'They're eggs,' I replied.

'They're what?'

'Eggs,' I repeated.

Then more silence.

Finally the sergeant lifted a phone beside him on the counter. He waited and said, 'Sir, you better come down here. We've got a situation.'

The station chief arrived and looked at the eggs. Eventually he asked me, 'Are they cooked?' Then he told me to break one. The yolk flowed over the counter, catching the edge of my arrest form before the sergeant quickly snatched it up. The second egg was carefully placed in a transparent plastic bag to produce as an exhibit in my forthcoming trial.

The cell stank of piss and shit. In the morning I was released until my next summons. I walked into the daylight. Pedestrians were busy along the Strand. Shops were opening as if nothing had happened. I wondered if I had imagined the masked anti-war ball that had squeezed normal life out of the city. But now London collapsed back into its habitual groan. Control had returned to its daytime owners. This cursed city had already obliterated our resistance. The relentless continuity of life, temporarily disturbed, spluttered on without thought. I hated its complicity, its acquiescence.

As I came out of the basement foyer of the police station, already filling with tourists asking directions and reporting lost wallets, I became aware of someone behind me. I pushed open the door and hurried along the street. 'Excuse me. It's me. Excuse me,' a woman's voice hailed me. I felt a hand on my shoulder. I started and turned. It was her. Her hair fell over her shoulders. She looked tired. The red scarf was draped loosely around her neck. She smiled. I could see myself in her eyes.

'Were you arrested?' I asked.

'No, I wasn't.' She leant on her hip, her jacket undone. The same insolent confidence I remembered from the demonstration. 'I waited all night in Charing Cross Station.'

I was confused. 'Was a friend arrested? There were quite a few of us.'

'No, I was waiting for you. I was worried about the arrest. I thought maybe I had encouraged you to do it. That I was responsible.'

I didn't know what to say. I felt silly. Exposed. Like everyone else crowding and pushing past us on the Strand, I was overwhelmed by the day. I felt as ugly under the morning sun as we had been beautiful under the Halloween moon.

She unfolded the newspaper she was carrying and opened it to the second page. Downing Street: a crowd of people. The loud-hailer pointed towards the police. She read from the article.

'One protester urged the crowd to tickle the police. Sixteen people were arrested. Six have been charged with public order offences.' She broke off and indicated the centre of the photograph. 'That's you,' she said, laughing. I was visible on Mark's shoulders. 'Do you want breakfast?'

She was concerned. I spoke about the arrest and told her that I could go down for five years. I said that I had got carried away.

'We all were, last night,' she said. 'That was the point.' She wanted to know what she could do. I thought she needed to assuage her guilt at encouraging my behaviour, write herself out of my arrest. I could feel the nausea rising in my stomach from the memory of the cell. I was nervous.

Then she spoke about herself. I drank cheap coffee. I was impressed by her insistence. In an hour I knew everything about Rebecca Siegfried. She had been brought up by her mother, Judith, in Brighton. Her father, Ronny, had left when she was two. He lived in Australia. Her mother was a clerk in a solicitor firm, where she did all the work and was treated badly. Judith's flat overlooked the sea and had wind chimes made of shells they had collected from the beach and strung together. Rebecca had studied music. She composed musical scores for audio books, lived near Edgware Road, and could hear the birds in the morning. She was having dreams about the end of the world and did tarot readings. She was a caffeine-fuelled talking CV. 'Before Afghanistan I had never been on a protest, but now I'm active in an anti-war group. I'm not political. I voted Labour, but now I wouldn't spit on them. I'm a Pisces.' Her words tumbled out, a tangle of life, lovers and war. 'I am so angry. I really wanted to break into Downing Street yesterday. I've just broken up with Duncan. He wanted to marry me. When can I see you again?'

'I don't need to. I know everything about you,' I laughed.

Our knees touched. She brought her hands to my face, leant forward and kissed me. Her kiss was like everything else about her that morning: adamant and determined. She did not hesitate. Rebecca pulled me out of the earth and held me. She wanted me; it was as simple as that.

2 November 2002

Dear Sir,

NOTICE OF PROSECUTION

Defendant: Yourself

Operational reference number: 01CX3327302

I am writing to inform you that I have sent a notice to the Clerk of the Justices under section 23 (3) of the Prosecution of Offences Act 1985, of charges against the defendant (Yourself).

Violent Disorder

On 31 October 2002 at Whitehall SW1 while present together with two or more other persons, you did use or threaten unlawful violence and your conduct taken together with that of those other persons present was such as would cause a person of reasonable firmness present at the scene to fear for his personal safety.

Sections 2(1) and 5, Public Order Act 1986

The effect of this notice is that you need to attend court in respect of this charge and that any bail conditions imposed in relation to this must be respected.

CAUTION: This notice only applies to the charges specified in it, and does not have any effect in relation to any others that may be pending or other proceedings against you. If you are legally represented you should contact your solicitor immediately.

Yours faithfully

Senior Crown Prosecutor

Southwark Trial Unit

Chapter Two

Stuntmen

8 November 2002

I was due in court soon. I had not told Jessica. I didn't want to burden her. I faced a public order offence. The police claimed to have film that proved I was inciting the crowd to attack them and pull down the gates to Downing Street, ferment revolution, beat up the prime minister. It was ridiculous. I saw Rebecca again. We met on Edgware Road. The restaurant was full of wealthy children wearing branded clothes and speaking private-school English. I couldn't enjoy the food. Rebecca was different from how I remembered her at the demonstration, tired and less confident. I tried to pretend that I was not taking the charges seriously and spoke quickly about politics.

'Now, of course I'm an anti-war activist, but ultimately I believe that the only solution is the overthrow of capitalism. I don't believe that the rich can be regulated or persuaded to hand over their stolen wealth. In fact, I would argue that it's the other way round. Take the rich—Warren Buffet and Bill Gates, for example. They actually tell the politicians, governments and lawyers what to do—not vice versa. That's the ruling class with their interlocking directorships and the monopoly control of big business. This class, they're completely unelected and unaccountable. Even the Queen in 1981, when she was valued at an estimated twenty billion pounds, took herself off the rich list and then kept her loot secret. So our solution is simple. Anti-capitalist strikes, demonstrations and riots are the beginning of our attempts to counterpose workers' power—to run the world exclusively for human need and not for unproductive and greedy wasters who make up less than one per cent of the...'

Halfway through my speech she put her hands on the table

and asked me, 'Are you spending the night?'

We left the restaurant. The night had collapsed onto the street. I was disoriented. We walked to her flat as though we had been drinking.

She had two rooms so small they seemed to be constantly defending themselves against disappearing altogether. A futon, a bookshelf stuffed with novels, a cheap Persian rug in the bedroom, an electric piano, a sofa.

I was the hard man of the anti-war movement who tried to break through police lines, but I was nervous, worried that I would be exposed.

Everything about Rebecca was beautiful: her eyes, her hair, her skin.

She took her clothes off.

We kissed in the lounge, then sat on her sofa. I pulled my trousers off. I cradled her breasts, took one of her nipples in my mouth. Pulled down her underwear. Esther was getting sick again, I thought. I knelt. Rebecca spread her legs and I teased her with my tongue. She reached down and grasped my hair as I began to taste her. I built up a rhythm, responding to her gasped orders to speed up, slow down, don't stop. Even as I drank her in I couldn't stop thinking about my big, little sister.

Rebecca's orgasm was loud and wet and beautiful, but I didn't get an erection. We were shy again, holding onto our naked bodies like kids, sitting on her sofa.

Rebecca suddenly sat up straight, tying her hair in a knot behind her head. 'I think these things are immediate. If you don't find that attraction straight away, then it's not going to work.'

'I'm just distracted. My head is full of nonsense,' I said.

'Well, that's what I mean. If it doesn't work like that—' she snapped her fingers together—'then it won't. If you don't find me attractive...'

Rebecca was curled up, her legs tucked against her. Her skin clung tight to her, speckled by brown freckles. Me, a fleshy pig next to her, my body sick-white, my shoulders dotted with red spots, and she thought that I didn't find her attractive?

'No, it's just first-night nerves,' I said.

'Nerves?' she said, thinking on the word. 'The Downing Street Tickler is nervous,' she laughed, sounding relieved. 'Then I'll turn the heater on and make you a cup of tea with a shot of brandy.'

'We haven't had a car accident,' I said.

* * *

1979

Our grey-haired aunt and uncle lived in a small village with their disabled son. Peter Marlowe sat in his electric chair like a king. We travelled from London for the day. Esther sat on her legs and I asked constantly if we were nearly there. Jessica drove; Stewart gave directions and read from the newspaper. When we arrived, Stewart rushed in and grabbed Peter, pulling him out of the chair and onto the ground. They rolled over, knocking the furniture around, the two of them hollering. Stewart was messy, breathless. The day was like this.

Stewart boasted: 'I can take my head off as well.'

'Please do it, please!' we shouted.

No one was going to remove their head in his presence, Peter declared, and hit his fist on the table, yanked his chair into reverse and screeched off.

We continued, 'Please do it.'

'No, I can't. I can only do it in front of a film camera. It's too frightening for anyone to see in real life.'

'Then pull your finger off again,' we cried.

Pushed out his chest, threw out his arms.

'Stand back, kiddos. Stand back.'

His hands came together, tangled in a strange embrace. He pulled at his thumb, moving one hand above the other. We let out another sigh, more for the theatre than the trick.

When we left Stewart drove, sinking deep into his seat. None of us spoke. We stared at the chalk hills dividing the motorway. Reaching London, we saw people hurrying in for Sunday night meals in high street restaurants. Stewart spoke: 'I thought you were showing off today.' Jessica remained silent. 'I said, I thought you were being a show-off. You put me down and contributed nothing to the day.'

Esther and I stared out of the window. We were driving faster now; the streetlights blurred.

Jessica didn't speak.

'I hate the way you never challenge anything your brother says. Why are you like that?'

'Can't you just be quiet? We had a good day. Why do you have to ruin it?' Jessica finally answered.

Stewart shouted, 'You ruined it for all of us. Didn't she, kids?' He half-turned to us in the back of the car. 'Didn't she, kids?' he repeated. 'Didn't she grind us down?'

Esther sat looking out of the window. I turned to him and nodded my head slightly.

'You see how miserable you've made the kids? I've had enough of you dragging us down,' he shouted.

'Pull up the car,' Jessica said, grabbing her bag. Stewart pulled over.

There was a row of restaurants and shops, with people on the pavement.

'Get out.' Stewart pushed her as she fumbled for the lever on the door.

Esther didn't move. Jessica climbed out, tripped on the curb. Stewart leant across the seat and pulled her door closed. We sat silently in the car, watching Jessica zigzag across the pavement. She slowed down and went into a newsagent. We waited. She came out a few minutes later, more composed, and began to walk toward us. Stewart put the car into gear and started to move out.

I saw Jessica running toward us, reaching the car, her face still streaked with tears. The car pulled out. She hit the boot with her hand, stumbled and fell into the gutter. Esther and I craned to see her from the backseat, staring at her out of the rear window.

We drove home.

Esther turned back to her seat and fixed her gaze on the traffic. I sobbed slowly, holding my breath to stop my tears. Esther slid her hand into mine. I held it so tightly she gasped.

* * *

Mark Ridgeway, 2002

Mark was big. His shoulders and back were wide, his chest a great muscular rectangle. His hands were huge and flat, as though they had been widened with a hammer. He exercised because his large limbs needed to be stretched and spread. He cycled uphill like I free-wheeled downhill. He ploughed up the water in the swimming pool like a tractor on land. He was a strong man, but not for himself—for the movement. Mark's oversized arms and placemat hands were public property. His size belonged to us.

For Mark there was no waiting for the apocalyptic moment, the utopian explosion, the *grand soirée*. For me life was revolutionary suicide; for Mark it was real and existing practice today—now. My appeals to the coming *real struggle* were incomprehensible to him. I thought Mark's beautiful bulk was evidence of the existence of the socialist republic today: he was an ambulating and invincible organism of huge and complex harmony. Mark was a human anthem to what we could achieve—but also how we could fuck up. How we destroyed our movements, divided our pathetic forces with endless squabbles and factions, scattered our unity with pedantic and abstract obsessions and divorces. I worried that Mark was in danger of bringing down his own towering life-force.

Mark was covered with hair everywhere except on his head. He kept his head waxed and tanned. I always liked sitting close to him so I could admire his new suits with their ironed trouser pleats and inhale his latest perfume. In the public toilets he sprayed the fragrance on his thick wrists and then dabbed it across his neck, just like I remembered Jessica applying her perfume when I was a kid. With tweezers he pulled out stray hairs from his eyebrows and nose. One finger pulled up his nose as he stared grotesquely into the mirror. All of this, I thought, to look pretty next to me in the courtroom. 'Can't you do that at home? It's horrible, Mark. We're going on a demonstration—why are you putting on perfume?' 'Aftershave,' he would mutter, barely bothering to correct me, never taking his eye off the tweezers and his reflection, his mouth contorted into a faint smile. He liked the attention. He looked good for the effort. Our sweet-smelling activist, about to ruin his life.

We would dance when we met; the excitement of seeing each other made us want to move, to gyrate a little, the restless, quick steps of our feet marking out the ground. Mark would tower over me, twisting his frame to an inchoate rhythm, as though he was about to devour me or make love to me. We spent our time together like this. Our joy and dancing sometimes exploded into torrents of screaming in the pub, touching on public highways, as I threw myself into Mark's iron-ready tall frame. He would hold me in his arms like a child sacrifice.

'You know, if you wanted me to give you a blow job, I would do. I hope you know that,' I said to Mark one balmy night last summer.

'Why would I want a blow job from you?' he asked reasonably.

'I don't want to give you one, but I would, just as a favour. For friendship.'

'To prove your friendship to me, you would suck me off?'

'Yes. The thought doesn't turn me off,' I said honestly.

'Should I be flattered?'

'Yes.'

'Well, I am. Thank you, Eddie, but it's not necessary.'

'Good. You can hold it in reserve if you like.'

'Lovely, I will. I'm very touched.'

'Well, it was just a thought. I probably wouldn't swallow, though.'

'Well, there'd be no need. No need.'

'Suck, don't swallow.'

I realised then that we weren't so subversive. We exchanged kisses and embraces when most men just slapped each other's backs with their flat hands as if they were hitting a kettle drum. Even my blow job declaration fell into a certain macho norm. My extreme feelings of friendship had to be expressed through the cock paradigm. The true crowned god of Western man: A large penis sitting on a gilded throne in the centre cortex of the brain. *I love you, Mark. I would suck your penis.* For all my liberation I ended up at the same place as everyone: our genitalia. Mark's penis.

'I don't understand what's wrong. You love Alicia. You've been together for more than seven years. You tell me that you get on with her better than anyone else. You still make love. You share a political outlook. Why do you want to leave her?' I asked.

'I don't. I mean, I don't know. It's the kid thing. I want kids and she can't have them,' Mark said.

'Because she already has a grown-up kid, Mark, and because she's older than you. I understand that you want to have kids, but why don't you try to adopt?'

'She's too old. Too tired. Why would a fifty-five-year-old woman want to adopt children? Anyway, I'd end up having to do all the child care.'

'I can't believe what you're saying. You're just a fucking misogynist who decides at forty-five that he wants children but doesn't want to look after them, so he ditches his older lover for a young one. I can't believe you said that. You must stay with Alicia. The rest is crap and children are no panacea.'

'I think it's more complicated than that,' Mark muttered.

This was a version of the conversation I had been having with Mark for about six months. His life had suddenly bunched up: his mother had died the year before and now he was in a hurry. He was smart only in his clothes and politics. The rest of his life was a mess, a great jumbled loud-hailer of chaos and doubt and duplicity. I knew he needed to exhale his dilemmas and catastrophes to anyone who would listen. 'You're like the fucking ancient mariner. If you keep talking, Mark, someone will have you shot.'

'You're right—and it'll probably be Alicia—but I can't help it.'

Alicia had come over from South Africa at ten and stubbornly held onto her Johannesburg-Indian accent. Alicia was in a rush to understand the world before it came to an end. She knew a lot about it, perhaps too much—she was an expert in massage, psychotherapy, political economy, literature, and law. Alicia could do stand-up on anything. 'Mark is having,' she told me recently, 'a midlife crisis. He needs intensive therapy, not CBT, but psychodynamic. He's working too hard. He needs to stop work on conveyancing, which is the worst, most lumpen aspect of the law, and retrain. He is also doing too much politics. This is avoidance and it's a familiar pattern.' Always a neat formula with Alicia—for Mark and all of his friends. I was: 'Eddie has solipsistic personality disorder. He has what Georg Lukacs described as the phenomenon of reification.' How could she combine psychotherapy and Hungarian Marxism? Irritatingly, she was normally right.

Mark went silent for a few weeks. It felt as though the world had shut down. I wanted to hear him again, always wearing his life on the outside, his thoughts and hopes and politics flashing on an advertising hoarding in the sky. Now that hoarding declared: I Am Going to Die.

'You're not going to die!' I exclaimed.

'Yes I am. We all are, and soon. So fucking soon.'

'Okay, but that doesn't really get us anywhere.'

'I've only got a few more years and there is so much to do. So much to understand and change.'

'Politically, you mean?'

'Yes. How can we change the world in a single bloody lifetime?'

'I don't know,' I offered pathetically, 'but we have to try. Understand. Analyse. Develop movements. Read.'

'Read! Eddie, reading is not the answer to death. Yesterday the lights changed to green when I was halfway across the road and I only just got to the other side. I'm already ebbing.'

'Rubbish. You're forty-five.'

'Forty-six.'

'Well, if our deaths are imminent, surely we have to hang on to the people we love. Alicia, for example.'

'But I want to have kids.'

'Well, volunteer in a children's home.'

'My own kids, Eddie.'

'We're socialists; it doesn't matter where they come from.'

He was quiet for a moment. 'I sometimes think, what's the point if you've got no time left? Soon we'll be on the front line. All dying. It will be our time to go over. To die. We will have reached the outpost and there will be no one in front of us. Nothing. All our friends and family dead. Just us. Me. Everything gone.'

'Fuck, Mark. You're depressed. You should leave the morbidity to me. I'm worried about you.'

'You'll be gone as well!'

'Maybe, but I'm younger than you.'

'Life feels too short. What is life, anyway?'

'I read that life is a short period of time in which we are alive. Does that help?'

'No. It makes me want to have kids even more.'

'I don't understand the connection,' I said.

He didn't answer.

It was as though he had already decided to leave Alicia. I think this was the reason he fell in love with Giuliana.

* * *

12 November 2002

Friends Meeting House was already full. People sold newspapers: *Socialist Worker*; *Workers Power*; *Hate Racism, Hate Imperialism*. They were shouting slogans, flapping their arms in arguments like featherless wings. I stood on the bottom step looking at the crowd, recognising faces, waving at people. I was waiting for Rebecca.

Tony from our anti-war group came up to me. 'What was wrong with you the other night?'

'I was arrested,' I said.

'Yeah, I'm not surprised. You were acting like a fucking anarchist,' he said.

'We were being jostled by people trying to get into the building. I was taking the initiative,' I said.

'You needed to get on someone's shoulders, shout orders to us, to take the initiative? That's crap.'

I could feel my stomach turn. 'I am facing a serious charge for inciting a riot. What's your idea of leadership? Passing a resolution on the Central Committee, comrade?'

Someone announced that the meeting was starting.

Tony came to meetings and spoke like an obnoxious schoolboy. He was a rising star, I was told, and he kept a blog. *God help the revolution if he's left in charge*, I thought.

He looked at me, a mocking smile across his thin lips. 'What did you achieve, Eddie? We're trying to help the movement grow, not stir up fruitless riots. This isn't Italy.'

Rebecca pulled at my arm. I wanted to tell him, *Rebecca found me on the march because of my anarchism, and she is beautiful, you mean, thin-lipped bastard.*

'I thought Eddie was magnificent. What were you doing?' Rebecca came up to us. She spoke loudly, above the rush to the doors. As he began to answer, she poked him in the chest and said, 'Selling papers?' She walked us to the door. 'Who was that idiot?' she asked.

It was easier for her; she was new. I had seen, in my short life, meetings before the first war in Iraq, the humanitarian bombing in Serbia and the liberation of Afghanistan. I felt I had been lucky to survive. The swell of activism, then its collapse. Each time the same thing: pounding on doors, stapling placards, posting leaflets, endless committee meetings. Yet the wars kept coming. The Trotskyists were right, I thought. We needed more than anti-war demonstrations. Something more solid. A way of arguing that these wars were linked to the library where I worked, my labour, the supermarkets, the government. Nothing separated the bombing from our routines. We were all working the same cogs. But what was the solution? Socialist blogging?

We pushed through the main doors and into the meeting. A semi-circle of two thousand people faced the stage.

Mark beckoned to us, impeccable as always in his suit. He stood and shouted, his jacket hanging off one shoulder.

Rebecca sat next to me. I whispered a running commentary into her ear. 'She's one of the Trust-Way Nine—they've been on strike for eight months,' and: 'He's a founding member of the Revolutionary Communist Party. He came over from Angola in the 1960s. Don't believe a word he says; he's all mouth, he says the same thing every time he speaks.'

Rebecca stayed after the meeting. We looked at the books arranged at the back of the hall and she stared at a pamphlet, *The Future Socialist Society*. The photograph on the front cover showed a small boy sitting in a factory smiling, the collectivised machinery behind him. There was a man kneeling by the child. Rebecca asked, 'Does the man control the child and the factory, or just the child? Or just the factory? Is that your socialist future, Eddie?'

'Like hell it is. To start with, it's in a factory. Secondly, the man in the picture is wearing dungarees. I don't want to go anywhere near a factory under socialism, and if I have to wear dungarees, I'll join the counter-revolution.'

'That's just as well, because I thought I was going to have to leave,' Rebecca said, laughing.

* * *

January 1976
Daddy's Two Moods

Stewart the monster
A rage louder than thunder,
Screaming for no reason (what did we do?),
Stamps, smacks and shouts,
Until we cry and our hearts break,
I want to take Eddie's hand and run away.
Instead we lie together whispering stories under the covers.
Daddy the champion (we can do no wrong)
He laughs at all my stories,
'Ice-cream sodas and cinnamon toast,' he shouts
Buttered children sandwiches on the bed,
Lovable and playful,
Everyone wants my daddy,
But he is just for us.

By Esther Bereskin (age 9)

* * *

1979

Stewart's office was ringed by tables lined with editing and recording machines. Huge reels of tape spun, feeding into each other. He sat on his desk chair, moving between machines, throwing edited tape into a pile in the middle of the floor, his headphones cocked over one ear. Tape flicked around on the still-spinning reels, muffled voices on low volume and lights flickering erratically. Stewart was operating a time-machine, I thought. In the library of reels that lined the room, he was the archivist of everything that had ever been said. We threw ourselves on the discarded edits arranged like a mountain in the centre of the floor.

Stewart stared down at us from the top of the stairs. 'Come up here. I want to play you something.'

We climbed the stairs, puffed up and proud to be invited into the studio.

'Sit down.' He pointed to a small carpet positioned like a raft on the floorboard in the centre of the room. 'Now listen to this.' There was a slow slurring as the machines sped up. The words caught each other. A voice emerged.

'Okay I'll sing you a few lines. I'll get in trouble, but fuck them.'

The voice was lyrical. It seemed put on.

'Thanks, John, but can you sing into the microphone?'

'That's you, dad!' Esther and I screamed.

There was a pause, then the sound of tapping on a table or chair.

Imagine there's no Heaven
It's easy if you try
No hell below us
Above us only sky
Imagine all the people
Living for today…

Imagine no possessions
I wonder if you can
No need for greed or hunger
A brotherhood of man
Imagine all the people
Sharing all the world
You may say that I'm a dreamer
But I'm not the only one
I hope someday you'll join us
And the world will live as one

His voice was slow, as though he was trying to remember the song.

'Well, that's it. It's my communist song. I'm quite pleased with it,' the voice said.

'It's powerful, John. Why did you write it?' Stewart's question triggered more giggling from us.

'Because the world is so fucking fucked,' he said.

Stewart stopped the tape.

'That, kiddos, was John Lennon, interviewed in 1971. Jessica was outside playing with you, Esther.'

'Wow!' I said. 'Where was I, dad?' I asked. Then after a second, Esther asked, 'Who is John Lennon, dad? Is he from Chicago?'

The kitchen caught the light in the morning. It was a kitchen and laundry. Our clothes would dry on a rack above the stove. When they were dry, our laundered clothes smelt of Irish stew and bread-and-butter pudding. Today there was the smell of homemade hummus that hung in a handkerchief over the sink like a breast in an old bra. Stewart made us cinnamon toast and ice-cream sodas. He knelt and held us, pulling us into his arms. The three of us sat on the counter blinking out the sun and drank in silent ecstasy, slurping and sucking in time.

Stewart took the empty glasses to the sink. 'When you grow

up, one of you will have to invent a potion so we can live forever. So we'll always be together.'

'I'll do that,' Esther said.

* * *

Eddie Kidd, 1979

We took turns. Last weekend Esther spent the day with Spikey Joe; she returned clutching a twisted nail removed from Joe's famous bed. Both she and Stewart were exhausted, Esther tripping over her words. Next weekend was mine. Stewart had managed to get an interview with Eddie Kidd. When I knew Eddie Kidd he was beautiful: tall, his face always a bit insolent, mocking. In my short trousers and my BMX I was a stuntboy, sharing the name of the man who made his motorcycles fly as he wheeled and skidded his way into fame in the 1980s.

Eddie lived with his stunt team in a disused parking lot in the middle of a scrubby field in Kent. His house was a mobile home balanced on loose bricks. The car park was full of wrecks, motorcycles and metal ramps that pointed into the sky like broken, upturned floorboards. It was the site of a strange war, with men flinging themselves into the air from metal planks. It was a bizarre ritual of late civilisation, a subversive and mangled 'fuck you' from the combustion engine. 'You are welcome.' An elderly man in leather with a dirty moustache and a limp greeted us at the gate. 'Let me introduce you to Eddie.' He led us into the caravan.

Eddie sat on a velvet sofa in his underpants with a woman rubbing his legs. He saw us and waved. 'Come in, come in.' Eddie's body glistened and undulated. His hair was smoothed back, run through with engine oil, I thought. He lounged with the post-climactic insouciance of a porn star. I wanted to touch him.

'I'm Stewart Bereskin and this is my son, Eddie.'

'Ah,' exclaimed Eddie to me, 'we must be related.'

'Eddie is already practising to replace you on his BMX,' Stewart said.

Eddie stroked my face. 'Hey Eddie,' he said, 'You can be my brother. I think we should conduct the interview on the track,' he added, turning to Stewart.

There was a new stunt. Eddie drove a battered car up a ramp, hitting the ramp with the side of the car. If the speed was right, the car would scuttle along on its side for a few metres. It was not mathematical; there were no charts, mercury measures or equations, just bricks, ramps and accidents. The stuntman had to be broken before the stunt could work, before they found the right angle, speed and expletives. The plan was to conduct the interview in the back of the car. Eddie now wore a leather suit that he'd pulled on like a skin. Stewart lay on the backseat, his reel-to-reel recorder held to his chest, the microphone near his mouth. I was wedged between his feet, his legs squeezing me into place. Eddie strapped into the front with a helmet. The engine started. My father began his narration.

'I am now lying at the back of Eddie Kidd's car. We are about to attempt his latest stunt: to travel a hundred metres on the side wheels of his car. I have my son with me. How are you feeling?' He thrust the microphone towards me.

'I'm scared, dad.'

'You don't need to be. I know this stunt back to front,' Eddie replied.

Stewart had made programmes about my birth and recorded my first cry, which he sold to the BBC sound archives. All our utterances were recorded and edited. He could not understand the world without the slurring and turning of his reels. He'd asked Jessica what she thought of the birth seconds after Esther was born. 'How did it go, darling?' he enquired. 'Fuck off,' she screamed. Stewart wanted to fix our words, fasten them to his tapes. They were markers on our way in the fury of time. He wanted us to hold something still.

We drove toward the ramp, my father speaking wildly, Eddie concentrating. Though I was only eleven, I knew that this was a stupid thing to be doing. There would be an accident. We hit the ramp; I was immediately pushed towards the door.

'We are now riding up the ramp and about—'

As the car pulled away from the ramp, tottering on its side, Stewart let out a howl.

'My god, we are now in the air. I can see the sky. Hold on, son. Eddie, are you in control?'

Eddie wasn't. We had crossed half of the parking lot. I saw in my upside-down world broken cars and scraps of metal. Stewart's commentary continued: 'We are now going at what speed, Eddie?'

'Thirty-five miles per hour.'

'That's incredible.'

I noticed some movement in front of the upturned window. A man running, then another on a motorcycle. Both shouting. I couldn't sit up.

'Eddie, how do we get down? How do we turn around?' Stewart's contrived journalistic nonchalance had dropped away.

'There's no way of turning back. We just go forward,' Eddie screamed in triumph.

I could see the motorcyclist waving an arm. We reached the end of the car park. I saw a dirt track and the start of ploughed fields—the uncertainties of the Kent countryside. We crashed through a fence, Eddie and Stewart now screaming in unison: Eddie in maniacal delight, Stewart in horror.

'Fuck! Jeeeeesus,' Stewart cried, his legs a vice around me.

I was calm. I made calculations. We were not travelling fast. The field was flat. It was a long way to the main road. We would live.

Stewart's work instincts were strong; he held onto his tape recorder.

I could see the fields and half of the sky. The car tore through the fence. We continued across the field, Eddie refusing to give up.

Suddenly our sideward assault on the world ended. The car paused momentarily, suspended for a second in the ploughed mud, and then fell, gently, onto its side. Stewart's side. There was a quiet thud as his head hit the door. I slid onto him.

'Jeeeeesus fuck,' he said.

Eddie hit the steering wheel. 'We should have come down sooner.'

Stewart craned his head, inspected the tape. The reels were still turning. I could almost stand. Mud and grass were smudged against the cracked glass.

'We have survived the stunt, perhaps even broken a record,' Stewart said into his microphone.

Stewart had run away when he was fourteen, learnt to fly and escaped with his small brother to Quebec in a light aircraft. The only place, he thought, where he could learn to think, away from his father's suffocating dogmas.

We were pushed to the ground, released and dusted down, given hugs for successful initiation into the stuntman fraternity. In the caravan we celebrated with sweet tea in dirty and cracked mugs. I sat on the steps of the caravan while Eddie spoke to Stewart, looking around at the cars and thinking that this was what I wanted to be, pretending already that I was: a feral kid brought up on petrol fumes and the roar of motorcycles. The car park was deserted. The fading light pulled shadows across the tarmac. The shapes of the cars, already twisted, stretched out towards me. The grey of the sky was now broken by the sun that cast its last light along the horizon.

I heard a car in the distance; it pulled up abruptly by the gate. From each door children climbed out. They saw me, waved, looked at the broken cars and the lines of motorcycles and let out a simultaneous gasp. They then, as if to some prearranged signal, leapt over the gate. There were five of them. They ran toward me.

Their courage exhausted, they stopped about ten paces from the caravan and edged their way slowly forward. The eldest, older than me, stood in front of the caravan and said quietly but firmly, 'You're Eddie the Kid, aren't you?'

'Yes I am,' I replied.

* * *

13 November 2002
Dear Eddie,
Your case at Bow Street Magistrates' Court
Date of Hearing 29 November 2002

We enclose the initial evidence which we have received from the prosecution in relation to your case (it is a lot of shit, to be honest, comrade). The prosecution will rely on this evidence, so we need to talk.

My advice is, you shouldn't show this evidence to anyone. We don't know who is working against us.

Anyway, comrade, see you Saturday in Norwich.

Yours fraternally,
Peter Tafe
Tafe and Associates Solicitors

* * *

14 November 2002

What little publicity there was around my case spoke of 'the anarchist.' This offended me. I received the first letter from the police two days after my arrest; eleven days later another letter came from my solicitor. The firm I'd contacted was experienced in working with activists. To be addressed as 'comrade' in my official correspondence helped, I suppose. Peter Tafe—Taffy, as he was known by his comrades—was a street fighter who could not stop speaking. At our first meeting he narrated his life. 'I must tell you about my name. I've long had to abandon my own research but I kid you not, I found Welsh names right across Africa from North to South, including in mid-Sahara, North Niger and Nigeria. In my village in Wales and both my grand-parents' villages—totally obscure, dead, dying hamlets today, but they were once centres of mining—a recent genetic survey by Dr Stephen Oppenheimer, yes, of TV fame, found ninety-six per cent of the genetic makeup of the population of these two villages is of absolutely pure African origin, with specific North African/Berber haplotypes and allelomorphs. Basically means, despite the white skin colour, my family—almost beyond a doubt—when its original arrivals got to North Wales about 10,000 BC we were very recently black Africans, who we now know spent maybe a generation or two in Galicia, North Spain and possibly Western Ireland, where similar genetic dispersals are found.'

I tried to follow Taffy as he traced his name through NASA satellite photos, African villages and the Breton and Irish countrysides. Then we were onto sheep.

'Anyway, this gets me to my name. For twenty-five years in England my nickname, which I gave up punching people about, was "Taffy," which means sheep, and I learnt to love it as I rose in stature in the eyes of my work mates.'

I wasn't sure how we got there but suddenly we were in the 1970s, in the strike wave that was almost a pre-revolutionary situation, he said. I thought that this must be another exaggeration. I didn't know what to believe.

'Remember the strikes that brought down Edward Heath in 1973? Those were our days,' he said. He had retrained as a lawyer in the 1990s after a strike in Liverpool. This small man with enough muscle-fibre for the entire movement had left school at fourteen. He was now my lawyer and spoke so deeply he sounded as though he was gargling rocks.

'There is something you should know about me, Eddie. You know about my conscious, intellectual comprehension of why struggle, organisation and party are vital, but there is also a personal, less conscious one. From sixty-eight to seventy-four I lived as one of the downtrodden, modest, quite honestly fearful members of the working class. I experienced the opposites. The power of organisation, the thrill of open strikes and struggles, the responsibility of being a steward and a public speaker at workers' mass meetings, and the totally personally enthralling joy of *victory* over the entire UK ruling capitalist class. Seeing them scared, running *scared,* is an unforgettable and indescribable *joy,* Eddie, it's fulfilment, it's liberation, it's like a dawn of your whole self, coming alive as giants. We are *all* under this lifelong crushing conditioning, brain-washing, this insanity-inducing stress, pressure, labour, frustration, time-wasting exhaustion!

'We had all of that then. The night the Vietnamese people sealed the abject, total defeat and surrender of the world's mightiest, most formidable, richest killing and torture machine in the mid-seventies, I and a few other young shop stewards proposed that as nine hundred stewards for seventeen thousand municipal workers we try by official or unofficial means to turn that evening into a celebration. A city-wide Imperialism Beaten Party in every pub in Coventry. It was passed. All we needed to do was go to pub landlords and ask them to simply defy licensing, serve all night and allow unrestrained dancing, bands, music and revelry. As far as I know not one landlord refused. We danced, drank, shagged and laughed till well past dawn.

'You have to understand, Eddie, that such experiences colour the whole persona of a young man of twenty-five. I was with the mother of my children, Jennifer. She's still a fighter too. We were lovers for thirty years! And that was because of what we experienced together. And know, Eddie, that it is the best thing we have ever known. Liberation, in the sense of workers winning, is the highest form of human happiness that all living generations can possibly know. At present, sexual shared orgasm and ecstasy is the only real solid joy we all know. What I cannot describe is that this is an experience, a liberation, a release that is beyond even that—not in such a personal, intimate or physically obvious way—but in a total, all-embracing way. Each of our victories—the miners at Saltley, February 1972, the lights going out as I was drinking my pint. I remember dancing around the pub in ecstasy. The dockers, and carrying those "convicts" out of Pentonville prison shoulder-high, hearing the deafening cheering and seeing older men weeping in joy at reliving workers' power on the loose—these are things, Eddie, that today, now, almost make me weep with joy, except that we haven't got them.

'These are what old fools like me not only live for, but want to go far, far further with. I want *total* global liberation for *all*, Eddie. I want to hack the whole capitalist class and every last one of their agents to death. Trotsky used to say, "When we've hanged the last capitalist from a street lamppost using the intestines of the last full-time trade union bureaucrat"—that'll be when ninety-nine per cent of the population will have won. And then we'll finally be free and we can throw off the shit of ages and rebuild society as we please!

'Sorry to ramble so terribly. My point, Eddie, is that I am "touching base" with you. I have a feeling that your case is really the start of something big. I've been arrested dozens of times. In the last war we had demonstrations in Norwich. The police started to muscle in. I squared up to one of them, he was playing with his truncheon, and I said, "If you even think of weighing in on our march against a terrorist war I will personally make sure that you end up in hospital. I will hit you so hard you will not be able to work for six months." I brought my fist up, waved it in his face. They didn't touch us after that. It helps to be known as a lawyer.

'Listen, comrade, I have heard that some people in the movement are calling you an anarchist, but to me you stand in the best tradition of our politics. People like us take the initiative. We're Leninists. We don't stand aloof from the 'petty' struggles of the workers, poor peasants and unemployed students. We seek to *lead* them. Shape them. From the front. Of course this means that the Eddie Bereskins are sometimes taken out and hung out to dry by the cowards instead of by the bosses. Gutless quislings and bureaucratic careerists and Mensheviks. Lenin had his share of cowards and traitors too. Zinoviev! Bukharin! Kamenev! And dozens of other academic, undisciplined fellow passengers. We're fortunate to have cadre like you as our general staff! Forgive me. I was in the army for three years.

'You face five years, but I am confident that with the best socialist defence, we'll get you off. If not, I will personally ensure that you disappear for a few years. If you know what I mean.'

I had no idea what he meant.

We met at Norwich station. I travelled from London. We had two hours together. I ate two bacon sandwiches and drank three cups of tea. Peter had coffee. He delivered his discourse above the din of the coffee machines and train announcements. I felt cheered. He sat next to me like a cornered bull, his bald head bobbing up and down as he spoke. His suit shirt fitted tight against his body. I was being represented by Popeye. His defence, I thought, would be a death threat to the judge.

'The first thing we have done is demand the videos the police claim they have showing you directing the crowd to tickle the police. Lovely tactic, by the way, comrade. When this comes, we will see what we have. We'll speak on the phone as soon as I get the videos. When we get legal aid I'll come to London. Hold tight, comrade. I'm proud of you. What fun it is to be back in battle! Thank you, comrade. Thank you for being a real Bolshevik and reconnecting me to what I live for! Remember, Eddie, the mere ensemble of our semi-organised efforts alongside the immeasurably immense power of the modern working class—if we can marry the two together, we will win.'

I left certain I would win, pleased with myself and determined to start weight lifting. The platform was wet, the day drizzled relentlessly. Our faces were sprinkled wet as we waited for the train to pull into the platform. Taffy kept up his fraternal banter. 'Fuck knows,' he said, raising his arms to the low-hanging clouds, 'why this island is so crowded. I would rather be a lawyer in Jamaica. I am moving to Jamaica after the revolution.' He stood motionless on the platform, smiling at me through the train window. As I shunted away, he punched a fist in the air and shouted something I couldn't hear.

* * *

February 1978

I had the small front room in the house, a rectangular window that overlooked the path leading to the front door. If the house could have been driven, it would be from my room. I slept under two duvets. My nights were complicated. Stewart would cajole me to bed, promising stories. I would wait for him to come upstairs, composing questions to delay him. He would tuck each errant corner of my duvet under the mattress and I would roll against the wall. Stewart would then lean over the pile of covers, find me, kiss me. 'I love you, Boyo.'

In the night I would hammer on my parents' door and scream. Jessica would come out to hold me and bring me into their bed. I would lie sleepless between them, not daring to move, longing for the creeping hope of dawn, for the light to seep under the curtain.

One year we travelled to Chicago.

'Boyo, I've brought up the caterpillar.'

Stewart bounded into the room, brimming with excitement.

He leapt onto my bed and hugged me.

'Here, cross it out. The last segment.' The caterpillar was a way to speed up time, make it disappear. It was drawn on a large sheet of paper with a series of circled segments making up its coiling body. Each circle represented a day, and each day was crossed off until we reached our departure: an Advent calendar for Chicago.

'You do it.' I knew he wanted to.

'No, we'll do it together.'

He took my hand. Together we crossed out the last day.

Stewart lifted me and we danced around the room. Before I slept I peered out of the window in the fading light. I saw Stewart's arms across Jessica's shoulder, smiles busting out on their faces. I pulled the curtain around my face and pressed my nose against the window. Stewart looked up and saw me, raised his eyebrows—his lined, concertina brow lifted—and mouthed, 'I love you, Boyo.'

A year later I was put to bed by Jessica. It was raining. I heard the rain slapping against the window as I lay cocooned against the wall. Stewart was out at the BBC. Jessica came in, taking Stewart's role. She lay down on the bed next to me.

'I wish you wouldn't sleep like that. It's unhealthy. You wake up completely soaked.'

I held on to my covers tightly, fearing a struggle to remove my second duvet.

I heard Stewart arrive. The door slammed. From his first step into the house that night, I knew he was angry.

I learnt about adults through doors and walls, crouching low to listen to their conversations. The world came to me through a filter of floorboards and bricks. I could hear what was going on. Stewart returned home hating himself after another project had been rejected. I was convinced that behind these walls Stewart would finally kill Jessica. Or they would both explode. Esther and I would discover their charred remains in the morning. I learnt how the world worked behind closed doors.

I knew something was wrong. My father's downstairs progress had been too heavy. No loving shout to Jessica, just a series of thuds. The door. His bag on the hall floor. His footsteps into the kitchen. I buried my head into the duvets. Unable to hear anything, I fell asleep.

I woke when something crashed in their bedroom. Stewart's screaming bellowed through the house. Nothing from Jessica. Then more crashing. I sat up, pushed away my covers, froze. Sickness rose in my stomach. I could not move.

'Turn the fucking TV off,' Stewart shouted.

'No, you turn it off.'

'Turn it off, for fuck's sake, when I ask you.'

Stomping. Another crash.

'You are a fucking bitch.'

I went into their room.

I should have run. Grabbed my sister's hand and fled. Pulled her along the road. Jumped from the top of the stairs and flown away with her.

I opened the door. My mother was in the corner by the bay window, bunched up. Stewart stood with the television lying by his feet, sucking in breath. He turned to the wicker clothes basket, seized it and threw it at Jessica. It hit her. She collapsed completely, crying. This beautiful and strong woman, her tears as pathetic as mine.

Stewart saw me and ordered me back to my room. I didn't go. He moved toward Jessica and she tried to keep him away with little jabs of her legs. He grabbed her, lifted her up and turned towards the bed. Jessica was unsteady on her legs. He pulled back his fist and hit her. She fell back on the bed, blood and snot running from her face.

I left the room, ran to mine, and closed the door, fastening it shut with my bed. I hid my head in my damp duvets. I heard Jessica running downstairs. *Please let her make it to the door. Let her get out.* The front door slammed. I ran to my window and saw Jessica running to the gate, the black raincoat over her naked body. She looked like a flasher, barefoot, clutching the coat around her. She ran down the street.

I slept well after the fight, not caring about anything as long as Jessica was safe. How different the world would be if women were stronger than men. If only I could grant physical strength to women. This is what it came down to. If women could dominate men, when husbands shouted, one blow would shut them up.

I was up early. I slid the bed away from the door, dressed and waited for the morning. Esther was already downstairs, sitting at the kitchen table with a bowl of cereal, book open.

'Where's mum and dad?'

'Still in bed,' I said. I made breakfast. Stewart came down. I studied the bowl.

'Kiddos, I'm taking you to school today.'

'Where's mum?' Esther asked.

'She had to go to school early.'

Esther had slept, impervious. I resented her for this. Sleep always saved her. It coated her, protected her from the night. Maybe without it she would have snapped earlier and not come back.

Chapter Three

Sickness

15 November 2002

Esther was sick again: pregnant and sick. 'You're going to be an uncle!' she announced, and burst into tears. I cried behind my hand. We were linked by blood and tear ducts. I held her on the sofa and she curled into me tightly.

I sang: 'Sergeant Higgins' march is a sentimental march and when you see them pass smile, smile, smile.'

She sniffed. 'Why are you singing that?'

'Because that's the song you wrote for us when we were small. You used to sing it to me when I was sad.'

She was still. 'I think I'm getting ill again, Eddie.'

Just when you are ready to give up, something tells you to keep going. It happened that day. I wanted to tell Esther about Rebecca—to swear her to secrecy and make her laugh. I turned off my sister's hill. As I made the steep climb to the park I felt my stomach turn: she was getting sick again. The street was lined with trees and identical terrace houses. Families with small children, the road choked on both sides with people-carriers. Young people doing well on organic food and the odd pop concert. I thought my sister's child could play with me in the park.

I passed an old couple. The woman had stopped. She was holding onto a garden wall to catch her breath. They didn't speak. The man put his bags down, beads of perspiration on his forehead. He looked at the woman and then ran his hand through her grey hair, pushing the fringe out of her eyes and combing it back with his fingers. She looked surprised. She stood straight, ready to complete the ascent. I stepped off the pavement to avoid them.

My sister was sick again. I must remember to tell her that I loved her. I could only tell her when she was ill, under the cover of her madness. I was a coward.

My mother's voice was faint last night. 'Esther's pregnant and keeping it. I told her, "Good—now you know you can have kids, you can get rid of it." She won't. She says it's already too late. She didn't even find out till she was a few months along. She's getting sick again and she's taken herself off lithium. She says it will damage the baby.'

Whenever Esther fell ill, Jessica shrank. Her hair whitened. Esther was strangling Jessica.

'I should have concentrated more on my work, Eddie, made something of my profession. I gave up too easily. I always have,' Jessica told me, embracing a mug of tea with her hands.

'How can you say that, mum? All my memories are of your work. Your dedication. The kids loved you.'

She was sitting on the leather sofa, the fat cushions lifting her off the floor. She waved away my words.

'Well, it's of no concern now. It's done.'

I looked around the room. The coffee table was stained with tea circles and piled high with novels, biographies and histories, as though they had been placed there to keep the table from walking away. My mother read at each corner, on the sofa, on the armchair and on a stiff metal chair dragged from the kitchen. She was untidy with books, but nothing else.

'You should come on the anti-war demonstration,' I said.

Sitting on the sofa, she seemed so small—bent forward, slouched, her hands ribbed with veins and old skin. She looked like a decrepit child. We had drained the life from her. We had left her white-haired and sad. Loving us had aged her. 'That's enough, Eddie. I want to read now. Off you go. I'll see you on the demonstration, but honestly, we don't need to speak every day. What is there to say? Familiarity breeds contempt.'

She pushed herself out of the sofa and jumped to her feet. She gave me a perfunctory kiss and kicked me out of the house. I was pleased.

Anything that disturbs Esther throws her to the ground and stamps on her. She is a mountain made of sand. In the day she reaches the sun; at night, when the wind comes over the park, she is levelled again. I think she is going to disappear.

* * *

October–November, 2002

I did something less edifying. I stirred. As I fell deeper into my own crisis and the aftermath of my arrest, I plunged into the diverting emotional whirlwind of Mark's dilemmas. I wanted to forget my own turmoil by stirring up his. I found companionship in another breakdown. I dug myself into his stem cells, sometimes urging him on, sometimes urging caution, sometimes both in the same text message.

`Be careful Mark. Alicia is everything to you—you won't get better. Giuliana is beautiful and I understand that you want kids.`

Mark's revelation was not unlike mine. Thrust like angry and disoriented soldiers into the same trench, with our strange meetings—mine with Rebecca, his with Giuliana—we were in the season of war, campaigning and love.

We turned up in early October to a meeting of Tooting's anti-war group. I was the first to arrive. A woman with long hair, olive skin and dark eyes walked in, saw me and smiled. I found the room in the community centre and set out the stall with papers and pamphlets. She came into the room. 'Hello, my name is Giuliana.' Her accent was heavy. 'Are you here for the meeting?' She sat down and we waited together. I tried to explain our activism to her and she nodded and smiled knowingly. 'I have been involved in the anti-war movement recently in Italy. I was a party councillor for Rifondazine Comunista in Florence.'

'Fuck,' I said. I always said 'Fuck' when I was surprised. 'Well then, I'll shut up, councillor comrade. Welcome to our humble anti-war group in South West London.' She laughed. Mark arrived wearing a suit. I didn't know why he dressed up. His shirt was unbuttoned at the top, nonchalant and smart. He was the only activist I knew who cared so much about his appearance. He had always been like this—beautiful and well-dressed, like Trotsky. 'Trotsky was the best-turned-out Bolshevik. Disciplined in appearance and politics,' Mark had explained to me.

'Maybe,' I had retorted, 'but he was also president of a soviet. Twice.'

Mark sat next to me and made some calls to find out what had happened to our movement. Giuliana talked. 'I haven't been very active since I left Italy. Stupid relationships. The last man was a dreadful nationalist. He was overbearing. I had to leave. I'm a researcher in dentistry.'

'That sounds boring,' I teased.

'It is. I needed to get involved again. I only feel alive when I'm active.'

'Welcome back.'

'I'm half-Palestinian.'

'It's okay,' I said, 'you already impressed me when you said you were a councillor for the Italian communists. Now you're showing off.'

She laughed loudly, her mouth open. Mark raised his eyebrows to me and mouthed something which I think was *Wow* or *Great* or *I want to have children*. I wasn't sure. The meeting had been cancelled, so we went for a drink: Giuliana, Mark and me.

Mark did most of the speaking. I had never seen him like this. He was ecstatic. Possessed. He spoke like a man who was about to die—as he had convinced me that he was—cramming words and jokes into every pause and gap in the conversation. I was jealous that he was doing this for Giuliana and not me. He had never made as much effort when I was the only company. I also wanted to tell Mark that for his own sake, he must pace himself. *If you want Giuliana,* I thought, *you shouldn't look so desperate. Getting older makes us desperate.* But I thought Mark's stories and jokes might manage to elbow time aside in his dizzying sprint towards Giuliana and youth and children. I could hear Alicia's diagnosis. 'Mark has a complicated psychopathology—he craves love and attention. He has an abandonment disorder.' Could it be possible that our entire species suffers from abandonment disorder? I was already edging towards supporting Mark's breakup before he even realised what he was doing. I would help him in his impossible race for more time.

'I can't believe this,' he said when Giuliana went to the toilet. 'She's incredible. Perfect. Political. Beautiful. What is the chance of this happening? The meeting cancelled. We are not told. You turn up. She does. I do. All of us at the same time. What is the likelihood, Eddie? What a beautiful coincidence. Beautiful. Christ, life is beautiful.'

The fundamental difference between Mark and me could be boiled down to this: when he was overwhelmed and delighted (which was often), he said 'Beautiful,' but when I was awestruck and amazed, I said 'Fuck.' Fuck, Beautiful. Beautiful, Fuck. Faced with revelation and change, Mark's world curled up while mine curved down. I sought solace in the earth; Mark, in the sky. I loved that about him. Maybe that was why I was always jumping on his big back and shoulders, so I could see further, ride on his complicated joy. There was even something uplifting about his current obsession with death. Death was a political question that Mark could answer with concrete practice, even if his answer was incoherent; Mark believed that speaking at five hundred words per minute was a solution to our imminent mortality. 'I can't believe this,' he said, hitting the table once more. 'It's beautiful.'

Later, afterward, we were in Mark's car outside my flat. Mark was speaking. The windows had misted over and the air was humid. Condensation ran down the windscreen.

'I can't believe it. All of this happening tonight, to me. To us. She's amazing, like Alicia only younger, better, single. She told you she was single! Amazing.' Mark was speaking to the windscreen, hammering the steering wheel with the palms of his hands. His seat-belt still fastened.

'But you're not, Mark. You're not single.'

Mark ignored my attention to detail. 'You have to admit, she was amazing. Councillor of the biggest radical left party in Europe from the age of eighteen.'

'An ex-councillor and a dentist. It can all be made to sound less exciting.'

'She's beautiful. I mean, politically, she's beautiful.'

'Yes she is, but you're in a good relationship.'

'But you know the issue. Alicia can't have kids.'

'You don't even know Giuliana's second name and you're already planning kids with her?'

Mark picked up my first point. 'It's true. I'm not single. Alicia is everything to me. We talk about everything. There's no question that this is the best relationship I've ever had. Seven years. But there are problems. You know them. We've been talking about them for more than a year.'

'So you're not getting on?'

'It's not that. We get on brilliantly.'

'You've stopped sleeping together.'

'Oh no, there's never been a problem there.'

'So you have a good sex life?'

'Very regular. Very sexy.'

'She can't have kids and won't adopt or think about alternatives.'

'No, no, she has said that she's happy to investigate surrogacy.'

'Fuck, Mark. What's the problem, then? Everything works. You're happy together. You talk about everything and you have sex regularly. You're not single and you're not going to be.'

He was quiet. I thought I had won. I wound down the window an inch so the car filled quickly with cold air. I was pleased to have refused Mark's ebullience. I had not entertained his glorification of a young woman. I had not been a cheerleader, encouraging his libido and restlessness. I thought, as the car cooled down, that I had been a real friend. I was pleased that he had listened.

After a while Mark spoke. 'I can't believe it. It's so beautiful. Such a coincidence. The meeting cancelled. You turn up. Me. Giuliana. No one else. It's beautiful. She is beautiful. Can you believe it? Life, Eddie, feels beautiful.'

I got out of the car. As I leant in to say goodbye, Mark spoke more calmly. 'Have you heard that there's a united call for a huge pan-European demonstration against the build-up to war? They fixed a date. Fifteenth of February next year. It has to be everything we do. It's very exciting. Imagine a global day of action against war. Beautiful.'

I smiled and slammed the door. I was impressed how Mark moved seamlessly from infatuation to politics. I wasn't sure Mark had an internal life. Everything happened on the outside: his obsessions, his politics, his lovers. There was no filter in Mark that decided what to say and what to keep in. How had he reached forty-six and remained so innocent about the world? Between his brain and his tongue there were no intervening layers, no dishonest mechanism to prevent catastrophe. I made a mental note to remain at the wings of his new obsession. As I climbed up the concrete stairwell in my block of flats, the lights flickering on as I ascended, I wondered how he was going to keep his new mania from Alicia.

* * *

20 November 2002

Somehow the great illusion has spread that the rich who have grown giddy on their wealth are hard-working. I am not sure how this lie has become so widely diffused. Paul, despite his laptop and mobile phone, was just a playboy. His work involved restructuring Eastern Europe (he called it structural reforms). Paul's model of banking, he told me, was drawn from Goldman Sachs. 'Essentially what I do, Eddie, is break them down into pieces. So they don't know what's hit them. I systematically dismantle what they were before I came along. Then I rebuild the banks bottom-up until they resemble the internal organisation and patterns of communications at Goldman Sachs. At the same time, Eddie, we tell the government to sell, sell, sell. Everything they have. This immediately gives our new banks huge opportunities, but only after they've been broken down. Basically it's an army job. The accountancy work I send back to the States. I am a prophet!' He laughed at this image of himself as an envoy from God. Paul was part of the new crusade that I wanted to smash. Four days after my sister announced that she was pregnant, he left her.

An army job. Break them down.

Esther lived with three friends. They danced together and had dinner parties. I liked the house, a mass of varnished pine floorboards that shone a glutinous gold. There was a choice of herbal tea and a wicker chair by the window. Possessions were limited, as far as I could see, to clothes. Even this ownership was vaguely perceived—they wore each other's. Shopping was arranged not by a formal, centralised plan, but ad-hoc Post-It notes stuck onto the fridge. They shared everything.

The garden in the summer was complete with the usual birds and squirrels and a family of foxes whose cubs frolicked insanely by moonlight. Sometimes I slept on Esther's floor on a white sheepskin, with a cup of chamomile tea growing cold beside me. I listened to the laughter as they got ready for bed, uncomplicated by men and fucking. They knew more about communism than me, bricked up in my flat alone.

As I made my way to the front door, along the short path from the road, I thought this would be a good place for Esther to get well again. I pressed hard on the bell. Nothing. I knocked and my knuckles ached under the skin. I heard a chair scrape across the floor, the sound of slippers sliding along the hall. Esther pulled open the door and stood with her dressing gown half open at the top, one breast exposed. Her eyes were unblinking and wide, as though they had been pinned open. She stood staring at me, her face impassive.

'Esther!' I said enthusiastically and moved forward to her, pulling the dressing gown around her, tightening the loose belt. She stood still. I put my hand on her face and kissed her quickly on the lips.

'Eddie,' she said and focused on me.

She hugged me, pulled me tight against her so I could feel her naked under the dressing gown: the contours of her body, the rise of her pubic bone, her breasts pressed into me. She kept hold of me. I thought I could feel her belly slightly bloated against me. I felt awkward and pushed her gently away.

We moved into the kitchen, past the stairs and a line of coats. I fumbled loudly in the sink for mugs. One cup slipped from my hand and broke. The noise hung in the air as I placed the pieces on the draining board.

'What are you doing in there?' She sounded better, irritated with me.

'Just being a clumsy wanker. Did you hear about the demonstration outside Downing Street a few weeks ago?'

Esther didn't respond.

I took the tea into the lounge. She was sitting on the wicker chair, her legs curled under her, an arm on the windowsill. The glass was wet; drops of condensation chased each other down the window, sinking into the soft wooden frame.

Esther was looking out, her eyes peeled open again.

'Did Stewart abuse us? I think he might have abused me on that weekend. We slept in his bed, didn't we?' she asked.

I put the tea on the table and sat opposite her. I could feel the pulse in my neck beginning to race. I breathed in deeply. Each time Esther was ill she returned to our childhood. Everything else in her life was irrelevant except this. Stripped back to her bones by the illness, the only thing that was left was that weekend and our dead father. Nothing else mattered, nothing else made a difference to her life. Why could our happiness not press down that year? If a whole life stretches out, it will still be that night that chokes us. I didn't want this conversation. I didn't have the strength, not now. I started to sweat. I could feel my clammy arms sticking to my T-shirt. I saw Stewart's eyes red with tears as he hooked us under his arms, pinned us down as he flicked through the photographs in the pile of padded albums stored in the cupboard under the phone, open and scattered across the floor, some of the photographs escaped from the transparent covers.

'Can you see us?' he shouted. 'We were a happy family. What happened? What went wrong?'

I wanted to say to him, dripping in sweat, my head aching as I saw Esther trying to flatten the chaos in hers, *You went mad, dad.*

'I don't know, Esther,' I said, finally shaking off the memory. 'I can't remember.'

'He had been such a loving father.' Esther drew a line on the wet glass, confusing the beads of frenetic water racing down the pane.

'He was a difficult man. Troubled,' I said.

'I still miss him,' she said.

'No you don't,' I answered adamantly.

Esther turned and looked at me. 'Don't I?' she asked. I had disturbed a tenuous order.

'No. You don't,' I repeated.

She looked relieved, thankful for the clarification. I was not sure that she missed him, that either of us did. When he had gone we felt free for the first time; we could breathe. He would not appear from behind a building, wouldn't pick us up suddenly from school, wouldn't kill Jessica. Did we miss him? If we could have pushed back time, would we have chosen to see him again? Could there have even been a reconciliation? I did not dream of a reckoning of son and father in the underworld. When I thought, by some slip of time and reality, of a meeting with Stewart, I could not sleep.

Esther's friends had stage names. Rachel Star, Jasmine Phillips, Ruby Holland. They had studied together in Bristol. Jasmine came in as I began to plot my departure. Esther sat with her arms wrapped around her bent legs, nestling her head on her knees. We stopped talking. I sipped my herbal tea. I wanted to go. I could see leaves falling to the ground outside, rocking from side to side on the still air. The fading light came through the half-open blinds, turning the room a brown rust.

'I'm here. Someone put the tea on. It's beautiful outside, still quite mild, and the light is glorious.' Jasmine was never depressed, never even sombre. I wondered at her perpetual ebullience. I thought it was an act. I was convinced she applied the joy in the morning with her eyeliner and took it off at night.

Jasmine came into the room, looked at Esther, rolled her eyes sympathetically to me. She kicked off her heels and pulled up a chair next to Esther.

'You've had a lovely day, but now it's going to change. I'm cooking, and you know what that means.'

She waited for Esther to respond.

'Catastrophe,' Jasmine said.

She laughed, sat up in the chair and put a hand on Esther's back and rubbed hard.

Esther suddenly stirred, realising that Jasmine had come in.

'Do you think I was abused by my father, Jasmine?' she asked.

She wanted to test her hypothesis on someone else.

'No, I don't think you were. You've never mentioned it before,' Jasmine answered.

Esther got up from the chair and it scraped backwards. She pulled open her dressing gown. She was naked underneath.

'Look,' she shouted, pointing to her pubic hair. The skin had been scratched raw. It was red and torn.

I jumped forward and tried to pull her dressing gown closed, embarrassed in front of Jasmine.

Esther pulled back. I reached for her. The chair fell. She continued to point and shout, 'Look, look. Can you see where he abused me? Stewart.'

'No, I can't see anything.' Jasmine's voice was calm; she put her hand on Esther's shoulder and led her to the door. 'I'm going to bring you dinner in bed.'

Esther tried to resist before accepting her guide. They walked slowly along the hall and up the stairs. Esther was still holding her dressing gown up.

'Can't you see anything?' she pleaded.

I could hear them enter Esther's room, and the insistence in her tone faded. I felt useless, usurped by her friend. My absurd dance in front of my sister to keep her covered.

The sky irritated me. It was still blue when I left the house. It looked cold. I automatically zipped up my jacket, pulled the collar around my ears. I began to walk, moving to avoid the bins that had been dragged onto the pavement for collection. I saw a child throwing himself off the pavement on his skateboard. I walked down the hill toward him. He fell off, stood up and stared at me, embarrassed.

'I used to do that,' I said. 'But I had a toothpick, a thin plastic board. Not this big thing you're using.'

'D'you want a go?' he asked. He must have been ten years old, with black hair and round cheeks. He wore a pair of jeans torn at the knees.

I got on the board and wobbled. My hands flapped. I pushed myself toward the curb but couldn't lift the board and crashed into a green wheelie bin on the pavement. The palms of my hands stung. They were red, small stones sticking out of the scratched skin. I brushed them off. The boy stood over me, his mouth open in a smile.

'You should try it again,' he said.

'No, I feel stupid already. I'll kill myself and break your board.'

He laughed.

'I don't care about the board. Here, I'll show you the stunt.'

He flicked the board up with his foot and caught it in his hand. He moved to the other side of the road and rushed toward me, face fixed, eyes on the pavement. He missed again and laughed. We sat where we had fallen, watching the board roll slowly down the hill, missing the parked cars and picking up speed. Neither of us got up to stop it.

'Do you want another go?' he asked.

My hands were throbbing. I could remember something, but it wouldn't hold still long enough for me to see it. Light had faded from the sky and the street lights flickered on above us. I got up and brushed my trousers down.

'Yeah, I'll have another go. I'll get the board.'

I unzipped my coat. I could feel the air rushing over me as I ran down the hill.

* * *

March 14, 1983

Dearest Eddie,

Your letter arrived this morning. I've read it three times already, including once on the phone to Grandma, who was very pleased with it also. Tonight I will read it to Grandpa and Uncle Max. Your letters are always appreciated. This most recent one took exactly ten days to arrive. Too long! Slow mail.

As I've already said, I will continue to send you gifts of money when I have some. My income, as always, is up and down. It is due to the sort of work I do: freelance journalism and peace work. Some months are good and some months are less good. But you—and for that matter, Esther—will share some of my income from time to time. Esther will shortly get her due. I don't want either one of you to feel that I have been neglectful in this instance. Or that I am playing favorites—I love you both, even though there has been so much time and distance separating us… not to speak of pain and the hurt which we all feel.

The work I am doing at the moment is for the Chicago Coordinating Committee for Disarmament. It is not like a regular nine-to-five job; it's a seven-day-a-week thing. All day and all night. During the day I'm at the office, which is in a church in the city, and at night I'm at meetings. The main purpose of the job is to educate the people in Illinois about the threat of nuclear war that hangs over all mankind. The central focus of my work is to help organize a disarmament rally in Chicago—every year a growing number of people join the all-day rally. Thousands and thousands. I also have my own TV show. I am the host and the producer of the show. Almost all of the above I do for free or next to nothing. To be a peace worker might be noble, but it is mostly unpaid. So this is the reason why I sometimes can't afford to send you money. I hope Esther understands.

Back to your letter, you speak of sports. I hated them as a kid. I remember playing American football. Whenever a guy got hurt—and sometimes they'd cry—the instructor often laughed at them, "Don't cry" or "Don't be such a pussy, a little pain is good for you." Stupid, stupid bullying teachers!! Oh yes, by the way, do they still get kids to go for 2 or 3 mile runs in the pouring rain? British stupidity! Don't ever think that this is right. It's dead wrong. It belongs to the Middle Ages. You say math is difficult. I must confess that I was very good at math when I was young. But

I was good because as a young boy, I used to work with my father and my grandfather (your great-grandfather Isaac) selling produce at a market, so I got real experience with numbers. But don't worry too much about math. The most important thing is to read. Reading is what separates us from the beasts. Reading is the key to the world of ideas.

Finally, I have a big calendar on the wall and every month I cross off the previous 30 days. (Remember how we used to do that when you were a small kid?) So yes, 26 months until we meet again. Because, as you say, when you are 16 years old, you will be allowed to travel. When you come you will be surrounded by a loving family who will shower you with adoration, good food, family, history and love as only a family can give. You will be like a reigning prince. We all desire your presence greatly! Most of all ME. I cannot tell you how I dream about that day when we will hug each other again. Maybe after you come, Esther will reconsider her anger and her upset—let the past remain buried in the dust and consider a visit here too.

Finally, you wrote in your last letter that you are not enjoying school and look forward to the end of it, but "I will attempt to pass as many EXAMS as possible (at the moment, the amount looks very small)!" I respond by saying, why keep beating your head against a hard wall (school)? If you are (as you yourself say) "under pressure" and if you "are not enjoying school" and that you are "looking forward to the end of it" and if last of all you appear to be going nowhere and "the amount looks very small"—why continue? Why waste your time in a school, in a setting, in a pressure-cooker that is so unattractive to you? Why not quit? Leave the damned place? Life goes on beyond school, you know! There are many opportunities outside!! And one of those opportunities is here in Chicago, USA, with your own flesh and blood, your father. If you want to, quit school and live with me. I can help you to find a job, or if you want to, find a trade, and best of all, become an activist in the peace movement or trade unions in my city which is more conducive, more attuned to your frequency. So quitting school in London doesn't mean the END, it could be the beginning of a new life, a new future.

I get a real lonesome feeling for you, Eddie, please try to reply NOW to this letter and in detail. We can in the meantime have a relationship—father and son—by letter.

I love you deeply, Boyo.

Solidarity, peace and love,
Your Dad

P.S. Have you been following the arrest of Klaus Barbie? The Butcher of Lyon, as your grandfather will tell you. We have to do everything in our power to make sure these psychopaths and murderers never come to power again.

* * *

22 November 2002

The first present I bought Rebecca was a vibrator. 'I was going to buy a vibrator when we met, but if you want to get me something…' So three weeks after my arrest and our first date I arranged to meet her outside Ann Summers. I arrived early and stood awkwardly outside the adjoining charity shop. Why hadn't I ordered the bloody thing online? The shop had two mannequins in leather underwear and riding boots holding whips. I stared at the shop, hoping to see Rebecca before she saw me so I could walk up to her confident and cocky, with a stride that declared that I was in charge and that I had done this many times before. Making sure that I did not betray what I was doing: fidgeting pathetically with my shrunken penis in my pocket. Being near all that public sex made me feel insecure and vaguely excited.

The bright neon of the shopping mall burnt my eyes. Everyone looked the same, poor and slightly crippled on bad food, cigarettes and poverty. I saw a woman pushing a pram into Ann Summers. The baby was snotty and smiling, his fat finger pointing the way into the shop. I thought maybe this pudgy, red-cheeked little human being had suggested the visit in the first place. What were a few vibrators and leather bodices to a two-year-old, anyway? No hypocritical morality about childhood and porn from me. Our society was about to make a porn show with a massacre of Iraqi children. So I told myself that a small anal plug and some lube were the real symbols of peace and love to a world in permanent and televised war. I wanted to tell the mother and child my thoughts but instead I continued loitering outside the Red Cross shop, playing with my testicles.

'What are you doing here?' Rebecca said. 'I thought we were meeting inside Ann Summers!' She put her arms around me.

'Oh, I was just having a look. These are good places for bargains,' I said.

'You weren't shy, were you, Eddie?' Rebecca pushed her body against mine. I could feel her moving, slowly pressing tightly against me.

'Are you getting excited, darling, for our vibrator'?

'Not *ours*. It is yours. I am buying it for you and I feel very odd.'

Rebecca took my hand and led me into the shop. I didn't realise how much I had wanted to see her. I had been impatient since I had last seen her. I thought I had been impatient for the weekend and the film that I had promised to take myself to, but now I realised it was because I needed to see her.

I didn't mind the vibrators, though I'd momentarily panicked that she wanted a plastic penis when she could have mine. She wanted, I calculated, two penises; double dick delight. I immediately thought that we could add a video link to a website and graduate in less than a month to 'AMATEUR COUPLE SHOW HOW IT'S DONE WITH VIBRATOR.'

'I want to ME as he MMWV when we get home.' Rebecca had

a habit of inventing acronyms.

'Isn't that a disease?' I asked.

'It means Masturbate Eddie as he Masturbates Me With Vibrator.'

We moved deeper into the shop, past the underwear hung on the wall like instruments of torture. 'I'm embarrassed. Can we have this conversation later—somewhere more appropriate?' I said.

There were four shelves in the middle of the shop, with rows of vibrators glistening and stiff like the models of historical monuments in tourist shops. I thought suddenly of the Eiffel Tower. Only these penises were not to scale—they were, apparently, real-scale, lifelike, huge shadow-casting pillars that could stand up like bedside lights or lightsabers, police truncheons, towers visited by bank-holiday tourists. I felt panic in my stomach when I realised that they must have been modelled by real men and their penises.

Esther came into my mind. Between my new lover and my sister there was a row of oversized plastic penises. I felt frivolous. How could I be wasting my time on sex toys when Esther was getting sick? I saw her thin, featherlight, trying to hold herself to the ground to stop the wind blowing her away. I thought how thin she was. Then I focused again on these large penises lined up like soldiers, and I thought that Esther was only the width, maybe, of five of Ann Summers' vibrators standing next to each other in a line. I could measure my sister by the width of the dildos that I was purchasing in the afternoon, in the middle of the week, months from a possible war, as my sister started her long slow meltdown again. I felt nauseated.

I pulled one of the penises off the top shelf. It was see-through, in pink glitter, the length of my forearm and almost as thick at the base. There was a small protruding finger and when I turned a switch the vibrator started to dance. Not vibrate, but shake and swivel backwards and forwards. I jumped and dropped it; it continued its pulsating dance on the floor, like a person trying to escape from a giant sock. I cried, 'My God, what is it doing?' Rebecca looked equally shocked. 'I think it's broken!' She picked it up with the tips of her thumb and first finger, then seized its shaft, which thrashed around in her hand like a trapped animal, and turned the switch on the base. The object finally stilled. 'Am I meant to put that up me? It would kill me.'

'I think you handled it quite expertly,' I said. We laughed, relieved that we had survived.

The shop was full of other couples who seemed more sure of themselves, browsing the shelves nonchalantly. 'How many of these people,' I said softly to Rebecca, 'have suffered a bereavement recently? Probably half of them?'

'At least!' Rebecca said.

'Well, it makes you think,' I said.

'What about?'

'How resilient we are as a species. Here are all these people, some still in mourning, many recently having buried their parents, aunts, uncles, brothers and sisters, probably even lovers, and here they are in Ann Summers. Like us. Buying vibrators.'

'Not all of them are buying vibrators. That couple, for example.' Rebecca indicated to a couple with a nod of her head, a man and woman a few metres from us staring at a box in urgent conversation. 'They're buying Velcro-fastened bondage straps.'

'But you know what I mean. Humanity gets up quickly.'

'And starts having sex again,' Rebecca said.

'Yes. I find it hopeful,' I said.

'Good. Can we choose now?'

I pulled down two of the smaller vibrators and held both in my hands. I ran a finger along the raised ridge along its middle and the texture of the rubber, like the contours and skin of a real penis. The large vibrators on the top shelf were scraping the light fittings on the ceiling. I doubted if my penis would even stretch to the blue erection in my right hand, let alone the larger cock in my left. I was suddenly aware of how empty and unfilled my trousers felt. I hurriedly put my small handfuls back in their place.

'What's wrong with one of these?' Rebecca reached for the Leaning Towers of Pisa on the higher shelves—the industrial chimneys, their peaks covered in clouds. I choked and blushed.

As I replaced the two penises I was holding, one fell sideways. It hit its neighbour, another forearm-sized vibrator, which also fell. Soon the entire shelf was collapsing like dominoes, some of them cascading forward and catching the larger vibrators below. Suddenly the entire display of plastic cocks, metres high, came tumbling down. I tried to catch them, first in my hands, then when they kept falling by wedging my back against the shelf. This only dislodged the tall loyalists, who had until this point steadfastly refused to give up their standing position. Rebecca stood back to watch. I had penises falling over my shoulders, through my arms: a crashing wave of cocks breaking and splashing through my parted limbs. When the falling subsided, I was in the same position, pressed against the now-empty display, my smile lost, with the two vibrators I had caught early on in my hands. The others piled into small mounds on the floor. A few had activated in the fall and now shuddered and slithered around my feet.

The shop had stopped. People gathered around me. An assistant, a broad, blond man who had no doubt been a model for some of these fallen cocks, came forward, smiling. 'If you would just step away, sir, I'll clean up.'

The onlookers laughed and turned away to other amusements. Rebecca came up to me, her eyes wet with laughter. She kissed me hard on the lips and whispered into my ear, 'Are you keeping those, sweetheart?' I was still clutching the vibrators I had caught. I handed them to her, smiling guiltily. 'I think we'll have to take this one to mark the day,' she said, holding a smaller pink penis. I still didn't speak. I just wanted to pay up and get out.

Rebecca said, 'I think you'll be able to laugh at what just happened in about three decades. Okay? So we won't mention it until we're an old couple.' Rebecca winked at me and walked to the counter with the money I had forced into her hand.

Until we're an old couple? I repeated this to myself. *She thinks we're going to get old together. Already.* I saw her at the counter, the dildo standing between her and the assistant like another party in the exchange. Rebecca and the cashier were laughing. She was standing tall, hair bunched back, fighting for freedom from the clasp that held down her curls, her face white and slightly freckled. Her lips were marked out sharply. She turned to me, the purchase almost made, her mouth parted broadly, showing the gap between her two front teeth. Her eyes glistened, wide and dark. I thought, *Is it too early to be in love?* I followed her out of the shop.

'We can take it with us on demonstrations,' she said. 'If the police attack us, we can turn our dildos on them!'

All I could think was that she had said *we* again. She had plans for us. *We* would defend ourselves against the police with our dildos. *We* would protest together and *we* would grow old, laughing together about our long-redundant sex toy buried in the attic, the battery having frothed and seeped over the idle motor years before. *How beautiful*, I thought. I could see her, a hand reaching back open like a star, her face eager. She was delighted and happy at all things. The ugly breakups and upsets of life hadn't seemed to hold onto her. How could she already be thinking that we were going to stay together and grow old? It seemed ridiculous to me. She was lovely, funny and sexy, and I was pleased now by the thought of spending all this time with her. Maybe she'd been joking.

I took her hand and she squeezed tightly. Here she was, open and sincere. It was strange for me not to suspect subterfuge. She didn't operate in a parallel world of secrets and half-truths. I knew then, that afternoon, that this was how Rebecca was: unremitting and honest, about the vibrator and old age. I didn't know what to do.

'I want you to use this on me when we get home,' she said. 'Remember, Eddie, your role in this relationship: MMWV.'

'As long as you're not hiding any WMDs,' I said, nudging her.

* * *

25 November 2002

My productive life has been very small. When I look back at what I've done, I suppose it doesn't amount to more than a few weeks of concentrated time: when I spoke well in a meeting, studied hard in the public library, helped to run a campaign. Putting these things together at the end of the day, piled up like a list on a job application, I realised they were not worth more than three months of my life. I wasted time: got up, made cups of tea and rearranged the furniture as though my existence depended on it. I was exhausted now, thinking about my profligate wasting of time, my journeys to the newsagent, the neurotic twitches of activity that brought me nowhere and left me tired. In my aimless rambling between my bed and sofa, through the streets of the neighbourhood, I had worn down the planet, created a slight divot in the world's pavements and carpets. There was a mathematics to my reductionism. All life reduced to time-wasting. An average person walks thirteen thousand steps a day, which over thirty years had carried me 334 million miles—to Mars. If I had walked that distance, across the galaxy, made that my life's work, I might have felt a sense of achievement at the end of my life. At least I could have said I had walked to Mars. Instead I had meandered and lost my only chance.

It was the same for Esther. She divided her life between sanity and insanity. Her wasted life being sick. 'That was the year I was sick. When I escaped from the hospital in my dressing gown. When I was sectioned. Then I was well again for five years, until…' The years of her sickness grouped up, so the world was separated by the periods when her feet were on the ground and when she soared above us on her broomstick. My sister, Esther, the witch.

Chapter Four

Lovers and Fighters

28 November 2002

The night before my court appearance Rebecca came over. I had to pretend that I was a street fighter and that I didn't care about the case. But I did and I was nervous. What had it achieved? The anti-war group was supporting me, but resented the waste of time. There were better, more important things to do with our precious resources, hours, and arguments. I sat on the sofa with my shoes off and turned the side light on. I had an old fan heater humming at my feet, puffing out hot, dry air. I drew circles on a pad of paper. Rebecca told stories from the kitchen. I loved this feature of the kitchen. All articulate noise came into the room incomprehensible. I intermittently said 'Oh yeah,' hoping that this would keep the evening going.

'So you won't get a chance to speak tomorrow?' Rebecca sat down on the sofa next to me with a plate of sandwiches. She was familiar and confident, as though we had spent years living together. I was already a fact. I stood up.

'I told you, tomorrow the police present their case. They'll give evidence and then Taffy will speak for me. This is just to see if there's enough evidence to proceed. I've already told you.'

I wanted to throw her out of the flat, with the plate of sandwiches and her shoes. She put the plate down next to her. 'Don't speak to me like that. I know you're stressed. Now come here.' She patted the sofa next to her.

'Don't bloody patronise me.' I stood in front of her.

'Eddie, calm down. I am not patronising you.'

'Oh, fuck off.' I took the plate and threw it into the kitchen. It broke on the wall and fell on the tiles. The echo of the broken china rattling on the floor of the kitchen faded slowly.

Rebecca sank back into her seat. 'Now you're scaring me, Eddie.'

'Then go,' I said and fell back into the armchair opposite the sofa.

Pulling on her socks in the hallway, Rebecca fell. I could hear her. She rushed through the lounge picking up her things, throwing them into her bag. The door slammed. *She thinks I'm going to hit her.*

I sat in the chair as Rebecca had left me. I thought about Stewart. The image of him, tall, slightly bent over, his freckled and spotted back and his receding hair and glasses. I thought about his anger, his shouting slightly muted through the door of his office upstairs while the three of us lived in terrified silence below. *I am my father,* I thought. *I am not even a copy of him, but an exact recomposition of each of his ways, his stoop, his spotted shoulders. We start empty and are filled up by our parents.*

The flat was cold. I curled my legs under me. The phone rang but I left it. My father was fifty-one when he died. I am thirty-four. Seventeen years ago I got a birthday card from Stella, who was a year older than me at school. I can feel it in my hands. Letters cut out from a newspaper to spell 'Just seventeen—time to start having fun.' I laughed to myself as I ran my fingers over the words. I think she wanted to fuck me. I could see her face. Those seventeen years were suddenly stirred up in the room. I could see them all. Stewart's death, Esther's first attack. Each collided, for a moment, in front of me. I didn't know any more in what order they had happened, but I knew that they had just passed. The last seventeen years had passed in the time it had taken me to get from one end of the day to the next. I had not noticed them, had not realised that I needed to be different now. The next seventeen years, until I was fifty-one, would be gone tomorrow. A life can pass in three days of seventeen years. Nothing properly marked and nothing learnt.

The phone rang again. I got up to answer it.

November 2002

When it all started I had no idea how catastrophic it was going to be. Did Mark have any idea that the destruction was going to be so great when he first told me how beautiful Giuliana was? When he made those ridiculous declarations about her in the car in October? Then it all seemed absurd and easy. Mark's eyes glistened and his heart pounded in anticipation of a fantasy. I teased him. Yet I should have understood what it meant as he hammered the steering wheel with rhythmic repetition—his decision to break up his life and change the course of Alicia's life, her daughter's, Giuliana's. His movement that night, the movement I took as a bodily exclamation mark to a good story, had been Mark finding a fissure in the ground of his life and smashing it apart. Separating its hairline crack. I don't think Mark intended such destruction. His meeting with Giuliana had been a random and insignificant collision of two beings who shared some ideas about war and socialism, but now this. People are predetermined, but we don't realise it. We make decisions that seem temporary and accidental, yet they fix our lives on new and inextricable paths that we never really wanted. I had started down my path of destruction on Halloween, and Mark had prised his life apart until it consumed everyone he loved. I knew he hadn't intended to do this—and like me, he had stumbled, clumsy and heavy-footed, into his own bad decisions.

* * *

July 1979

Jessica's friends had leant on her to let Stewart have us for the weekend. We were not consulted. Neither of us wanted to go. Instead the decisions were left to the adults who were busy ruining our lives. The rented house was small. Flowers grew up a wall, two steps from a park and fields. Summer was good. Stewart turned up in the small red family car. We were outside.

Jessica came out and they stared at each other. Then she came over to the car. Esther and I held our breath, desperate for them to stop hating each other. Jessica looked in the car and commented, 'I'm just checking that you haven't brought any of your psychos with you.'

In the back of the car, we saw them mouthing insults at each other. I knew that we were going to pay, that Stewart would hate us for the row he was having with Jessica. I knew that they shouldn't be doing this around us and that this wasn't our fight.

On the journey to London we sat nervously, not moving. Stewart looked back at us, shouting. Thumping the passenger seat next to him, working himself up into a frenzy. He was always a cautious driver. He did everything in his life cautiously, except hitting his children.

Our house loomed over us, huge in our childhood, with its rusty bricks and bay windows, its front garden with two rhododendron bushes. It was a place of infinite possibilities, limitless space and spare rooms. My father's office, where we would bounce in the mounds of rejected tape and sit on his lap as he edited his broadcasts. It had everything for us, hallways lined with radiators where we could drape sheets to make tunnels. A garden that ran from the front lounge to the coal shed at the back. A willow tree we climbed, swinging on its tough, stringy arms, embracing its fine bark.

The weekend started in the dayroom, along the hallway that led from the front door. It was the room where we ate, watched TV and measured ourselves against a wall. Stewart parked the car quickly and hurried us away from our neighbours' gaze. There was a sandy corduroy sofa in the dayroom that unfolded into a bed and he dropped Esther and me onto it. He started to cry, screaming at us, perfectly coherent.

'Why have you done this? Why has it happened? Don't you realise what has been lost?'

Stewart was average height but he boasted at being six feet. If he was, he only just made it. He had a large head, with short, receding black hair and narrow shoulders. His screaming became louder. Esther and I sat waiting for him to stop. Both of us were crying. He targeted Esther. I had always been his ally, the one privileged with 'I love you a tiny bit more than your sister' as I sat obediently on his knee and followed him around.

He grabbed Esther under her arms and carried her across the room. In the corner away from the window there were cupboards. On the wall above the phone was a notice board; below it, a small table. Stewart placed Esther on the table and started to shake her. He lifted her up so that she was pinned against the wall, the notice board behind her, and shook her again, more violently this time, so that her head cracked against the wall again and again. Stewart repeated this as though he had discovered a new trick. I did not try to pull him off her. I didn't run over to him, hit him, drag him off her. Anything would have been better than sitting on the corduroy sofa and watching him smash Esther's head against the wall. Esther was now limp and whimpering, struggling to breathe. He hooked her under his arm and lifted me up under his other arm. He carried us to our rooms upstairs, dumped Esther in her bed, carried me to mine. My room was at the front of the house. Across a long hall at the back of the house was Esther's.

Stewart disappeared. I could still hear Esther's sobs. He started to rage again, crying to himself and muttering curses.

'Do you know what we have lost? The family is broken.'

His violence recharged, he went into his bedroom then came into mine, his brown belt in his hand. He turned me over and started to whip me. I cried loudly, but not because I was blinded by pain. I cried because I thought he expected me to. When he finished he left the room and marched across the house to Esther's. Her screams were real howls of pain. He turn the belt around so she was thrashed with the buckle.

He left her room. I could hear him, leaning against the hall wall, catching his breath. Panting. Esther was now silent except for barely audible tears. This went on for a few minutes as Stewart revived himself again. His anger rose. He scooped us up again and dragged us from our rooms.

'I want you both to see what you have lost. What your mother has done to us. What has been destroyed.'

Esther hung in his arms, limp. We were in the dayroom again. In the fading light he flicked the lamp on next to the phone. He opened the cupboard, pulled out the photo albums and chaotically flicked though the pages, the two of us propped up under his arms.

'Look, see this. This is us. Our family. Can you see? Can you see how happy we are? Can you see how much we loved each other?'

More albums were pulled out, more photos pointed to. Together in Chicago, the four of us smiling two summers before on the last trip to the States. Another photo, taken in a studio on Lake Michigan, the family in 1970s fancy dress, kneeling on a white fur rug, smiling out our joy.

'Look at us. Now nothing. Destroyed.'

He took us back to our rooms and left us briefly, then came in calmly and held us in one of his enforced hugs, rocked us in his arms, sniffing up tears. He told me what he had planned for the weekend. It would start that evening with *Jason and the Argonauts* at the Welling Odeon. Stewart already knew he was leaving, that he was going to lose the custody battle, his escape to Chicago imminent. This was his farewell to us: the last weekend he was going to spend with us. So he left in style, the climax of his fatherhood over forty-eight hours. The pyrotechnics of our childhood. Stewart, in his valedictory salute to us: 'Bye-bye, children. Off I go. Don't forget me.'

A few hours later he fed us and took us to the film. Stewart was exuberant, excited to be with his kids, full of anticipation for what we would eat, where we would go. At the film Esther had trouble sitting, her bottom and back bruised and throbbing. Stewart tried to haul her up onto his lap. She refused. He turned to me. I jumped up and watched the film sitting on my dad.

I don't know if we can date Esther's fall to that weekend. Some fibre keeping her together was broken. A knot of despair unravelled in her head that would become the illness. Stewart snapped her that evening; he broke his daughter. Perhaps it did something to us all: set in motion his sickness, Esther's madness, my violence.

Stewart used to quote Lenin at the breakfast table: 'Hey kiddos, you must understand that there are decades when nothing happens and then days when decades happen.' I wonder, when my mother screamed at Stewart, sent us away for the weekend, had affairs in front of us, if she thought that we were too young and would forget, or that like her we would bury it with a shrug and refuse to talk of it again. And when Stewart attacked us that evening, did he think his anger was justified?

On Saturday night we had a shopping spree at Harrods. We were whisked into town and ate club sandwiches and hot chocolate with whipped cream in the Harrods Food Hall. For a few hours we were the spoilt children of a rich father. In the toy department he bought us space-suit dungarees. Both identical miniature movie stars from *Staying Alive*. Esther picked out shoes. Disbelieving sales staff followed us around. My father charmed them, flirting with his booming North American baritone: 'I haven't had such good service since I was in Chicago. You've been marvellous.'

We travelled back to the house in a black cab. The three of us sat again in the back of the taxi, my heart ticking in time with the counter, worrying how Stewart could pay. When we got home Stewart made us ice-cream sodas and cinnamon toast. He leapt around in a buoyant mood, tossing us up, hugging us, loving us, a comic-book dad. He took us up to his bedroom, onto the double bed, and made a human sandwich with us. Buttered us, his hand a make-believe knife. He put layers of cheese and turkey on us. Esther played the bottom slice, me the middle, Stewart the top. We wriggled and laughed and tried to erase the previous night. Stewart spoke to us separately. He took Esther to bed, kissed her and asked her to promise that she would not tell anyone about what had happened. She promised. He asked the same of me and I promised too.

Stewart lay on the bed and spoke to his brother in Chicago, in front of me. 'Listen, I'm coming over and I will have nothing. Can you find work for me? Can I stay with Mom and Dad? I really need to set something up.' I noted each word and remembered his frown and the way his furrowed forehead raised long horizontal lines on his brow. We were incidental players, shunted around the stage in an epic and pathetic tragedy.

On Sunday Stewart drove us back, repeating over and over in the car that we mustn't mention the beatings, that we might not see him again if we did. When we arrived there was another standoff with Jessica. Stewart unloaded the bags of presents and disappeared. *Farewell, old man. Good night, good night.* I unpacked the bags, showed Jessica our presents and told her what we had done. There are decades when nothing happens, and days when decades happen.

The divorce generated in Jessica a relapse. A craving to fuck, to be needed. She was beautiful, only forty. Sexy. Large curves. Clothes always carefully chosen. I was proud of her when she picked me up from school looking so pretty. I felt like her date. She knew she was attractive and desired. Jessica fell into the arms of several lovers. One man was ridiculous: short, bald and fat. He hovered around after Stewart left. I wondered how Jessica could insult us by sharing her bed with such a man. Our mother's explosion of lust was her riposte to the misery of the divorce—an escape into carefree fun, and a way of underlining her separation from Stewart. Stewart knew what was going on and he managed to find us. To track us down in our boltholes. In a lovers' maisonette in Greenwich, he rang. We smothered the phone with a cushion and we played in the park. The phone still rang. In the evening as we tried to sleep, we could hear the smothered ring of our father telling us that he was still there. That he knew where we were. Violence was Stewart's hallmark. The slap was the syntax of our childhood. Play too loudly—slap. Break a glass—slap. Argue—slap. Don't answer—slap.

After Stewart beat her in the bedroom, Jessica appeared at our school for our first escape. She wore dark glasses like a Dallas divorcée. Even as a battered woman she was beautiful: beaten and glamorous. I hoped that she was wearing her antique black boots with pointed toes so she could defend herself from Stewart. They would give her the possibility of counter-violence; she could kick my father away.

* * *

29 November 2002

I woke up oddly triumphant. I put on a political T-shirt and my raincoat and stood in front of my bathroom mirror before I left the house. I opened the coat to look at the message. The T-shirt was sky-blue. On it a man was crouching, staring into the distance, crudely drawn, with a keffiyeh across his face. He was pulling back a slingshot. In black above the squatting man were the words, *Whenever the working class are exploited there will always be working-class resistance*. I liked the idiocy of the T-shirt. The squadism. The working class in guerrilla fatigues resisting capitalism with a catapult.

I closed the door and put up the hood of the coat. It was cold, but I was exaggerating. I felt good. Insolent. Tough. *Fuck the court. They don't have anything on me.*

I swaggered to the train and sat with my legs apart, my hood still up. At Charing Cross I jumped over the barrier even though I had a ticket. It was still dark and the tops of the buildings I passed billowed steam. The night cleared slowly as I zigzagged up the Strand towards Aldwych and the Court. People looked the same, stumbling along to work, the occasional tourist turning lost in the middle of the pavement. *Everyone is lost in this city*, I thought.

As I turned into Bow Street I recognised figures in the distance. A banner. Familiar coats. I lost my cocky confidence, lowered my hood and flattened down my hair.

There were about thirty supporters. I walked into the court. Inside were X-ray machines and a glass counter, three-metre-high ceilings, neon lights buzzing and flickering. Four police cars lined the pavement outside the court. I was flattered. The police always think we are better organised than we are, that socialists are organised into terrorist cells. My supporters bundled peacefully into the lobby of the court, refurling their banner. In the middle of the lobby was Taffy, absurd in his suit. His arms seemed caught in the tight hold of his jacket. The collar across his neck looked like a noose. When he saw me, he shouted, 'Comrade, you've arrived! I have everything in order. You're up next. The pigs are presenting the evidence against you, but I've seen their testimony. They've nothing. They're scared. Look at us today,' he said, indicating the small group of supporters. 'The anti-war movement has occupied Her Majesty's judicial system.'

I was grateful for his exaggerations.

'Only thing to do now, comrade, is to speak to your supporters.'

I was surprised. 'You think I should speak in *here?*'

Speeches were a tradition, made at every event. I was the master of the dramatic mumble, with a fanfare of waving arms, interspersed with 'Now comrades, the key point is. . . The central argument is. . . ' My speeches left the impression of a great revelation never satisfied, full of gesticulations substituting for content. Three policemen stood in the corner with their phallic hats and folded arms. I hoped we'd be called into the court, but instead silence fell.

Taffy spoke first. 'Comrades, welcome to this court, where criminal incompetence and occasionally justice are handed out. We know that the only real answer to this ridiculous arrest is what the anti-war movement does on the streets. But we are determined to see that the accusations of the police against our comrade and my client, Eddie Bereskin, are thrown out today. Eddie is an activist and a socialist. We will defend the right to protest!' He finished with his arms out, ready to crush the British state in his embrace.

I spoke. 'Thank you for coming. I hope that this absurd waste of money and time will come to an end today. I am charged with inciting a riot when we were trying to stop a war.' Taffy hissed into my ear, 'Mention the demo on 15 February.' I stopped speaking, lost by his prompting. I saw Rebecca at the back of the group. She was smiling. I picked up Taffy's hisses. 'And, friends, we need to remember to build the demonstration for 15 February, when we can really stop this illegal war.'

The tannoy announced, 'Mr Bereskin to Court Two, please.' Someone from our crowd shouted, 'The Downing Street Tickler!' The crowd erupted in laughter. We pushed our way amiably into the court.

My problem had always been that I wanted everything over when it had just started. I couldn't bear the waiting, the patience and discipline that life required. I couldn't stand the constant repetition—that nothing was ever definitively finished. I was bored by working as a librarian. After I had catalogued a trolley of books, lining them up neatly by their class-marks, I would have to do exactly the same again tomorrow. And as a socialist—I knew there would be another newspaper to read, another book to understand. We made small gains today, but had the same fights tomorrow. We could hold our ground, slow down the wars, but never stop them from happening. I saw Rebecca find her seat in the public gallery. I was surprised that she came. I thought our fight would have broken us up and ended the relationship. I didn't know how I felt that she was there. What would happen now? This was the end of the beginning of our relationship, I thought, and now it had to finish. It couldn't last. It shouldn't go on. Like all things, it had to finish. This was probably the first of many court appearances, and the thought left me exhausted; all I wanted was for it to be over. I didn't want life to last so long.

Taffy was sitting next to me on the bench. He nudged me and whispered, 'I love these things. Don't tell anyone, but I get more of a kick from being in court these days than from demonstrating.' The stone-hard court was Dickensian. The magistrate came in and we stood up. He peered at us over half-moon glasses. He wore a heavy tweed jacket and a black cape that flared out at his shoulders.

'Sit down,' he grunted. 'I can see that the accused is a popular man. I recognise your rights to be here,' he said addressing the public gallery, 'but please respect my court and do not speak, heckle or make speeches. We are going to see where this case is going and that will require patience. Right, to business. Can I hear the charges against the accused?'

Taffy popped up. 'Sir,' he said, his voice rough and deep, 'I want to request that this ridiculous case, which is a waste of time and politically motivated, be thrown out.'

There were exclamations from the public gallery.

'That is why we are here, to see if there is a case. Please sit down.'

Taffy sat down slowly and muttered, loud enough for me to hear, 'Bastard.'

The magistrate ordered the prosecutor to make the charge. A man sitting in between the three policemen stood and read from a sheet of paper: 'On 31 October at Whitehall SW1 while present together with two or more other persons the accused did use or threaten unlawful violence, and his conduct taken together with that of those other persons present was such as would cause a person of reasonable firmness present at the scene to fear for his safety. The accused is therefore being charged under Sections 2(1) and 5 Public Order Act 1986.'

He sat down. The magistrate asked one of the policemen to stand, and both stood up. The audience tittered. One policeman sat down, leaving the other standing, his black palm-sized notebook in his hand. He flicked open the hard cover and started to read.

'I am Adam Hill, and on 31 October, I was on duty in full uniform in the custody suite at Charing Cross police station. At 01:00 hours I was present as the charging officer for a man I now know to be Eddie Bereskin, who was charged with the offence of violent disorder. We were following and watching the crowd from the middle of the road to identify agitators and any known activists. At 19:25 I saw a man I now know to be Eddie Bereskin. He was a white male, late twenties, approximately five feet ten inches tall, shoulder-length black hair, goatee beard, thin-rimmed glasses, black leather jacket, black T-shirt with NOT IN MY NAME written in red, blue jeans. He was carrying a black bag. There was a white badge on the left side of his jacket. He had an earring in his left ear. He was shouting into a megaphone, "I will lead the charge." He then said, "One, two, three, push." There was then a violent struggle with police being attacked with flying pieces of wood. The crowd calmed down and with PC Hill we stepped back and recorded what he said in our pocket books.

'I stepped back into the police lines and again saw Mr Bereskin shouting into the megaphone. He was shouting, "Come on, let's move up where the police lines are thinner, up here." He then shouted, "A bit further now, we're nearly opposite Downing Street." The crowd all followed him. He then shouted, "Come towards me, I'm going to lead the charge. One, two, three, push, push, push." The crowd all then attacked the police line. Again wooden sticks were thrown at police. There was a violent struggle as the crowd again tried to get through the police lines.

They were all pushed back.

'I kept watch on Mr Bereskin and saw him walk away. He handed over the megaphone to another white male and disappeared into the rear of the crowd. The whole crowd then moved north to Trafalgar Square. I saw Mr Bereskin appear from Whitehall. There was no doubt in my mind that this was the same man as earlier identified. As he neared a police line this became the safest point to arrest him due to the large crowd nearby. I ran behind him and grabbed his right arm. We then ran him toward the police lines. He was struggling to get away. We took him to the railings. I placed him face to the railings. I then handcuffed him rear stack, double locked and checked for tightness due to hostile situation and struggling person.

'PC Kelling and PC Emment joined us. We arrested him at 21:45 hours, the first available opportunity. "You have been seen in Whitehall and heard to incite the crowd to attack the police lines on a number of occasions. You are under arrest for inciting violent disorder." No reply. He was walked to Charing Cross police station. The other officers kept on fending off a crowd who wanted to get to him. One young woman, a presumed friend of Mr Bereskin, had to be cautioned to stay away.'

The account was read flatly, without intonation. It was hard to understand. He finished with, 'That is all,Your Excellency.'

'You can call me sir,' the magistrate corrected.

Taffy laughed.

The second policeman stood up and repeated exactly the same account from his own notebook. There were only two variations. In his account I was described as five feet nine, an inch shorter than the first account. This irritated me. I am sure that they did this on purpose. I am five feet eleven. The police knew the importance of these measurements. The second difference was that Policeman Two read his notes with great intonation, giving each character a separate voice. Cockney for me: "The suspect then cried 'One, two, three, push.'" Posh for the police: 'I then said to Mr Bereskin, 'You have been seen, sir, in Whitehall.' At first the magistrate seemed impressed and leant back, but as the voices assumed more colour and pathos, he interrupted the account.

'This is not *Jackanory*. Please just read.'

We laughed again. Taffy prodded me once more.

'As I was saying, I was aware that other Forward Intelligence Teams were deployed in the area, as were several Evidence Gathering Magnet Teams. The manner of a number of protestors was extremely aggressive. I saw several small objects flying quickly at police lines and then noticed three Duracell C-cell batteries lying in the roadway. Then I saw Mr Bereskin, who was shouting again, 'One, two, three, push, push, push.' The police lines came under immediate attack, which required the police to force the crowd back to prevent them getting nearer to the gates of Downing Street.

'Afterwards Mr Bereskin was spotted at the south side of Trafalgar Square. We ran up behind him. PC Hill took hold of Bereskin's right arm and I took his left. We then started to run him towards the police line at which point he attempted to resist us and escape. He tried to grab hold of a lamppost and struggled to get his arms free. Whilst on route, there were still other protestors attempting to intervene, requiring us to fend them off.

'Throughout the incidents described in Whitehall I was fearful for the safety of myself and my colleagues.'

The second policeman sat down and another policeman jumped up. This looked choreographed.

'I assume that your account won't depart radically from those of your colleagues, or at all. So spare us a repetition.' The magistrate turned to the barrister. 'What else do you have?'

The barrister stood up and tapped a pile of videotapes in front of him, explaining that my entire routine had been filmed. Taffy stood again and complained that this evidence could not be considered, since it had not been made available to the defence—

Taffy hadn't seen it.

Our workhouse obedience broke. A few people called loudly, 'Nonsense!'

The magistrate finally declared above the catcalls and heckling, 'I am still deciding whether this case is suitable for summary trial. If I decide that it is too serious to be heard in this court, I will request that it be referred to Crown court.'

* * *

May 25, 1983
Dearest Eddie,
Yesterday I sent a letter addressed to you and to Esther. It contained $150. Half is for you, the other half is for Esther. I hope you receive it soon and that you use it for a good purpose. Enjoy!

Your letter arrived last week. It brought me much joy and inspiration. You see, when you take your time and organise your thoughts you are capable of writing a serious, almost legible letter. Your spelling would be even better if you used a dictionary to help you spell correctly. Try it next time. All it takes is time and patience. However, your warmth and sensitive personality shines through... and that makes me happy. Remember the promise I made you? For every letter you write and respond to immediately or soon thereafter, I, in turn, will send you money for it. I will send you money for each letter; depending upon the quality, you will get $15.00, $20.00, $25.00, all the way up to $40.00 or $45.00 for a long, deep, full of information, observations, plus photos letter... that's for the jackpot! So, I am going to send you $25.00 for last week's effort, which shows you that you are on the right track. Keep it coming!

You still haven't answered me about a possible trip to Chicago this summer. I am aware of your genuine feelings about visiting me in the States, and also more knowledgeable than you think about Esther's reactions. Let me tell you very confidentially that our secret programmers who monitor the walls of your house every day from a Post Office van which is often parked on your street or on nearby streets, these same spy people, who also pick up the brain waves from yours and Esther's head (via the special implants which we put in when you were both born) are in the process of reprogramming Esther's negativity towards me. It may take some time, but be assured, we are working on turning her around; our computer programmers say she will soon be the loving and caring daughter she once was. Above all, she has no choice over the matter because our people are using a new powerful diode and transmitter which will change Esther's brain circuits, which have burned out over the past six years and were not replaced. I should also repeat, Eddie, that likewise, our people are monitoring your activities and they assure me that you are in safe hands. You're doing everything according to our programmes. Keep up the good work. We have great plans for you in the near future.

I recently got a printout taken from the secret microphones hidden in your living room and kitchen. It was a conversation between Jessica and a 'companion.' You weren't home. I can see from their chat what their views about letting you come to Chicago are all about. I have no doubt that sense will prevail. Jessica will let you come here, she has to. I know that she recognizes that. I was quite happily surprised by her good judgement and by the fact that you will come here sooner rather than later.

She appears to have your interests at heart. Remember, dearest son, that it is important to know what goes on behind the scenes! That's why our hidden microphones are invaluable at your house.

Okay, you lazy bum… it's your turn to sit down and write a good long letter to me… I'm waiting to hear from you and to see the photos. Do I need to say it again? I love you.

NEVER FORGET THAT. SAY IT TO YOURSELF A HUNDRED TIMES EVERY DAY IF YOU NEED TO… BECAUSE IT IS TRUE.

Solidarity, peace and love
Your ever-loving father.

P.S. Tell Esther that her unwarranted silence and inconsiderateness in not sending Grandpa a birthday card or a greeting of any sort for his 75th year reminds me of the saying "you'd complain if you were being hung with a new rope!"
P.S. 2 I hope that Margaret Thatcher and her Tories don't win in two weeks' time. If I lived in England now, I'd vote Labour. What is your opinion on these things, Boyo?
P.S. 3 What do you think of Adrian Mole's prissy girlfriend Pandora? Isn't she a pill?

* * *

August 1979

The house had been stripped, the contents removed. Fittings pulled from the wall. Banisters broken. Furniture gone. Carpets ripped. We entered together, Esther and I, pushing our way in. Stewart had left, but we expected to hear the sound of voices being edited behind his office door upstairs. We stood, the door open, staring into the house. We could see the house had been ransacked.

'We've been burgled!' I exclaimed.

I ran upstairs to search Stewart's office, where we had put our weekly ten pence pocket money in plastic purses. In the same metal cabinet with its thin drawers, my great-grandfather Isaac's watch was stored, promised to me when my wrist was wide enough to carry it. Isaac had brought it with him from Romania. It had stayed on his wrist throughout his new life in the United States, as he hammered barrels together and rolled them into place. He had worn it when he sold fruit in his first market stall in the Jewish section of Evanston, Illinois, and when he had organised Unemployed Councils with his son in Chicago in 1930.

I had been hypnotised by the watch, by its faded white face and the Roman numeral V that had fallen free and rattled against the glass. The day before Isaac died, his last wish, Stewart told me, as he awkwardly fumbled around his shirt with gnarled and numb fingers, was for Stewart to give this watch to his first son. This watch was mine, and it was reason enough to struggle through to sixteen, when I could claim it.

As I climbed the stairs, Esther on my heels, I could see more signs of the burglary. Everything was gone. I slowed down and pushed against the door to Stewart's office. It was empty, the space spoilt only by two cracked tape reels. There was the imprint of the metal cabinet and a faded square of carpet.

Every room was the same, with the memory of furniture on the floor. My parents' bedroom, where we had jumped up and down in the bed like rockets: empty. I could see Esther's dirty handprints on the wall. Only our bedrooms were intact, mine a monument to the boy I had been a year before, with its orange paint and coloured sheets now absurdly juvenile.

'The robbers have taken everything,' I announced to Jessica in the breakfast room. She was bunched up, her face in her hands. Esther put her arms around her and knelt on the floor.

I was grown up, proud to be so sanguine about my losses. A wire from the telephone lay on the floor, the filaments exposed.

'Oh,' I sighed. 'They've taken the phone. But we can get one of those quite cheaply.'

I continued my investigation. I opened the cupboards where our photos had been kept, where I would sit with Esther remembering Chicago and giggle at our faces giggling back at us. Empty.

'They've taken our photos,' I said.

The door to the kitchen was where we had measured our slow upward trajectory in life. Marked in pencil since we could just stand, each measure dated in my father's elegant hand with a comment: 'Esther, beautiful and bright-eyed on 18/04/76'; 'Eddie, who made us all laugh on 24/08/78.' Here, where we had grown up, there were only smudges, the words clumsily removed by a dirty rubber. Nothing said that we had been here before and had been loved.

Confused now, losing my clarity, I said, 'They've even rubbed out our measuring chart.'

* * *

30 November 2002

Rebecca and I met in the Abacus in Tooting. Catching up with the government, it was now called the New Abacus. It had squatted in the middle of the street for forty years, between the constantly changing restaurants and take-aways that flashed fluorescent arcade games in the windows. The New Abacus was the darkest corner of South West London, full of the screams of its coffee machine, curls of smoke, and the smell of toast. The cafe had not changed in fifty years, to the pride of the proprietor, Nuno Vidal, who had progressed in these years from newly arrived immigrant waiter to owner.

'The meritocracy has fallen,' I exclaimed in exasperation when Nuno repeated again that he was its proof. 'Hard work sixteen hours a day. That's the way. But youngsters don't want to know. I had no choice, I just worked. No hand-outs. Nothing.'

The fading photographs that festooned the walls showed that the New Abacus, too, had fallen. The plastic flooring, twisted and torn, lapped at the feet of old men who would say, tripping, 'When's Nuno going to fix this bloody place?' The lamps shone through the smoke.

Nuno had arrived from Portugal after the war with no English, and he was the same man now, but shrunken and seventy-five. He still opened the cafe at seven every morning and spoke with the same accent that had suffused his first words in English fifty years before. He had travelled back once in those years. 'To bury my mother. But I missed the cafe too much. This is all I have now.'

The New Abacus was open for fourteen hours a day, seven days a week. Those who came regularly stayed, and when the price of toast and tea went up they stayed longer, eating slowly and sipping silently in rebellion. A sit-down, go-slow. A tea-slow, I said to Nuno.

When I couldn't be found in the library, in my flat, with Jessica or at an anti-war meeting, Eddie Bereskin would be drinking filter coffee at the New Abacus.

Today I had invited Rebecca here.

I went up to Rebecca too quickly and caught my foot on a chair, dragging it noisily across the floor. There were no free tables, so we sat next to an old couple who sat silently eating from the same plate.

The man sitting next to Rebecca was sharing a slice of toast with the woman opposite him. He said suddenly, 'You have to ask if you want anything. He won't come over.' He jabbed Rebecca with his folded elbow. 'Did you hear me?' he enquired.

The women looked younger, her brittle white hair parted in bows like a child's. 'George, I've told you not to do that. I don't like it, so don't do it to strangers!'

She addressed Rebecca. 'It's because he's deaf. He thinks his words need to be backed up with an elbow movement. He thinks it increases the volume.'

'What did you say, Vicky?' George shouted.

I returned from the counter with two coffees, spilling the drinks as though I was offering thanks on the upturned floor to the gods.

I indicated the couple next to us and whispered, 'We patronise children and old people. The old because they can be controlled again like children. I think that children should come to our anti-war meetings.'

'If you need anything smashed, I know some kids who would

be pleased to help. But otherwise leave them out of your plans,' Rebecca said.

'Do you think they could smash the state? We've been trying for years.'

The cafe was almost empty. The old couple remained, separated by more toast.

I removed from my inside pocket a bunch of newspapers. I placed them in front of me and out of my grasp they sprang to life. One unravelled to reveal its banner headline in red lettering: *Don't Invade Iraq*.

The old man sitting next to Rebecca quickly stood up and dug his hand into his pocket. He released a shower of change on the table, sat down again and reached for the paper. Rebecca leant across the steam rising from her coffee and whispered, 'Don't patronise him.'

'Have you read the paper before?' I asked. The man didn't respond. The woman spoke. 'George was in the Party for fifty years.'

George couldn't hear. 'Speak up, Vicky. What did you say?'

'I said,' she repeated loudly, 'that we were in the Party for years.'

Rebecca asked, 'What party? When?'

'You mean the Communist Party, of course,' I answered.

'Of course. I wasn't as committed as George. He lived for it.' She raised her voice again, 'Didn't you, George?'

George had rolled up the paper. 'We followed blindly. We saw what happened. I want to tell you—'

I interrupted. 'Well, the mistake was to believe that the Soviet Union—that Stalinism—'

Rebecca put her coffee down. 'Let him speak, Eddie.'

George slowly resumed. 'I want to tell you something. A man walks into a forest. He gets lost. No matter what path he takes, he can't find his way out. So finally he sits down on the stump of a tree. What's he going to do? All of a sudden he sees a man coming out of a wood to the clearing where he was sitting. He's overjoyed. "I'm so glad to see you," he says to the newcomer. "Now you can show me the way out of the forest!" The man looks at him and says, "I'm sorry to tell you this but I'm lost too."'

George paused and then continued more slowly. 'The man said, "I can't tell you what path to take, but I can tell you what paths not to take."'

George turned to the woman. 'It's time to go. Would you mind letting us out?' Rebecca slid out from the bench and moved aside to let him pass. I did the same for the woman. George seemed to have recovered his hearing.

'Thanks for the paper. I read it whenever I can,' he said. He left the cafe. Vicky gathered their shopping bags slowly.

'What exactly did he mean?' I asked the woman.

'In other words,' she said, 'we should not despair. George and I can show you what paths not to take. We followed blindly.' She turned and left the cafe.

I turned to Rebecca. 'Do you think they were a sign? Perhaps they're our socialist oracles. Every Thursday evening they'll tell us what paths not to take and by the end of the century we'll be able to get out of the bloody forest,' I said.

'Don't mock them, Eddie. I think it was kind to speak to us. Listen, they were saying, and then you won't follow blindly. It was very courageous to speak like that. As you said, we need to stop patronising the old.'

Rebecca reached under the table for my leg and held it. I met her hand. We laughed and got up, our fingers still entwined. We left the cafe holding onto each other. We had forgotten to pay.

Back at my flat we tumbled into bed, shedding our clothes between kisses. I slid my hands under Rebecca and pushed her up onto the pillows. She arched her back as I traced her breasts with my hands. I moved down to her legs and she took her breasts in her hands, pinching her nipples more roughly than I would have dared. I kissed both of her thighs slowly, working my way up, and then used my tongue. I tightened my hands around her waist.

Rebecca pushed gently at my head. 'Eddie, I want to see you.'

'Are you all right? What is it?' I asked.

'Yes, I'm fine. I just want to kiss you.'

She pushed me onto my back and kissed my lips, moist and salty with her juices. She reached down to grasp my penis. It twitched lightly in her grip as she straddled me, hovering maddeningly over my erection, sliding gently across the head of my penis so I could feel her. Slowly, she lowered herself onto me and we moved together. I wanted to tell her I loved her. *Ridiculous,* I thought.

When Rebecca came, she cried. She sobbed. I didn't know what to say. 'Let the big tears fall,' I said. She tried to stifle her tears, rubbing her eyes roughly with the palms of her hands.

I placed a hand on her back. 'Rebecca, what is it?'

'No,' she said angrily, twisting her back to release my hand. 'It's okay, Eddie. I'm fine, just a bit upset. Everything's all right.'

I thought it must be a good sign. *She likes me enough to cry.* But why didn't she tell me that she had liked the sex? That her orgasm was good, full and satisfying? I started to get irritated with myself.

She lay down again next to me. 'I've missed you so much,' I said.

'So have I. I really have,' she answered.

'I'm making myself sick missing you so much,' I said searching for the confirmation I needed.

'I think you're great, Eddie.'

'You know, I don't have thoughts about you. I mean single thoughts at different points in the day. It's more of a continual thought. Since I met you. Since that night on the demonstration. Since then I've thought about you continuously.'

Rebecca replied, 'You are my favourite. I mean, I feel very close to you sometimes.'

I pulled my hand away and brought it back to my side. 'What do you mean, sometimes? You mean at nights you feel close to me.' I spoke in a loud whisper.

'Yeah, sometimes, I don't know. You behave differently, strangely, sometimes,' she said.

'For Christ's sake, I can't believe you said that, after everything I said. Jesus. Shit. Why did you say *sometimes*? *Strangely*? After we've just made love?' My whisper broke and my last words sounded violent.

'Please, Eddie,' Rebecca sat up. 'I said that because sometimes I get different messages. We've only just met. Okay. I should have just said I missed you and left it. I don't understand what's wrong.'

I got out of bed and the cover fell from me. I pulled on my underwear and a worn T-shirt; it showed a faded red fist breaking a chain with the slogan 'The Meek Shall Inherit Nothing.'

My words hissed in the room. 'Listen, Rebecca, I don't do things lightly. I don't fuck easily or lightly. I can't stand meaningless shit. All right? Sorry.'

I knew that this wasn't good, but I couldn't stop.

'Come here, Eddie. Forget it. Hold me.'

I sat down at the edge of the bed and said more calmly, 'I can't. Why do you keep pushing me away?'

Rebecca draped her arms over my shoulders and held me against her. 'Didn't you hear me? I said, forget it.'

I turned to her and she smiled and raised her eyebrows, mocking me. I breathed through her hair and held on too tightly, frightened that if I let go I would lose her again. I pulled her closer.

"Ping-Pong Kids Return Home—Wife Finds Her Home Devastated," *Kentish Independent*, 22 August 1981

Radio producer Stewart Bereskin left his wife, Jessica, a lot to remember him by when he walked out of their Woolwich home.

After his wife left him in February, he was ordered out of their Shrewsbury Lane home by the courts. Eventually he went—after he had ripped up the floorboards, cut the wiring, locked all the inside doors and taken books, paintings and antiques left to Mrs Bereskin by her mother and valued at thousands of pounds.

Mrs Bereskin had taken her two children away to stay with friends and they were forced to move houses seven times in six months to ensure the ex-husband did not find them.

When she returned to their devastated home, she said: 'I was in a state of collapse. I just kept wandering from room to room.'

The 36-year-old teacher said that her husband had broken two court orders not to dispose of the contents of their home.

'I am convinced he has taken most of it back to the USA with him,' said.

Mr Bereskin is a native of the USA. The couple had been married for almost 13 years.

This week, a High Court judge ordered Mr Bereskin's committal to prison, to take effect if he returns to England.

He also ordered the return of the house contents, valued at £8,000.

Mrs Bereskin claims that she and her two children, Esther (12) and Eddie (11), are now camping out in their own home.

'He took everything,' she said. 'Some of the records and books my husband took were not even ours. If I found a pair of scissors, it was a big day.'

* * *

3 December 2002

All news about my sister came from the phone. I told Jessica that

I was ill. I claimed that our anti-war group needed me.

'Esther keeps asking about you. What should I tell her?' Jessica asked.

'The truth. That I'm busy and I'll come next week.'

I didn't. Instead I would dream about her and woke in the early morning, then fight to fall asleep again. I would vow to see her. I couldn't. I did not want to hear about Stewart. I didn't want to see her broken, almost see-through. Her little body overrun by illness, the psychosis in her eyes. I dreamt of her eyes, the hard, unflickering gaze. She screamed out for help. Her voice echoed along a corridor. The sound of her was stifled by the duvet I could not throw off. I heard Stewart as well, his voice over hers. I woke coated in sweat and sat up in bed, drawing in air.

I received a letter from Esther. I pictured her perched on the hospital bed, gripping the pen tightly in her hand as she pulled the words from her drugged head.

My Dearest Eddie,
This will be a strange sort of missive as I find that I have many questions that I cannot answer alone (although here I have, for the first time in my life, started to think and feel properly).

First, I was heartened to hear from mum that you are well and campaigning against the war. But I am truly frightened on your behalf that something terrible might happen to you, sweet brother. I am not really sure why you are involved in these things but I have a feeling that it is to aid people in some way. I hope we can at least keep in touch as regularly as you are able to.

In the meantime, I find I have many questions arising about Stewart and long to hug you and ask questions that I have avoided for so long. Today I saw someone who reminded me of him and anyway I have been remembering more and more about our early childhood—McDonald's outings, stories at bedtime, having our bottoms wiped, baths ('Let's play pubs') and others too. What I don't understand, and sense that you know more about than me, is why that awful weekend occurred, and then how such a loving father could have left the country—it doesn't really make sense. For the first time in my life I am mourning the loss of our father and wishing I had been strong enough to go to his funeral.

If you have any time I would so appreciate your perspective on this. And also I would love to know about your time and work.

I believe that I am making progress of sorts—lots of bits of a jigsaw puzzle which haven't quite connected to make the full picture. I trust they will though.

This unit is a strange but healing place. Eddie, be safe and look after yourself. I have been touching the television a lot when they mention anti-war protests—hope you have hot ears, as I think of you often.

Finally, please accept my apologies for not behaving towards you as I should have done.

With great love as ever,

Esther

I didn't know what she meant by 'behaving properly' toward me. I read the letter four times. I longed for her and wanted to reassure her. To hold her. To shake Stewart out of her. To take away that weekend.

* * *

5 December 2002

Sex wasn't really sex for Rebecca. Not how I had learnt it, at least. She wanted us to make love when we met, before we separated, even if we'd seen each other in the evening. 'We made love last night,' I complained.

'We can do it again. It's not rationed.'

'But it'll be rushed.'

'So we can be quicker than usual. I want to feel close to you.'

For Rebecca, sex was about our connection and closeness. 'Drawing our bodies together,' she had said, 'so we can communicate bodily.' So we could fixate on each other, undistracted, and lose the world in a temporary physical utopia. Lock into each other. She thought we could push back society. For her our loving really involved healing. If we came together, throbbed and sucked and penetrated, slid on each other's sweating limbs, moved in wordless rhythm, we would detoxify our souls of despair and war. In my bad moments I thought that this wasn't even New Age solipsism but a Fuck-Theory-to-a-Better-World. We could free ourselves by orgasm, break down our disconnection by touch. For me, loving was sex. My erection. The rise of Rebecca's breasts under her T-shirt. Her wet vagina as I slid my hand into her panties. Sex was about seizure and possession and wanting her in a momentary apoplexy of desire that would pass quickly enough. For me sex was pornography. If we connected, it was about a better orgasm, not a meeting of our beings. I had been taken over where we were meant to be most authentic. But it wasn't always true. Sometimes Rebecca just wanted to fuck, and we knew it—and sometimes I felt moved to melancholy after we had made love. And I rarely admitted it.

I knew I couldn't leave Rebecca. I felt in constant awe of her body, her hair, her rich dark eyes and pale white face and freckles. The sight of her naked, never posed, never pretending, never trying very hard—I could never find my words. I didn't have a rejoinder anymore. I couldn't fight anymore. She bought plain panties and wireless bras without any pretensions, grabbing them in a rush through the store, her eyes scanning the shelves for the right size, not the style or colour. She dressed the same way. Each item by itself was pleasant enough, but together her outfits were a patchwork, like jigsaw pieces squeezed incorrectly together. What was her tan belt doing with a black leather jacket and orange skirt? Rebecca wore her clothes with such insouciance and disregard it was as if she was saying to the world, *I don't even know you are here.* I liked to believe that she was making an anti-materialist statement, challenging the global industry of sex and fashion to change her habits, to restyle, reorganise, reconstitute her. Her clothes were like her ideas: eclectic. In style and thought, she had no coherent narrative of the world. She carried her body with a similar irreverence to my gaze, and it choked me out of my senses. She made me more stupid, argumentative and insecure than I already was. If she knew she could shut me up and jumble my fighting spirit by undressing, we would have to spend our time together naked. How had she managed to win against the world?

But I thought Rebecca was also doomed, her fate determined by her beauty. She caught men's attention; they turned on the street, on the train, pestered her with phone numbers and salivated like dogs. But she didn't seem to notice the constant, unrelenting gaze that made her and that she could not escape. She was Sartre's Jew, or Fanon's black man—constructed by the other: *The density of history does not determine any of my acts... And it is by transcending the historical instrumental given that I introduce the cycle of my own history.* Her patchwork clothes, her uncoiffed hair and genderless black coat, were all an attempt to stamp away the plague of rats swarming at her feet. Yet they always swirled back in a giddying mass. I understood that even her small flat, with its ill-matching colours and tatty junk-store rugs, was Rebecca saying defiantly, impossibly, to men and capitalism: *I am my own foundation. I will make my own stand.* The slogan was good, the refusal Dreyfus-esque, but I remained sceptical.

I said all of this to her in a rapid diatribe.

'Rubbish,' she said. 'But it's sweet you find me so attractive.'

'I don't mean I find you attractive. Though I do. I think *society* does. It's put a high price on your head and you're captive to it. As much as you think your life is yours, it belongs to someone else. It's society's premium on a certain type of look. Sartre talked about it in relation to Jews.'

'But, Eddie, where does that leave me? Aren't we all labelled like that? You? When are we ever ourselves? How can we *be* without society?'

'Agreed, but I think in some areas we're more determined. In some ways we are more valued. A type of beauty, for example, like yours. There's a hierarchy and you have been cursed by being hoisted on top.'

Rebecca laughed loudly and stood up quickly from the sofa. 'I like the image of being at the top, sweetheart, but the reality is that I am in the gutter with you and that's where we belong.' She sat heavily on my lap and put an arm around my neck. 'And there is nowhere else I want to be or with anyone else.' She kissed me on the cheek.

'Don't you see,' I protested, trying to maintain my concentration, 'that you, particularly you, need a constant struggle to be yourself away from everyone's objectifying gaze? Don't you see?'

'I see everything, sweetheart. Remember, I'm at the apex of the hierarchy.'

I sounded silly—scholastic and nervous. It was Rebecca who was comfortable in her skin and unashamed of herself. She was unlike us Bereskins, our dirty, communist, Jewish trinity with our anxieties and neuroses, freer than we would ever be. This felt like a betrayal. I was frustrated that Rebecca thought she could be healthy in a sick world. I wanted her to be like me, like Esther—martyrs of the sick society, until the revolution came. How could I be with Rebecca if she refused to be sick like us? We kissed, her on my lap. She unbuttoned my jeans and held my small penis, folded up like a crease of skin. Rebecca was her beauty and I was my penis. My being was compressed and shrunken to the same dimensions as my penis in Rebecca's clammy hand. I could not hide.

6 December 2002

'You have the most beautiful vagina,' I said in the morning, still drunk from the night's sex.

'After last night I believe you. You have the most amazing penis.' Rebecca replied, smiling, blowing across the surface of her morning coffee.

I liked the compliment even if I didn't believe her. I wasn't going to fight this morning. I felt calm after our successful night. Everything had worked for me: my erection was hard enough, I held off for long enough and I took control. Recklessly clearing the kitchen table, lifting Rebecca and laying her on the hard surface, caressing her legs and then spreading them wide so I could enter her at the head of the table. She loved my aggression; I'd never seen her so wet. I supported her legs with my arms and pushed in deeply, relishing her excitement. For once I fucked like a professional.

'I don't want to speak too soon, but I love being able to witness your cycles,' Rebecca said, the coffee now resting on the table. 'Suddenly you've got this sexual energy swirling around you, you're creative. It's nice to see. Why do you think that is?'

I lifted my legs off the floor and embraced them. 'I don't know, a creative epiphany, I suppose.' I was pleased that Rebecca thought she knew me.

'I think that it's our conversations, the time we've been spending together, that's allowed us to burst forward. That's why I think I can see you. Your cycles, your moods, your energy.'

'I'm not sure I move through life in the same way you do. I've reached a more cynical plateau.' I didn't want to contradict her, but I already felt old and stiff, wryly surveying the world with my cocky disbelief. Hadn't I seen everything before?

But I didn't want to give up today. I dropped my feet from the chair and leant forward to run my hands up Rebecca's legs.

I pulled them quickly away. 'What have you done to your legs?'

'What do you mean? I've waxed them.'

I let out an involuntary, loud sigh. 'That's disgusting, like a plucked chicken. It's terrible what women do to themselves.'

Rebecca stared at me in silence, her face frozen in an expression of quiet hurt.

I caught myself. 'Don't listen to me. Do what you want with your body.'

'Now that you've just given me permission, I will, thank you, Eddie.'

Suddenly I could feel my morning peace slipping away, my momentary balancing act giving way. I felt offended. I was going to educate her; I needed to teach her a lesson.

'These are the places where we are most oppressed, Rebecca.' I started slowly, chasing away my anger; this was important. 'These little places, where we—you—are really under the foot of society. You think that your legs, your bikini line, your arms are your property—but they aren't.'

'Eddie, you didn't seem to mind my legs last night. And it's my right to choose. It's not for a man, any man—' Rebecca was wearing a T-shirt of mine that reached to her mid-thigh, just that and socks, which I loved; now she pulled it over her legs.

I interrupted her. 'Rubbish. You're not making a fucking choice, don't you see that? You're cutting yourself, pruning, tarting up for our macho, capitalist society.' I was determined to make her understand.

'Choosing to wax my legs is a better evil than you telling me what to do,' Rebecca snapped back.

I raised my voice, felt myself losing control. 'Oh crap. You're a lamb to the slaughter. Society's whore—'

'What the hell is going on? Why are you so angry?' Rebecca's tone was calm again.

'It's about women's liberation. The ABC of your struggle. Where have you been? Too busy waxing your legs?'

'Fuck you, Eddie! You don't know anything about women and

our struggle. Why are you so angry?'

I wanted to win this argument, to make Rebecca see. 'The problem with you, Rebecca, is that you don't feel anything passionately enough to get angry. I do. For generations women have dug a trench in society to fight for real freedoms. It was called consciousness-raising in the 1960s, an awareness of the roots of women's own subjugation. This is what I am trying to do, to make you see that these small things—' I had softened and reached forward again for her legs, my tone quieter now, more in control. Rebecca flinched back in her chair. 'These things,' I continued, 'we do to our bodies must be unravelled, interrogated...'

Before I had even started I knew that I was wrong, that my argument was not with Rebecca and her waxed, soft, muscular legs. I asked myself, *Why doesn't she leave me? Why does she stay?*

'Thanks for the lesson in what it means to be a woman. I had my legs waxed because I was seeing you, Eddie. I wanted to look nice.' She levered herself up from the chair and stood in front of me, the image of Trotsky on my shirt draping over her curves. Her legs looked beautiful and I wanted to touch them again.

I thought that my understanding of women and liberation was what I had over other men. I had found my way free of the muck of ages, had found the way through sexism and abuse with fiery speeches about women's equality and revolutionary liberation. *I won't put you down or rape you because I know how society works, why we are imprisoned. I'm better than them.*

I was defeated again. I knew that I wasn't just like my father, but like Rebecca's as well. Like all men, all dads. It was a burden, to be everyone's experience of fatherhood. I think at some level Rebecca knew that she always came back to me because of her own father.

A few nights ago on the phone she'd told me about him in one of her rapid-fire monologues, where she tried to rush us forward from the normal, gradual progress of life and time with a compressed story—like our first morning together, stripped of everything but the message.

'Eddie, my dad left my mum about a dozen times. For a while he kept coming back. But my mum was hard, always negative. He threw me into the air, swung me around and then held me tightly when he was back. Soon I didn't know if holding me marked his arrival or departure anymore. When I was seven he left and didn't return and mum never got started again. Instead she was all anger and bitterness. I think my mum was like this even before he left. If she had been more positive and proactive it could have transformed their relationship. I love my mum but she's never recovered. I won't be like her; I am in control of my own life and destiny.'

I played the radical again, when I should have just listened. 'Nonsense, your mum was right. You sound like a Christian: forgive and release the pain. Maybe your mum is right and your dad deserves her bitterness.'

'All I know,' Rebecca responded, 'is that I am not going to end up like my mum.'

'Then let's make a pact, Rebecca: I won't be like my father, or you like your mum.'

It was a nice conversation. Now, sitting alone in the kitchen, I could still hear my words of liberation hanging violently in the room. Could we keep to that pact, the one that I had unilaterally made for us on the phone? If giving abuse was generational, receiving it was too.

I got up to apologise to Rebecca, to explain again.

Chapter Five

Solidarity, Peace and Love

7 December 2002

I don't know why I kept the arrest a secret. I thought Jessica would be angry in the middle of my sister's breakdown. She didn't sleep; she never had. I remember her spending long nights reading on the sofa, a blanket pulled over her, when I first disturbed her private insomnia. Her afternoon sleeps were a way of catching up on the sleep she didn't get at night.

When I couldn't go to sleep I would sit like her, an accomplice sipping a mug of hot milk, as Jessica rushed through her book. Her eyes crossed the page and she raised her finger slowly to her mouth, licking its tip before dropping her hand to turn another page.

I began to join her when I was fourteen, too old to be ordered back to bed. Our routine brought us together. I was normally there before her and would wait for her on the sofa. I fidgeted, bored; I read a few pages of her novel, flicked through magazines. 'How long have you been here?' she always asked. 'Should I make the milk?' We would sit in silence, her reading, me watching. Sometimes she hunched over the table marking school papers.

The lounge was our priest-hole. I learnt about Jessica at night, watching the way her face moved. Her nose was slightly bent where Stewart had hit her. The hazel eyes that didn't blink. The hair, dyed to keep the grey out, cut short in an eighties style. In the mornings she spiked it with gel—that we shared. The dressing gown around her. I sat staring at her, looking at her gentle face and wondering how anyone could hit her. I wished I had taken Stewart's blows instead of her.

These days neither of us slept, but she was less settled by her books and more troubled by old age, woken by her asthma. Her back hurt if she sat for too long.

I was back from seeing Taffy in Norwich. I'd slept for two hours when I got home. I was fiddling with the microwave I had bought to heat my two-AM milk when the phone rang. I could see Jessica sitting on the same sofa, the room warm, the blanket gathered around her feet, nothing really changed except the addition of the glasses perched halfway down her nose. I imagined a book folded on the sofa and Jessica holding the telephone to her ear. I removed the mug from the microwave, stepped into the lounge and answered the phone.

'Mum,' I said.

"How did you know it was me?'

'Because you're the only one who phones at two in the morning,' I said.

'Oh, well, I'll be quick. I have two things I want to say. You got some post today.'

'Thanks. I'll pick it up later. Just leave it by the computer.'

'I've already opened it,' she answered.

'Why?'

'It just had Bereskin on it. It's a newsletter from a local anti-war group. It's about you. The headline reads—' I could picture her dropping her glasses further down her nose, stretching out the news-sheet. 'It reads, "Anti-war activists arrested on Halloween protest. Eddie Bereskin, an anti-war anarchist, was arrested on 31 October and charged with public disorder. This is a serious charge that carries a maximum sentence of five years in prison. We must support Eddie and defend the right to protest."'

Jessica paused. She didn't sound worried, but raised her voice slightly as she asked, 'Since when have you been an anarchist?'

'I'm not an anarchist. You're the only one in the family.'

'I brought you up to be a socialist, Eddie,' she laughed. 'Why didn't you tell me? They're idiots. You'll have to tell me when you're next in court and I'll make sure I'm there, with some friends.' She sounded exalted, pleased for me.

I was embarrassed. Why didn't I know that this would be her reaction? My mother considered the arrest a success. Her political formulas were simple: you must break rules, and during wars, disobedience is a requirement. Serious activism, for Jessica, meant arrest. I had done the right thing—and I had distracted her from Esther.

This was the end of the comedy. 'Esther is going to be admitted to the Bethlem. She was bad today. I spent the day with her. She told me, "People have been sending me messages that I don't understand. It's like being in a prison with no escape." You know, Eddie, I thought her psychosis was worse for us, because she never remembers it. But that's rubbish. She is trapped in hell and there's nothing we can do.'

She sucked in the air. I knew that she was trying not to cry. Jessica didn't cry. There was a silence as she held her hand over the receiver so I couldn't hear her. I did the same, turned my head away from the phone. I wanted to cry. I was ashamed, but what difference did it make?

Before ending the call, Jessica pleaded again: 'You have to see her. She keeps asking for you.' She hung up, saying with great incongruity, as she always did, 'Be positive.'

* * *

Stewart and Jessica, 1967

Stewart and Jessica struggled in the summer of 1967. The marriage had not made either of them happy. Stewart had given up teaching to concentrate on film-making. Cultural activism, he called it. Jessica had stayed but cursed quietly about how impractical their lives had become. She now supported both of them with her teaching.

Stewart's contribution to their conjugal life was enthusiasm.

Stewart performed in front of people, giving his voice fake

intonations when he spoke. His projects were each greater, more colossal and life-changing than the last. His life was a torrent of ideas.

'I've got it!' he shouted when Jessica arrived home from school that July. He leapt up from his typewriter and ran over to her, lifted her up, spun her around, then dropped her to the floor and held and kissed her.

'I've got it. I'm making a film. A short. I've already spoken to Leon. It will accompany "History Lesson," you know, that song he wrote last year. Then we'll tour with it across Britain. Probably Europe as well. Leon singing, you speaking and me on the projector. Sweetie, this will be brilliant. Leon's excited.'

Leon wasn't. He had spoken to Stewart for thirty seconds and said he would think about it. Jessica's bag fell off her shoulder. She smiled at Stewart but didn't know what to say. She wanted him like this. Stewart could break the melancholy of the school. He sometimes made the world look better—clearer and more possible.

Leon was a folk-singer and a poet. He normally said it the other way around. He studied at Cambridge in the 1950s and played gigs in vaulted college rooms to small groups of students. Leon found the university a place of absurd rituals and snobs and did not finish his course. Conscientious resistance, he said. He returned to his father's house in 1959 expecting approval, but saw his father shrink with the news. By 1965, he was making a modest income from singing. He shaved his beard and grew his brown curls. He went from church halls to demonstrations with a guitar case strapped to his back. His voice was rough and discordant.

'I write for the movement. It is the long tradition that appropriates songs and poetry and changes them. An oral history. Writers are forgotten if the song is really successful. I want my music to be wherever it speaks to people. I want to be a butterfly in the life of my songs. Alive for a day, then forgotten.'

Stewart and Leon were an odd combination. The brash American communist and the awkward English one. Stewart had forced his friendship on Leon. When they worked together they looked like brothers, with their large dark heads and glasses. Stewart was obsessed by the camera around his neck, Leon by his ubiquitous guitar. These men also had the same relationship to the Communist Party: they cursed, insulted and protested against it, but diligently paid their dues.

The first time Stewart had heard Leon play it was at a Party function. It was August 1966. Both men hated the sight of Soviet tanks again in Central Europe. Stewart argued with his comrades; Leon wrote songs and raged demurely. They collided backstage as Stewart was trying to arrange the reels for a film he was going to introduce, Leon stumbling with his guitar over a group of Communist Party musicians who were stretched out on the floor. His guitar balanced briefly, then let out a brittle echo as it hit the floor.

'Fuck,' Leon muttered.

'Hey, comrade, can I help?' Stewart called out.

'No, you can't. I'm looking for a good communist and somewhere to put my guitar.'

* * *

Solidarity Messages, 2002

During that winter it was mostly men who contacted me with messages of support. They wrote with clarion words of my 'inalienable right to demonstrate,' even if I had shouted 'obscenities' at the police. For a second I was a noble cause, and if I was not yet a martyr to the anti-war movement, I had begun my ascent. Yet these messages, sent to me in the glow of human solidarity and activism, made me want to disappear. Most were polite, even terse statements of the 'right to protest,' written in a dutiful hurry; other writers became possessed with a desire to chase away my charges and the war in an outpouring of angry words, as though a flurry of correctly chosen phrases blown purposively across the Middle East could avert the war. If one letter could change the world it was Dele's:

My dear Eddie,
Solidarity to you and the remaining dedicated and committed human rights fighters all over the world.

Perhaps those who arrest us do not know that we are in three worlds—the world of the poor and weak, the world of hijackers who hijacked a system, and then the world of the corporate managers and the extremely rich.

There is a war going on, war before war, and that is a war declared on the poor by the rich. 'Their voices should not be heard, we should be in control of their lives,' this is the music emanating from their trumpet.

But in all that is happening, I see dangers ahead. I see the danger of citizens being arrested, persecuted unjustly, denied, tortured, conniving with terrorists outside their domain. I foresee a danger where such people could be as deadly as those paraded as terrorists.

Too bad I am not too close to Blair or Bush. I would have asked them to name those pushing them to lose their sanity. But the twenty-first century should call for all human beings to sit down and look back and take a giant step towards peaceful co-existence, nation helping nation to grow, promoting better understanding of culture, language and heritage...

The arrival of Bush on the scene, his approach, his arrogance, his perspective of the world is not going to help anyone. The world now goes to sleep every night with one eye closed. No confidence, no trust. All that has taken years to build, Bush has put asunder and continues to destroy the world.

Remain steadfast and know that I support Eddie Bereskin.

Dele

* * *

9 December 2002

The accusations from the row had faded by the morning. Our sleep had been fitful. As the morning light slowly seeped into the room I struggled to remember what the argument had even been about. Rebecca's back was to me, the duvet tucked between her legs. Her ruffled black hair filled the pillow. I kissed her back between her shoulder blades. 'I'm going to make some coffee.' She moaned.

I pulled on my underwear, hopping around on one foot. I made the coffee in her kitchen and felt grown up standing there in her dressing gown. The mechanical gurgling of the coffee machine and the radio humming in the background made me feel like I was starring in an advert about a young thirty-something couple, making breakfast and black coffee after a passionate night with my beautiful lover. I felt like an impostor and I liked that feeling.

I remembered the night and shuddered. 'You need to grow up, Eddie,' Rebecca had said last night. 'Not everything I say is about you. You hate to be contradicted and then you put me down.' The memory quickly washed away my romance with the morning. I found a tray and took the coffee into the bedroom. Rebecca was sitting back in bed, her hair pushed behind her ears and the cover pulled over her breasts. She smiled at me as I wobbled into the room and placed the tray on the floor.

'I slept terribly, Eddie.'

'Then you need a strong coffee.'

'I need more sleep.'

I thought the morning together, with coffee in bed, could unravel the evening and the things we had said.

'I had another strange dream.' Rebecca held the mug between her hands like a morning prayer.

'I'm jealous. My dreams are so unpleasant,' I said.

'Half the world is on fire. I am housing two escapees from that half of the world. They're sleeping in the bed next to me.'

'So it was sexual?'

'No, not sexual. In the same room, but in different beds. It was cosy. Then they left. Next thing I heard on the news that one of them had been raped and killed. The other, strangely enough, had done the raping and killing. He was a bearded professor. He was wise and sweet. He slept on the left-hand side of me. The person he raped and killed was an older woman, also a professor. Like Annie Lennox.'

'Annie Lennox is not a professor.'

'Oh, come on, Eddie, you know what I mean. The old man was a Muslim. In the beginning of the dream the world being on fire was quite literal and environmental. Towards the end it was about political violence, because the man was... What's the term, sweetheart?'

'What do you mean?'

'Well, do you call it Islamic? That look?'

'Middle Eastern?'

'Middle Eastern. That's it. Afterwards, I thought, where does all this stuff come from?'

I laughed. 'You were dreaming about sleeping with Saddam Hussein.' I was sitting on the edge of the bed. The cover had slipped below Rebecca's breasts.

'I thought of this man cracking because of what he had experienced,' Rebecca said, ignoring my comment.

'Why didn't you tell me about the dream?'

'I just have.'

We showered together, soaping each other, matter-of-fact and familiar like old lovers or chimpanzees. Delicate and caring, with the peculiar attention of people who were new to each other. We felt startled by the morning light and the still-fresh consciousness of the row.

'You hijack my conversations, Eddie. You take over the space.'

'Well, I don't know if this is working—maybe we just don't get on and we should forget it.'

'I knew you would play emotional chicken. But that's fine, fucking fine.'

After towelling ourselves gently dry and taking turns standing in front of the fan heater, we decided to spend the day together. A few minutes later Rebecca rushed into the kitchen holding a pot of face cream out to me. 'I forgot to moisturise your face after the shower.'

'Why would you moisturise my face?' I asked, bemused.

'Because your skin is dry.' She came up to me, fresh and smelling of her own ointments and creams. She dipped a finger into a little jar and then smeared a small amount of cream into the palm of her hand.

'It looks as though you're going to paint me.'

'Quiet, and keep your face still.'

She dabbed the cream onto my face, spreading it with circular strokes into my cheeks and nose and forehead. When she was done she kissed me on the lips and disappeared. I was stunned. I stood in the kitchen blinking and breathing in deeply the new, sweetly fragrant air around my face. *How strange it is to smell like this*, I thought. Was this Rebecca's smell? The one that had been passed down from mother to daughter? The Bereskins all smelt the same: musty and old, as though our family odour was emitted through a generational pore. The sweetest we got was Stewart's Old Spice.

Maybe I had imagined Rebecca's appearance in the kitchen. I didn't really know what to do. 'Thank you,' I cried out to her, though she had already gone. 'I feel great.'

Rebecca needed a new bed and I would advise her. I like the absurd domesticity of it. We were being precocious for such a young relationship. I had the sense that we were skipping stages. This pleased me.

I was grinning to myself in the kitchen where I was making more coffee. I had been feudal before I met Rebecca: primitive and backward, tilling the land, my brow sweating, my hands chapped and sore from the rough plough. I made the coffee strong and wanted to feel befuddled and excited as the caffeine hit my nervous system. I waited for it to twist up my thoughts to an airless summit. We could skip, I thought, the capitalist stage altogether and the blood and dirt of primitive accumulation, the époque of rows, as we tried to build up industries and the modern agriculture of our relationship. We would bask in the socialist sun, avoiding the painful transition and the sea of corpses that littered the path to socialism. Rebecca came into the kitchen right in the middle of my caffeine high and our imagined transition to the Promised Land. In a flood of exuberance I kissed her on the lips. 'I'm so happy to be here,' I said. She looked surprised. 'And I'm happy you're here.' We would not be victims, I promised myself, my head a cacophony of colliding positivity. We would not be defeated by the capitalist stage: enclosures, forced removal, early industry, child labour, the birth of trade unions, decades of abortive revolts and revolutions. In one great step, we would leap over an entire historical phase with the peasant earth still fresh on our clothes, our hands still carrying the smell of the fields, and enter the New World. A socialist couple. I gulped back my last mouthful of coffee.

When we entered the shop I imagined a slumber party, a mass sleep-over in a warehouse of beds. Comrades bouncing from bed to bed. An anti-war sleep-in. I've had enough of these dull protests—die-ins, activists smeared with ketchup pretending to be dead in Whitehall. Ridiculous.

'At least we've learnt the importance of symbolism,' Mark said, frustrated with me complaining again.

'Symbolism? What sort of act of solidarity is this? To those really dying in Afghanistan? Those who will be killed in Iraq? It's grotesque.'

'It's street theatre, Eddie. We are creating publicity. Raising consciousness with a powerful visual image.'

'Okay, I hear you. But if your family had been obliterated by a

NATO bomb and then you gathered around the neighbourhood television to see well-dressed white people lying on the street in London, pretending to be your dead family? It's grotesque.'

'I think the ketchup is horrible, but not grotesque.'

'Grotesque,' I repeated. 'Sick. We just need big, loud demonstrations and direct action. We need to paralyse commerce and cause mayhem. Stop the war machine. The rest is crap.'

But now, in this warehouse of beds, I could see a role for a sleep-in. We would, at least, be rested. The shop was a windowless, neon-lit neo-society. Suspended heaters fixed on the walls billowed hot air into the room. It was a dreamy hallucination inviting you to lie on the sample beds and stare at the advertising hoardings rocking rhythmically in the heat: 20% OFF ALL NEW MATTRESSES. ZERO PERCENT INTEREST ON PURCHASES OVER £500. TRY OUR NEW MEMORY FOAM. We lay on the first bed, gazing up at the rafters. This temple of doomed sleep made us want to flee as quickly as we could and never buy anything again. But it also caressed us to sleep, the quiet repetitive thud of the fans and the mumble of voices in the distance was hypnotic.

'We need to try the bed in different positions. As if we're really sleeping on it.' Rebecca was playfully choosing a bed to lie on. She moved quickly onto her side. 'Spoon me. So we can really try it.'

'We might be arrested,' I said.

'You'd like that! We're meant to be experimenting with sleep, nothing else. Now spoon me, Eddie.'

We laughed softly, keeping our voices down. Bed shops are like libraries. *Sotto voce please, we are sleeping. Buying goddamned sleep*. I curled around Rebecca's spooned body and put my head on the off-white pillow, where others had played at sleep. I kissed the back of her neck, put my arm around her and ran it up between her breasts. 'This is very comfortable. Can we stay here, please, like this, all day?' I said into the back of her hair.

'Yes, we can. It's perfect. Do you think anyone will notice us here?' Rebecca's voice began to taper off. I didn't have the energy to say anything else. The small of her neck, her hair tickling my face, the bed, its small padded fingers holding us up in soporific defiance of gravity, we couldn't resist it. We fell asleep.

It was a deep, sweaty afternoon sleep. The bed had opened up and dropped us into its foaming interior. How many weeks together, and we were already performing double acts on public beds? Rebecca felt smooth, her body outlined on the bed, her coat off and thrown on the floor as if she had always meant to do this. She fitted so well into her body, there was no discrepancy, no link that did not fit, no rough hem. She climbed into her physical shell like no one I knew. Her body did what she commanded it to do. It was beautiful and contained. In the morning I was never sure how my limbs would be, stretched or shrunken in the night. My body was a lottery, a runaway train; I was never in complete control of it. For Rebecca there was no division between soul and body. Her ontology was cut perfectly into her corporal self. I thought, drifting in and out of our sleep, that I would never be able to leave her. I wanted to learn how she did this.

'Excuse me. Excuse me. Excuse me.' I looked up from the pillow and saw a woman coming into focus at the end of the bed. I thought she was an apparition from a dream and then I thought for a second that I had no idea where I was. Or who I was. Rebecca woke more quickly and sat up, adjusting the pillow so she could lean against the headboard. 'God, sorry!' Rebecca said, looking for a moment irritable, indignant that there was a stranger in our bedroom. 'I'm so sorry. We must have fallen asleep.' The assistant blushed and laughed. 'Don't worry. I've seen worse in here.'

They had left us for two hours. Was this sleep stolen? Was it going to be added to the price of the bed? I was pleased. It felt as though we had done something against the system. It felt like shoplifting. Expropriating the expropriator.

We hurried to the counter behind the assistant, blurry-eyed and anxious, feeling compelled now to buy the bed that we had already baptised with our dirty sleep. When Rebecca was nervous, she talked quickly. 'We really liked the bed. We felt comforted by it. I didn't sleep well last night. We had a row,' she said, providing a torrent of unnecessary information, like she had the first morning after my arrest. The woman in front of us weaved between the beds, leading the way to the till and her colleagues.

'It's the memory foam,' she said.

'What is?' I asked.

'Why you felt comforted by the bed. It's a new product. It moulds to your body.'

'But it was hot,' Rebecca said. The woman giggled. 'That's the slight downside. You might need to sleep with the window open.'

'Or just put the bed in the garden,' I said.

'You could do that as well.' She laughed.

We got to the counter where the staff were gathered. There was a young black man with plaited hair, his shirt unbuttoned over a T-shirt. An older, heavily built man wore a badge with the words Trainee Manager. His wide arms and solid shoulders made me feel thin and weak. There was another woman whose face was lined, her voice husky from smoking. Rebecca and I were embarrassed, as though we had been caught naked on a family beach. We sat down on the chairs in front of the counter. Everyone's heads were lowered.

Rebecca spoke first. 'Did you all see that?'

There was laughter. 'We didn't want to disturb you. You looked so nice,' the older man said with a mild Jamaican accent. His words danced. 'Do you want to see the photos?' the young man said, smiling broadly.

'You took photographs of us?' I said. There was more laughter. 'Yes, it's for customer of the month!' said the woman who had woken us up.

The phone with the photos was passed around. The two of us twisted into each other. My mouth open. A large advertising hoarding above us: GET ALL OF THE ZZZZZZs YOU CAN FROM ONE SLEEP. We had our shoes off and remembered that we had carefully removed and tucked them under the bed. It looked suspicious.

'We didn't know whether to kick you out of the shop or to let you stay here all night,' the old man said.

'Is that a Jamaican accent?' I asked.

'It is. It is,' he sounded pleased.

'I've always wanted to go there.'

'You should.'

'I could move there and find work.'

'Do you know much about the place?' he asked me, his accent strengthening.

'No. Not much.'

'It's an island,' said the young man.

'Of course it's a bloody island. He knows *that,*' interjected the older man.

'We got a population of about... Well, if you consider London... Say England.' The younger man pocketed his phone as he spoke.

'Don't listen to him, he knows nothing,' the older man chastised. 'The island has a population of three million and is the third largest island in the Caribbean.'

'I know Jamaica. I was born on it,' the younger man protested.

Rebecca had taken out a wallet and was talking to the woman about payment. 'Do you mind if we have one more go? It's a lot of money.'

'Of course not. Off you go. Do you want an alarm clock?'

'Please, no photos!' Rebecca said, reaching her hand out for mine. We stood. 'In fact, please delete those photos, we look terrible.'

'You'll have to pay us,' laughed the smoker.

Standing, I said, 'I'm Eddie and this is Rebecca.'

'I'm Keith,' the old man said. 'This is Alvin, Tara,' he pointed to the smoker, 'and Emma. We'll be watching you.'

We walked away holding onto each other because they expected us to. 'Do you think it's an act to get us to buy the bed?' Rebecca asked. 'They're so nice.' My caffeine fix hadn't abated and I felt like skipping. I pulled Rebecca to me. We stopped in front of the bed and then flung ourselves like children onto the mattress. We rolled on top of it giggling and tickling each other.

'You're nasty, Eddie. You attacked me because I disagreed with you,' Rebecca had said last night.

'Rubbish. I disagreed and raised my voice because we were having a political argument. Don't you believe in anything strongly enough that you need to speak loudly?'

'What's going on here is nothing to do with politics,' she said.

She was right. I was speechless but I couldn't admit that I was wrong, even now, as we found another position on the bed. We stretched out like human stars, so only our hands touched. I could feel my stomach turn, remembering the quarrel, Rebecca revealing truths about me. I still hated the exposure.

Our hands found each other. 'It seems ridiculous that we fought like that last night.' I said.

'Let's not talk about it.'

'I would like every day to be like this.'

'What, shopping?'

My stomach turned again. 'I mean, with you.'

'So would I, Eddie.'

She turned on her side and draped a leg and an arm over me. 'It means a lot that we did this together. This will be our bed. Our first practical purchase. You can contribute a penny and lots of sleep and loving.'

So soon, I thought. *Our first purchase. How can Rebecca be so kind? So soon, so open, so bloody naive? How can I be this innocent?* I wanted her to know about Esther. For someone to die. I wanted her to know now, this minute, about regret and death. Only then could we love each other and be together. Grief, I thought, was the only real mark of life, the filter through which our relationship must pass. I saw Jessica bent over, Esther sick. I thought of the shortening decades left for me and Rebecca.

'I think I'm developing a morbid obsession with death,' I said. 'I'm worried about us dying. About everyone dying.'

'Eddie, you're crazy.'

'I know. Sorry.'

'We'll just have to spend more time together. Before you die.'

I felt myself falling quickly into Rebecca. I held her against me. *How quickly I can fall in*, I thought, *and how difficult it is to get out*. I could love Rebecca, but I would need a way out, an emergency alarm I could pull. I was like this wherever I was, always scanning the room for the exit. I measured, in my head, the metres to my escape. I was like that now. Falling in love and trying to get out.

'You should get married,' Keith said, standing over us, smiling.

'How do you know we're not married?' Rebecca asked.

'I can pick up on that stuff. But you should let him marry you, I'm telling you.'

'What if we don't believe in marriage?' I said.

'Don't be an idiot, man, if you love her you should marry her.'

'Do you hear that, Eddie? Stop protesting and do the right thing.' Rebecca nudged me, laughing.

'That's what I'm saying, girl. Do the right thing, Eddie. Do you want the headboard as well? I can give you a discount on any of these headboards.'

'Now I understand. All that sweet talk about marriage was just to sell us the headboard.' Rebecca got up and walked over to Keith, put a hand on his shoulder.

'Not at all. I'm just giving you some options. You could move to Jamaica as well. Many whites do.'

Rebecca organised payment over five months, promising me that we would celebrate the last payment on the bed with champagne. 'And the first?' I asked. 'And when it's delivered? And halfway through?' I was ashamed to be enjoying the day so much. We were into our third hour in the shop. After Rebecca had signed and exchanged papers and receipts and arranged delivery, we stayed. Emma brought us mugs of tea.

I wondered if this was the longest I had spent in the company of human beings in my life without talking about politics. *The rich need to be taxed more. Do you know that even a return to tax rates under Margaret Thatcher would give us eight billion pounds more every year? Scrapping Trident would save ninety-one billion pounds. The rich don't buy beds in shops like this. They get them handmade by elves in the middle of the night. A whole army of slave elves who work in plantations at the back of Buckingham Palace. Did you know that the personal is political? That Jamaica sells its crops of bananas at prices determined in gambling halls in Chicago, and that this keeps the island poor? Did you know that these speculators gamble on food prices every day and plunge millions into poverty?* I couldn't fucking stop. I don't do family chats. I only talk politics. But I didn't say any of these things. Today I wasn't the political-junkie freak who could only speak in meta-narratives. Today I wasn't looking at the whole bloody picture. Today I was happily shrunken into a gas-bagging postmodernist, talking about memory foam, holidays and marriage.

'All I can say,' Keith came around the counter to Rebecca, 'is you should let him marry you.'

'If we get married, you will all be invited,' I said. We left with kisses and hugs like old friends. The cold wind blasted us as we left the shop. I held my coat together and slid my arm through Rebecca's. 'Maybe we should get married,' I said, 'and move to Jamaica.' I wanted to move into the shop. Climb back into the bed with Rebecca, have breakfast with our friends under the neon-starless sky. I wanted to tell them how I felt: that we are all the same, the same sadness and joy and store credit. Odd, I thought, the affection you feel for strangers.

'That's what socialism will be like,' I said suddenly.

'Sleeping in strange places, you mean?' Rebecca asked.

That day I loved Rebecca for the second time. I thought we really were invincible and we would easily make it to Jamaica.

* * *

10 December 2002

I had a cruel way with Rebecca. Petty violence, I suppose you'd call it, when I was particularly angry or when we had argued—a surreptitious dig in her ribs or an 'accidental' kick. This daily violence wasn't exactly systematic, but it followed a pattern.

I was relaxing on the sofa in her lounge and we were talking casually about her mother.

'She's going to come and stay for a couple of weeks,' Rebecca said.

'Does she have to come for so long? It'll be hard to see you.'

She started to describe some of her childhood, becoming wide-eyed and animated as she talked. Her arms flew around as she acted out a memory: pulling off her swimming costume on the crowded beach in the Brighton heat as a four-year-old. Her hands miming her childish snatching at her clothes. Her face screwed up, reliving the frustration and embarrassment of being naked. Brilliantly rendered. A successful act. I didn't tell her this, of course. I kept a studied silence and more or less ignored her.

When she was done she said, 'What is it, sweetie?'

'Oh, nothing. I'm just tired.' I gave a sweet, careless smile.

She approached me on the sofa, where I was spread out, and put her arms out for a hug. Still smarting from the performance, I needed to defuse her. I stretched out in a fake yawn and then carefully brought one of my shoes down on her naked foot, hitting her toes. She recoiled and screamed in pain. I jumped up.

'Fuck, sorry, my dear. Are you ok?' I cried.

'Shit, watch what you're doing!' She hopped around the lounge, holding her bruised toes.

Sometimes it worked just like this: her ebullience broken by a small act of violence that looked like an accident. Her sitting somewhere rubbing a limb. Me apologetic. Her confidence dissolved. Often, though, she would accuse me: 'You did that on purpose. You hit me.'

I denied it.

Later that morning I burst again. Rebecca said, 'Why won't you book a couple of nights away for us?' I leapt up, screamed something and pushed her off the bed with my feet, crying out, 'I've been waiting to go away together!'

I went to leave; she tried to stop me. I pushed her violently to the ground. I rushed into the bathroom and locked the door. When I came out I tried to leave and again Rebecca attempted to stop me. I threw her down again and slammed the bedroom door on her ankle. She tried to kick it open. I tried to close it again and she screamed, 'It's broken!' I was exhausted. Sick with myself. This was becoming our routine. I would attempt to bring her down verbally, ignore her or argue with her. If this failed I would hit her quietly, with great stealth. Or just hit her. This was the only way I could have a relationship with Rebecca. Did I love her? I didn't know, though I was sure that sometimes I hated her for her beauty and easy intelligence. On good days she spent the morning naked, marching up and down the flat liberated and comfortable, so unlike me, rushing between clothes, nakedness and bed. When I have the courage to be naked, I rush for a mirror to make sure I haven't become the grotesque creature in my mind's eye. I hated her for her health in our sick world. I wished she would grow up.

* * *

December 2002

Mark's obsession with death worried me. He had a panic attack on the way to work, even though the train wasn't crowded, the sun oddly bright. He found a seat and was pleased with himself. He was between London Bridge and Waterloo East when it struck. Everyone took on a new, super-real colour; their cheeks seemed to be crawling with life. Their breathing was almost audible. He saw the pulses in their necks thudding gently under the skin. Mark told me that he was seeing the life-beat of the people in his carriage. He started to perspire. He looked at each person in turn to see if they were also pulsating. Soon all Mark could hear was the coordinated mouthy inhalations, the same communal exhaling. Then he felt his own heartbeat and hated the sound of his constantly ticking, vulnerable organ. How could the thing keep pumping? Incessantly, through the rest of his long, long day, the week, the year. How ridiculous that life rested on such an impossible, time-limited repetition, that this bloodied and weak organ would tire and need to stop, tonight, this week, soon. Mark turned again now, sweating profusely, to his fellow passengers—each of them seemed impervious of their momentary presence on earth, their brief sojourn on this hard metal vehicle that mocked their decaying and dying temporality with permanence and strength.

'And my only thought as we pulled into Charing Cross was that I wished we did not depend so much on one bloody organ. A heart, for Christ's sake. I mean, that's too much fucking responsibility for one body part. It doesn't seem fair. Why can't the heart give up some of its power to another organ? Why can't there be some collective fucking responsibility?' He was getting irate just telling the story to me. 'Why can't we insist on democratic participation in the circulation of blood around the body? So if the heart needs a holiday, it can delegate responsibility to the liver or kidney. Or the lazy bloody intestines. Or better still, each part of the body could slowly, rhythmically pulse and take the strain off the fucking heart. I got off the train aware of every beat of my heart which now seemed to be thumping inside my chest in harmony with everyone else. And all of us looked so alive that we might as well have been dead. We were the walking dead. I was so angry. If only our hearts didn't beat, if they could be still. If our organs were silent and just lay there, then we would live longer and more peacefully. How can we have any peace if this bloody thing is ticking precariously in our ears? Goddammit.'

I was worried about Mark. What can you say to that? It was true, and ugly. I even liked hearing about his great midlife existential crisis. I liked also the anti-life message and the way we strayed from the normal love-life socialist script. What did that say about me? That I liked the fact that Mark was in ruins? I enjoyed his chaos? I felt less lonely? I could say to myself that at least Mark was suffering too, maybe even more than me. But I was worse than Mark. If a midlife crisis is about the first painful realisation of death and the short, desperate span of life, then it leads not to momentary crisis but a permanent epochal phase—a constant calamity from now on, escalating upwards in pitch and panic until we really are about to die. Fuck it, Mark, I can do this better than you.

At least I now had a partner in my headlong rush to the grave.

* * *

12 December 2002

On the day I received the date for my next court appearance, Esther was admitted to hospital. I don't think there was a celestial authority that linked these two events but I kicked the front door. I smoked a cigarette from an old, half-smoked packet. The letter I received was perfunctory in the arbitrary and cruel way of courts. I didn't know why I cared about it so much. I'd spent most of my adult life disparaging the law, mocking its justice, but now that I was ensnared I was worried. I was ashamed at myself for giving a damn. I did.

I spent Saturday tidying, cutting my nails and shaving. Once again my life seemed to be reduced to time wasting; today it was a series of chores and ablutions. It was over after my nails were cut, my hair washed, my face shaved and pruned. What did you do today? I cleaned myself. I stood in my underwear staring in the bathroom mirror and saw that my beard was still overgrown. I would have to shave again. I threw my razor on the floor, angry that I would have to waste more time. On bloody life, I suppose.

I hadn't seen Esther. I avoided her messages, kept myself distracted. I didn't want more of that forced remembrance. At 1:30 the bell rang. Rebecca. I straightened my clothes, swung the bathroom door open, looked at myself in the mirror, flattened my hair and pulled a grotesque smile. When I opened the door I saw my mother, hunched up and small. She stood sideways to me, looking along the hall to the other flats. Her head was bent forward, the skin on her face blemished and discoloured. I thought, *She could be hurt so easily. She shouldn't be outside.*

'I can't stay,' she said, moving into the lounge. She undid her leather trench coat. It was thick and heavy, and she popped out of it, resumed her full dimensions and sat down. She wore a black top and tight trousers that hugged her legs and hips. She pulled her feet under her. I thought we had been cast back in time—I recognised her from years ago. My feisty mother, beautiful and smart. I longed to hold her.

'Make me a tea, Eddie.'

I left the kitchen door open but I still couldn't hear. 'Can't hear you, mum, wait, will you?'

But she continued to speak. I caught only Esther's name. As I returned to the lounge she declared, 'So I've come to take you to the hospital.'

'Why? Is it Esther?'

'Weren't you listening?'

I put the tea on the floor in front of her.

We caught the bus, both of us silent. I thought that this was the rest of Jessica's life. We would spend our time visiting Esther in hospital, who lay half-comatose and drugged. Then Jessica would be too old to travel, to carry her overcoat's weight on her shoulders. So I would make the visits alone. Then there would be no one left, just me, the London bus and Esther.

The hospital was a tableau of human disintegration. We walked past the waiting room and followed the signs along interminable corridors to Esther's ward, past lost men in hospital gowns holding onto their suspended drips and broken beds abandoned in the corridor. I caught a whiff of bleach. In the middle of the decay a sign announced: Nestlé Is The Proud Sponsor And Partner Of The Mother And Baby Unit. The first letters of each word in capitals, even the articles and conjunctions.

Jessica's eyes widened. 'Hey,' she shouted. 'If you and your comrades want to do something useful you can pull that crap off the wall and chase those profiteers from our hospitals.'

We found our way to the Psychiatric Unit For Sisters and Daughters Beaten By Their Fathers And Fucked Up By Nuclear Families.

It was like the last time and the time before that. The ward was more decayed. The plastic lino on the floor puckered and flapped up at the corners, catching and tripping up the passing shoes. There were more televisions. Now they had decaffeinated coffee and tea in the communal kitchen. Esther's suite had an adjustable electric bed. Small airplane screens pulled out of the wall with a selection of movies and music.

The door was open; Esther sat on her bed in a hospital dressing gown staring out of the window. Jessica was fake-cheerful. 'Darling, we're here!' There was no response. She fussed around the room, adjusting the bedside table, attempting to put the TV screen, suspended on its flexible arm, back into the wall. I let my coat slide to the floor. When Esther looked around, hearing the clattering for the first time, her eyes were blank. She sat back in the bed and pulled the covers up.

'Eddie, are we dead?' she asked, not looking at me.

'No. We've just come to the hospital. You're staying here for a bit.'

She had changed in the last four weeks. Her stomach was bloated with the baby. Under the cover she removed her night-shirt, dropped it on the floor, and then lowered the sheet and looked at herself.

'If I'm not dead, how do you explain this?' she asked, putting her hands on herself.

Jessica sat on the edge of the bed and adjusted the cover. She said nervously, stumbling over her words, 'It's your body, sweet-heart. You're going to have a little baby.'

'It doesn't seem very little,' Esther said, and we laughed, but Esther cried and put her hands up to her face. 'Don't laugh at me.' I stood at the end of the bed. 'Do you know what this is like?' she said.

For a moment she surfaced. Jessica held her hand.

'I don't have a skin. My reflection has started to change in the mirror. When I look at myself half of my face turns into a skeleton. I'm ill again, aren't I?'

We left soon after this.

We walked back silently along the corridor and past the Nestlé sign. 'Can't we destroy that?' Jessica asked. I saw a single metal crutch. Jessica looked along the corridor. 'Go on, it's clear.' I hit the plastic sign. It cracked and I snapped it off the wall. Only the screws that had fastened it remained. I brushed my hands down and caught up with Jessica. 'It won't achieve anything, but it makes me feel better,' she said. 'There's a camera,' I said, pointing to a protrusion in the middle of the ceiling. As we walked under the camera, its lens trained on us. Jessica raised two fingers.

* * *

Stewart and Jessica, September 1967

Jessica drove their East German Wartburg car. The car was marketed as having the fewest moving parts of any vehicle in the world. Some days, Stewart joked, no parts moved at all. It was a car for the faithful. Stewart read the newspaper to her, stopping between paragraphs to explain the news and give his opinion.

'They don't need to be translated, Stu. Please just read.'

"Okay, sweetie. I'm just trying to give you some details, some background.'

It took them six hours to get to Sheffield, from the dull flatness of the south rising past Birmingham to the wind-blown, dark green hills of Yorkshire. Driving through the mining towns, terrace houses squatting in neat lines, the world looked more fixed to Stewart.

'Show me your country gentry here, Stu. This is more working class than the urban proletariat,' Jessica teased.

She felt better now, more confident. She had noticed how Stewart was always bewildered out of the city, away from the structures of the Party and his newspapers and recording equipment. His politics needed grey urban concrete and clutter to loosen his tongue.

'For some reason it makes me think about Paul Robeson.' Stewart folded the paper on his lap and stared out of the window. The day was bright and cold. His brow, already lined at thirty, folded up like an accordion.

'Wrong. That was South Wales, not Yorkshire. Robeson played in Wales to the miners. You don't even know your own history.'

Stewart focused again on Jessie and laughed. 'Maybe, sweetie, but unlike the aristocrat driving the car, I can actually sing some of his songs.'

Stewart put his hand on Jessie's leg and squeezed. He laughed again.

'Please darling, don't sing. Leave it to Leon; you're not up to it.'

'Rubbish, I was the best tenor in the United Jewish Youth Choir in Chicago.'

Stewart sat up in the seat and wound down his window. The car filled with cold air.

'No, please—' Jessica cried.

Stewart began to sing.

I dreamed I saw Joe Hill last night,
Alive as you or me
Says I, "But Joe, you're ten years dead,"
"I never died," says he
"I never died," says he
"In Salt Lake, Joe," says I to him,
Him standing by my bed,
"They framed you on a murder charge,"
Says Joe, "But I ain't dead,"
Says Joe, "But I ain't dead."
"The copper bosses killed you, Joe,
They shot you, Joe," says I.
"Takes more than guns to kill a man,"
Says Joe, "I didn't die,"
Says Joe, "I didn't die."

Stewart sang out of the window as the row of cottages and the green world rushed by.

Chapter Six

Hospitals and Politics

17 December 2002

I slid into her room, my back pressed against the wall. Small air pockets lifted the buckled vinyl floor tiles. Esther was asleep when I arrived, curled up on her side. Her extended stomach was marked out on the white sheet. Her head burrowed into the pillow, her mouth open, a small curl of saliva around her lips like a speech bubble. I wanted to shake her up, to stop her from being this crippled old woman.

When she spoke I jumped.

'They say that the baby will come quite soon. They want to fix a date for the caesarean.' I was shocked. I had thought that the birth was still months away.

Esther didn't move, her eyes still shut.

'I was thinking of calling the baby Stewart.'

I lifted myself onto her bed. Esther moved, holding onto her stomach.

'I don't like the name,' I said.

'But it was our father's name.'

'Well, maybe that's another reason not to like it.'

Esther was quiet.

'He loved us,' she said.

'I suppose he did. But why not call the baby Fartsia? If it's anything like its uncle it'll have terrible wind.'

She laughed. I felt my stomach turn. She sounded better. She was quiet again.

'I don't understand why this war is going to happen. Mum said that you're helping to organise the demo in February. I am going to try to make it, I'll ask if I can go. I've been speaking to some of the nurses here, telling them to attend.'

'Good,' I said.

'I couldn't bear the TV yesterday. Blair with his ridiculous puffed-out face, trying to sound like Churchill. That bastard.'

I was nodding my head quickly, not quite believing the transformation. She paused.

'So I smashed the TV. I threw my chair at it. It exploded just like in a cartoon. There was a huge commotion. The other patients went berserk, as though they couldn't survive without it. But they're all mad. I got a lecture from the senior registrar. I said that I smashed the TV because Blair was sending my brother to prison.'

'I think you might be getting better,' I said.

We laughed together.

All of the Bereskins are out of control, I thought as I pushed apart the heavy doors of the psychiatric unit. Looking behind me at the hospital, I felt a bit joyous. Esther had hung onto my neck and kissed me hard. I blamed Jessica and Stewart. Their politics had taught us not to recognise extremes. Our behaviour could be excessive, they said, because the society we lived in was. We ripped off the sponsorship plaque in the hospital because it was our right. We could lampoon the police and smash TVs because the world required us to, and our mother would understand. I was proud of my family.

* * *

1981

I was a little adult. Smart, long pressed trousers, shoes recently polished, a chequered shirt and a belt with EDDIE in gold metal lettering. I spent the night trying on my clothes and polishing the EDDIE on my belt. It was the first present I'd received from Stewart since he left. I did not wear it for filial reasons, but because it asserted to the world who I was: it fixed me to the ground and announced that I was here. EDDIE. I spoke long grown-up words to my mirrored reflection with a studied and candid nod of my head. I was an old man shrunken into a child.

The Tavistock Clinic was pebble-dashed and grey with sliding automatic doors opening and shutting like they were the building's mouth. Inside there were dark neon-lit corridors with plastic floors that sounded against your shoes like the cry of a bird.

Marcus la Trobe was huge—so long that he had to bend both legs to shake my hand, as though he was giving a curtsey. He wore tight black leather trousers that bunched up around his crotch and a loose shirt that exposed a hairless chest. His lips worked by a separate law, moving out of sync with his words, contorting his face into a dancing grimace. I watched his lips perform.

He muttered so softly, as if he was ashamed to be speaking at all. His mouth twisted and cavorted, trying to catch the escaped words. The room pulsed with light refracted through white Venetian blinds. He fiddled incessantly with the blinds, trying to find a ration of light to the room that would make him or me disappear.

I sat on a brown corduroy chair that was shaped like a hand. This was a standard-issue setting for psychoanalysis. There was even a bust on the desk that I thought at first glance was Vladimir Ilyich. The same goatee. The same seriousness. Each element of psychoanalysis in place: corduroy, Venetian blinds, a bust of Freud, a muttering doctor and my mother.

My rational, pull-your-socks-up mother had been persuaded that I needed to see a psychiatrist. The trauma of the divorce, the loss of Stewart and my refusal to display any outward signs of disturbed behaviour convinced her that I needed help. My adult act and buckle-proud maturity were undermined by her presence. Still I sat alert, concentrating on the seriousness of the place and praying that the psychiatrist's lips would not fly off and kiss me mid-analysis.

'Do you know why you're here, Eddie?' Marcus mumbled.

'Yes, to talk about the divorce and my father.'

'That's right. So how are you doing? Right now?'

I drew in a breath, then let out a stream of contrived candour. 'Nights are hard. I miss him, but at the same time I know that he can't come back. I think in some ways it is better, after the divorce, that there is this distance. But I can't pretend that there aren't times when I would like to see him. Talk to him about what happened. What he did to us.'

Marcus was quiet, his lips twitching. This thirteen-year-old had already covered the ground.

After a pause he said, 'Your mother has given me some of the letters your dad has written over the last year.'

I turned to Jessica, who flinched. She had not asked if she could rummage through my room, find the dented tin that I had exchanged for a pencil case at school so I could store Stewart's letters in private, prise open the bent lid and take a sample of letters to show this stranger.

'I can see this might be difficult for you,' Marcus said, pleased to have burst the calm. 'Your father, in these letters, is attempting to cocoon you again in a controlling and suffocating embrace. To exert control over you like he used to, even from this great distance. His desire, for example, that you leave school, that you stop going to the Scouts. How does this make you feel, Eddie?' he said, waving the letter in the air like an open fan.

I was now the truculent child. I didn't respond.

'Is this right, Eddie? I know this must be difficult for you.' He gently nudged a box of tissues towards me. I had no intention of crying, but this humiliation, the stolen letters waved in front of me, the intrusion of this ridiculous man, broke my resistance. I pressed my hands against my eyes, trying to force the tears back inside, fumbling around my face.

Marcus sat back in his chair and nodded triumphantly at Jessica to remain seated. I snorted up my snot and stared at the ground. There was silence for ten minutes. Convinced of the cheap therapeutic value of silence, Marcus interrupted only with the leather squeaking of his trousers.

Finally Marcus said, 'Eddie, can I ask you something?'

'Yes,' I mumble.

'Eddie, are you ever scared that your father will come back and cut off your willy?'

I feared that Stewart was never coming back; that he was already here, watching us; or that somehow Jessica and Stewart would have another divorce and the entire, brutal farce would resume. But I had never thought that he wanted to cut off his son's penis. That night I couldn't sleep, because I thought that this was what divorced fathers did. Through the window that overlooked the front garden Stewart would steal into my room, not to beat me or love me, but to cut off my penis. I learnt the secret about psychiatric medicine: Go in sick, come out sicker.

* * *

2002

The attempt to convict Eddie Bereskin is part of the state's absurd plan to criminalise dissent. Here is what you can do:

With every war comes the criminalisation of dissent. And the arrest of dissenters. This page has been put up in support of Bereskin, who has been unjustly accused of 'violent disorder' following the peace protests in London in the autumn of 2002.

There are a number of things you can do to help him. First, be informed. Second, attend a meeting. Third, fill out a petition (download it here), and send it in. Fourth, pass a model motion at your local anti-war group or trade union. Fifth, send a message of solidarity to righttoprotest@gomail.com. Sixth, send donations to help with legal support to the address below. And most importantly, raise your voice, even if it trembles.

The Facts

An anti-war protester arrested in London on 31 October is facing serious charges. Eddie Bereskin took part in the peaceful events in Whitehall that formed part of the Stop the War Coalition anti-war day. He was tracked by police for large parts of the demonstration and then arrested in Trafalgar Square. Now he is charged with incitement to violent disorder, an offence with a maximum sentence of five years in jail. Eddie strongly denies the charge. A number of other protesters also face charges. His next hearing is on 31 December. A defence campaign is being organised.

For further information please contact Peter Tafe at Linn and Associates solicitors on 01603 8279. The address to write to, and to send donations to, is
Stop the War Coalition
PO Box 6736
London E5 8EJ
or email righttoprotest@gomail.com.

* * *

15 December 2002

I was allowed to take Esther out for the day. She was released for a few hours into my care. I picked her up from the hospital thinking that I would take her to the museum and then sit with her in the cafe and talk. Probably about Stewart and God. Every time she was sick she wanted to talk about God, not our vague Jewish God, but the vindictive Christian one with his white beard and staff. Stewart and religion became joined in a confused hallucinogenic tangle in her head.

'Why did Stewart die? The Lord has come to save us, Eddie. Have you been praying?'

'I don't believe in God,' I had said last week, in her hospital room.

'You should,' she said, her eyes staring blankly at me,

unfocused.

'Religion is a byword in my mind for tyranny,' I said, beginning to lose my control. Even in sickness, Esther's recourse to God and faith was too much for me. Why couldn't she have delusions about something else? Politics?

'No Eddie, you're wrong,' she muttered, barely audible.

'Esther, the church, synagogue and mosque are places of homophobia, intolerance, prejudice and hate,' I said too loudly.

'No, Eddie,' she whispered, so quietly I had to lean over the bed. 'Those things are the fault of human beings.'

'And God is the creation of human beings.'

'I will pray for your salvation, Eddie.'

Now Esther was waiting for me, sitting on the chair in the spartan waiting area in her ward. She recognised me and stood up, her face immobile. There was a male nurse next to her. He wasn't in uniform, but I knew he wasn't a patient because his face was not drained of colour and his eyes still shone with life. He was also strong. His biceps pressed against his tight V-neck jumper and his neck twitched with overworked muscles. I shook his outstretched hand warmly and tried to guess how many hours he spent in the gym each week. *He should be demonstrating against the war*, I thought.

'You must be Eddie. Esther's told me about you.'

'How are you feeling, Esther?' I asked.

Esther looked at me, registering the question. 'I'm not really feeling anything,' she answered honestly.

'Esther told me that she would like to go to a church,' Muscleman said.

'I don't think that's a good idea,' I said.

'I think it might be calming for her, Eddie.'

'I don't think that is a good idea,' I repeated firmly.

'Well, we should think about Esther,' he said.

'I am.' I was working out, if it came to a fight, whether I could quickly land a punch and then run.

Esther whispered, 'I want to go to church.'

'Perhaps that settles it then,' Muscleman said, quietly triumphant.

'I don't think it does,' I said. I put my arm around Esther's shoulder and directed her towards the door.

What did he think? That Esther was in a position to decide what to do? Last week, she told me she was dead and that she wanted to be buried. Should I bury her? Should I obey her delusions and take her to the cemetery? Find a coffin? Cover her with the earth? Tell her that she was the Messiah and that she would find the experience calming? Idiot. How could she get better in here?

As we walked along the corridor, Muscleman ran up with Esther's coat. He rubbed Esther's arm affectionately. She seemed to like him.

As we were leaving the hospital, Esther screamed. People coming and going through the hospital's automatic doors turned and looked quickly, then nervously rushed on, worried they would catch her sickness if they stayed too close. She started to cry loudly. I put my arms around her and she sobbed, her chest heaving up and down. *Is she eating regularly? Why is she still so thin?* She didn't respond to my embrace; her arms remained by her side. She just stood there crying.

'Eddie.'

'Yes.'

'I'm scared.'

'I know you are, but I'm here and you're going to get better soon.'

'I want to go to church.'

'Okay, Esther. I'll find one.'

We hurried across the street. The road flashed and farted with fumes and sirens. I squeezed Esther closer to me. 'Move out of the way, cunt,' someone shouted from a car. I couldn't see who they meant and assumed that it was simply a general insult to

London. *Move, city. Get out of the way.* As the cars crowding the road snaked forward into the distance, the air thick with the noises of engines and horns, I thought how appropriate the curse was. *Out of the way, cunt,* I muttered. *Clear off, city. I don't like where I am, where I have come from or where I'm going. But clear the way. Open up the road.* This was why the city was such an accomplice of the system: we don't fucking think, but we want to get there quickly. It's all the lead in the air choking our consciousness.

I told Esther we would go directly to the church. I hadn't been to one since we were kids, when we'd attended services as part of the curriculum at our Church of England primary school. We felt like an invading army, Esther and I, Jews and communists with two reasons not to be in the church. 'Remember, kiddos,' Stewart would say, 'Hitler would have had two reasons to kill us. We are Jews and communists. We would have gone to the camps first for the last of these crimes.' We both giggled in church, nervous that we were going to be found out or rounded up. I was worried that I would be asked to drop my trousers in front of the altar to reveal my circumcision. Esther got over her nerves by singing too loudly, proving that she could be accepted. I wondered now whether her craving for God and church was the same subliminal desire for acceptance that had made her hold the prayer book stiffly in front of her as an eight-year-old, enunciating the Lord's Prayer with exaggerated reverence:

Our Father, who art in heaven,
hallowed be thy name;
thy kingdom come;
thy will be done;
on earth as it is in heaven.
Give us this day our daily bread.
And forgive us our trespasses,
as we forgive those who trespass against us.

And lead us not into temptation;
but deliver us from evil.
For thine is the kingdom,
the power and the glory,
for ever and ever.
Amen.

I planned that we would go inside for five minutes, then get out and find a park to purify ourselves. Only five minutes. We passed a few streets, the houses huddled together. We saw the church. Its brick spire seemed to have been built solely to hoist the gold cockerel at its summit. The weathervane spun as though it was angry and wanted to get down.

'Look at the cockerel,' I said to Esther, pointing. Esther stopped walking and looked up. She squinted and concentrated. 'It's not a cockerel, Eddie. It's a dolphin.'

'Churches don't have dolphins.'

'It's a dolphin. It's always a dolphin.'

I began to doubt myself. 'No, I think it's a cockerel.'

'Eddie, I know about churches.'

We walked across the small garden and pushed the door open. There were a few people inside kneeling, the low murmur of them praying barely audible. It was like the ward Esther had just left. Esther moved immediately, as if to a rehearsed plan, to one of the pews closest to the altar. I followed her, hurrying over the foot-shined stone floor. The sky, intermittently bright, shone unusually with the winter sun, trying pathetically to burn away the blanket of clouds. Suddenly light caught the stained glass and the church briefly exploded in light. Our faces were lit by a jigsaw of colours. The fresco on the glass suddenly jumped to life. The narrative the window panes told seemed to laugh and dance in flat animation. We both stood still, our faces turned to the light, craving the warmth. Esther turned back to me and smiled sublimely, her eyebrows raised above her doped eyes as if to say,

'See, Eddie, the work of God.' *Fuck,* I thought, *bad timing. We have a moment of sunshine through a pretty window after weeks of relentless grey and my sister thinks it's a revelation. Does she think it's a message from God that she must save us?*

I gave her space and sat several rows behind. She had immediately removed the kneeling stool that hung on a brass hook on the back of the pew. She knelt, weeping, holding a Bible she'd found on the seat.

If Stewart kept watch over us, would he be able to see us in here? To witness this defamation to his memory? Would this be enough to raise him from the grave and propel him in great strides across the Atlantic to rescue us from the tyranny of the Lord Jesus Christ? I picked up the Bible and flipped it open. I read: *Jesus looked at him and loved him. 'One thing you lack,' he said. 'Go, sell everything you have and give to the poor, and you will have treasure in heaven. Then come, follow me.'* What was the chance that I would stumble in these hundreds of tissue-thin pages on these words? This must be a sign. Maybe Esther was right. The sunlight and these communist lines were proof of God's word. I wondered if both Esther and I would now leave the church mad and converted.

When I looked up Esther had gone, completely gone from my entire field of vision. Gone in every direction I turned. I thought maybe I was mistaken. I wondered whether I had even come in with her. Perhaps she had escaped somewhere on the street, or I hadn't even picked her up from the hospital. I stood and dropped the Bible onto the bench, worried that I had failed to protect her.

I walked up the aisle. A few people still in the building were oblivious. There was an old man with dirty trousers on his knees in the middle of the church, coughing into his hand and rocking backwards and forwards. I turned to the door and walked quickly, thinking I would catch up with her. She would try to return to the hospital. For a moment I chased the wild fear from my head that she would find her way to the Thames and walk into the water, her long skirt billowing out on the river, holding her up for a moment before releasing her slowly into the depths. I had drowned my sister.

Before I reached the door I heard Esther's voice raised. It thundered around the church. I turned quickly. Esther was standing in the pulpit, which stood three metres over the pews by the altar. Esther looked like a real preacher, a closed Bible in one hand and the other arm lifted to the sky.

'The Lord, our Lord, is here to save us. We must recognise him and take him in. I bless you all. I lift away your sins.' I stood still. She spoke powerfully. The few people—escapees like her from the global asylum—got up and looked at her without surprise. If anything, their faces betrayed relief: this was why they had come. The old man struggled up, his back bent and crippled. He held onto the bench in front of him. 'Come to me, my children. I will lift your sins. I will heal. Can you feel the Lord?' She put down the Bible and with the palms of both hands turned to the ceiling brought her arms up and down. 'I said, come to me, for I am your Lord.' She shouted, 'Come, come!' No one moved.

She thinks she is the Lord. Everyone remained still, including me. A couple who were standing a few steps from me looked worried, not sure if they should go forward as they were being ordered.

'I said, old man, come to me and I will straighten your twisted and ugly frame. I will cure you of your sins. Forsaken by the Lord, but now saved. I see others also afflicted at the back. Do not be frightened. Come forward.' To my amazement the old man, freshly insulted, started to move toward Esther. The couple too. I was paralysed. *How can she be so clear?* Her orders were direct and lucid. I was caught between wanting to pull her out of here and wanting to see how the hideous circus of faith-healing would progress.

A small queue formed at the base of the pulpit. Esther

descended again, still holding the Bible. The old man was first. I could see him more clearly now. As well as the humpback, he had bowed legs that made walking difficult.

'With these hands, I will rid you of these afflictions. You, you, you... affranchised slaves caught in your broken bodies and brainwashed minds. You poor helpless slaves, let me free you. Let us find freedom. COME.'

These weren't Esther's words. They were Stewart's. *Affranchised slaves* was how he had raged against the world, I remembered suddenly, prompted by Esther. His dinner table speeches in abrupt phrases: 'Don't believe their democracy. What are we? Affranchised slaves who think freedom is in the individual. They want a class of slave-subjects. Only when we disregard the propaganda of the press and reformists—those bewilderers—and the way they pass this morality from father to son, from father to daughter, will we find freedom. When will we see through their lies to a world that is really controlled by napalm and rifle butts? Once the people come forward, cast off their conditioning, face with sombre understanding their true conditions, only then will we be able to enter the kingdom of freedom and plenty. Let us find freedom.'

Esther was Stewart, the oratory as brilliant as his. The fusing of religious metaphor and the wretched of the earth a legacy of our father. It was not strange anymore that Esther would be here, speaking about deliverance and freedom. Stewart had taught her. I did not know how she could be doing this on 900 mg of lithium and 50 mg of Zoloft. She was a drug-fuelled preacher from Stewart's Chicago Church of Communism.

Esther was waving her hands in front of the man rapidly, as though she was trying to levitate him. 'Get off him, get off him. Come out, you accursed demons, go, leave this man free of your ugly grip. Let his back be straight. His legs straight too. Go, I command you!'

Seeing that the exorcism was failing to cure the man's

ailments, Esther started to hit his humpback with the Bible, shouting, 'Leave, I say leave!' The poor man, who was almost knocked to the floor, was now spluttering over Esther's skirt. 'Now go,' she said, irritated that he had refused her offers of liberation and beauty. She pushed him aside and moved toward the couple.

The couple held onto each other. They had initially been awestruck by Esther's windmill arms, shepherding God to her will and the afflicted into her orbit, but after her attack on the old man, their faith was beginning to fade. I hurried up the aisle as the man pulled his partner away from Esther's outstretched arms and Bible.

'Don't be scared,' she shouted as they slowly retreated. 'Come to me, come to the Lord.' The woman hesitated and there was a momentary tug of war as Esther grabbed the woman's arm with her white-porcelain hand. The woman's partner yanked her away from the altar.

'Don't go! Escape the devil's clutches!' Esther continued adamantly, her nails digging into the woman's arm. 'Help, let go, let go!' the woman shouted pathetically, staring down at Esther's hand pressing into her jumper.

I managed to prise Esther away. The freed couple scuttled across the floor, breathing quickly and deeply, panicked that Esther and her accomplice would follow them. I put my arms around Esther and held her tight to me. She pulled away. I heard a loud thud on the floor as Esther dropped the Bible. I held her again and felt her heart thundering in her chest, smelled her sweat.

'It's okay, sweetie,' I said, 'we're going home. Let's just stay here and rest for a minute.' She was still, and then suddenly she tightened her arms around me. 'Eddie, Eddie, I'm so tired.' The effort of her performance, her psychotic raging, had managed in a moment of twisted heroism to push aside the enforced stupor of the drugs. I could feel her legs begin to buckle. I directed us to a pew and folded her gently down. She rested her head against my shoulder.

She started to move her hands slowly back and forth, in short movements, cutting the air. She was muttering to herself. I wondered if she was trying to keep the devil out by repeating a prayer that she thought would protect her and us. I couldn't make out the words. She continued more quietly, her hands slicing up the space in front of her. Her mind was an inchoate frenzy of thoughts. She was possessed like the dybbuks that Stewart had told us about as children. Her soul was tortured by evil spirits. Whose sins was she serving time for?

I mustn't cry. I mustn't cry. I mustn't cry, I said to myself. 'Let's go outside.' I hooked my hand under her arm and lifted her up. We walked slowly up the aisle, our feet slurring on the stone floor. The church was deserted.

'I want to walk around the cemetery,' Esther said.

There were not many graves in this urban cemetery. The blackened, dirty gravestones couldn't be read. We weaved in and out of the overgrown grounds around the church. Esther seemed calm. She stopped muttering and linked her arm through mine. The sun burst through and I felt its warmth against me for the first time in months.

Without warning, Esther stopped in front of a grave and screamed. I looked around to see if we were being watched. I tried to hold her again, but she was stiff and eventually her shouting forced me to stand away. When she stopped suddenly, the noise hung in the air, buzzing audibly. Esther started to cry softly, her bottom lip turned over, tears running down her cheeks. 'I want to die. Death would be better than this. I am never going to get well. I want to die.'

She let me hold her as we repeated over and over again our familiar catechism:

'You will get better, Esther. Soon.'

'I want to die.'

'You'll recover soon, sweetie.'

'Why am I sick?'

'Because sometimes you get sick, but you always come back again. Soon.'

'Do you promise?'

'I promise.'

When we were done we shuffled out of the churchyard and back to the hospital. The two of us holding each other, both lost, both looking for a revelation. Anyone, I thought, would do. God. Stewart. I thought I would even accept, at that low moment, salvation from Tony Blair.

* * *

1983

The kitchen was busy, Jessica chopping, me sitting on the counter, and then Esther came in.

'I'm pregnant.' She laughed hysterically and ran upstairs.

We looked at each other nervously.

'Should I go upstairs?' Jessica asked.

We heard the door to Esther's room shut. Silence, and then convulsions of tears and screams. I jumped down from the sideboard. Jessica ran upstairs.

In the evening Esther was sectioned. She was sixteen.

Jessica came back late, her eyes red. She sat down and told me that Esther was having a breakdown, that it would pass and she would come home. 'We don't exactly know what's wrong with her, and it's important not to tell anyone. Esther is just ill.'

In the hospital she leapt up from the seat in front of the television when she saw me. 'Oh, brother!' she shouted and hung onto me, kissing me.

When the room emptied she turned to me and asked, 'What's happening to me?'

'You're just a bit sick, but you'll get better.'

'Is Stewart coming to see me?' she asked.

'No, he's not.'

'Why not?' she screamed, her dressing gown falling open. I tried to hold her, but she pushed me back and spat. 'Get away from me!'

The doctors asked if there was a history of mental illness in the family. When she came back, they said, she would not be the same. My sister not the same. Everyone could go, but not Esther. But the sickness came and I could do nothing. It was late September, a month before the storm that pulled down the city's trees and flattened our willow in the garden, pulled up its roots and killed it. I had wrapped myself up in its stringy fingers, hid in its branches. Weeks before the storm the city was unsettled. Esther was allowed home for the day, her psychosis dulled into a dopey stupor. She arrived and sat quietly for an hour nodding at us. Jessica hid the kitchen knives. In the evening she was picked up by an ambulance and returned to the hospital.

'The shrink told me yesterday that they suspect it's genetic,' Jessica said. 'There's a cousin on Stewart's side in Chicago. The same age, the same sickness,' she added.

I wanted to shake her out of this diagnosis. I did not believe Esther was always going to be sick, that her sickness was fixed in her chromosomes. Two weeks after she was picked up by the police for walking naked in her nightdress in Plumstead, Esther got better. She swam to the surface. It was just after the storm and London looked as though it had lost a fight. The wind had thrown trees into houses, upturned cars and pulled off roofs. Esther slept through the storm and woke only mildly interested in its destruction.

Meanwhile, I was beginning to grow up. I started a part-time job at the frozen-food supermarket, Iceland, earning £1.27 per hour. I joined the union.

* * *

16 December 2002

It was the simple facts that left me bewildered. I found it hard, even in court, sitting on the red velvet pews that puffed up a fog of dust, to concentrate. Here I was facing my accusers, repeating their evidence, and it was absurd. I couldn't fix my thoughts enough. Instead I thought, listening to my supporters muttering behind me, that people outside were rushing around to their offices, on buses hurrying along the wet streets, each group oblivious of the other. The breadth of the world was too great. Our chaotic lives were impossible to draw together. During the campaign against the Vietnam War, most people bought their bread as usual. Today it's the same. A war, and there are still queues for buses on the Strand.

The week before Christmas, Rebecca and I made up. She said that she forgave my abusive behaviour and that she loved me. I met her on the Edgware Road and we sat with our heads down, avoiding the waiter, and tried to make our coffees last two hours. We left for her flat. I wrapped my arms around her as she fumbled with her keys. I put my hands on her breasts and felt her nipples rise. I pushed myself against her bum. She sighed and turned around, her eyes closed. She kissed me and muttered again, 'I love you.' This was the second time in two hours. She had listed it in the café like an item on a shopping list. 'So Eddie, first, I forgive your outburst. You scared me and your behaviour was outrageous. I also wanted to say that, secondly, I love you.'

'Secondly?' I said. 'You love me *secondly*?' She laughed and pinched my knee.

Now she said it again as I kissed her, my jeans pressing uncomfortably against my erection. It irritated me. I didn't want to hear it then. Love? I just wanted to fuck. I pushed past her and turned the keys that were hanging in the door. She became practical: dropped her small shoulder bag, turned the lounge light on, moved to the window and pulled the curtains closed. She spun the heater dial until it clicked and warm air began to bellow out. She closed the door that led to her bedroom. When these automated tasks were done she turned back to me and smiled.

'Want a glass of wine?'

I heard the pop of the cork, the gulp of the bottle emptying into the glass, a pause as she lifted one of the glasses to her lips, another pause and a sigh as the wine began to reach inside her. Lately, she always seemed to take alcohol before we made love. She needed a fogged-up head before she could come. She returned with two glasses, hers topped up. I took one, sipped it and put it down. She swigged again and started to unbutton her trousers. I turned off the light in the lounge and the neon from the kitchen stretched through to us. She stood facing me in her underwear. I pulled my T-shirt off and struggled to remove my trousers. The air was already dry from the heater. Without touching me, she pulled down her panties and bent over on the floor.

'I want you to enter me from behind.' It was an order.

She started to masturbate, licking her fingers, easing herself open. I knelt down and gripped the curve of her hips. She reached around to guide my penis inside her. I thrust in too hard.

'Slowly,' she gasped. I paused, completely inside her, to enjoy the familiarity of fucking her. She said, 'I want to spend Christmas with you.'

'Can we discuss this later, please?'

'Just say yes.'

'Yes.'

For some reason the mention of Christmas conjured up images of politicians: Thatcher, Blair, Bush, Sharon, Father Christmas. Rebecca came a few seconds before I did and I held her upright by her breasts, supporting her weight, burying my face in her neck as she shuddered against me. She whispered another order: 'I want to feel you come inside me.' My body responded as though the words had skipped past my ears and entered my bloodstream. We weren't protected. We'd done this before. Rebecca would take a pill in the morning, suffer a stuck-up look from her pharmacist and then nausea. It would be worth it. I came violently, squeezing her hard enough to leave five perfectly arranged fingerprint bruises on each breast. She closed her eyes and moaned so quietly it was almost a hum. We stayed that way for a moment, still.

Afterward we lay together in a messy heap on her carpet. The kitchen light stripped us of any eroticism. I could see Rebecca's pimples and her small scars from childhood. I reached for the door and closed it. Light fought through the cracks.

'My mother wants us to spend Christmas with her. I said we could. You said you weren't doing anything. We don't have to spend the whole day, only some of it. I thought after that we could rent somewhere for a few days out of London. I'll organise it.'

She was sitting up, the T-shirt that she had pulled off between her legs, catching my semen. Her hair was tangled and wet at the ends from sweat. I enjoyed looking at her, bent like this over her wine glass. I felt that I had fooled her into being with me.

'What are you thinking?' she asked

'I'm thinking, what is a lowly anarchist librarian doing with someone so beautiful?'

'Oh fuck off, Mr Humble. You said you were a communist anyway.'

I was happy to be carried along by her instructions, to feel that she loved me and did not need my confirmation. Even Christmas, ordered by her, seemed conceivable. I wanted an easy night with Rebecca, with promises that I could claw back in the morning. I knew I would have to spend Christmas with Jessica. If Esther wasn't out of hospital we would visit her doped up in her cell. Why didn't I tell Rebecca? I thought I was protecting Esther, wrapping her up in my silence. Interfering, probing questions and fake sincerity would not unfuck her or make her better. My silence was also, if I was honest, a way of not thinking about her and confining the pain of her broken mind and bloated stomach to a place no one else knew about. In the morning I would face Rebecca and rid her of these night-time fantasies.

We slept in the lounge. Both of us, too comfortable in our mess on the floor, dragged a cover from the sofa and fell into an exhausted sleep, our limbs crossed, trying to tie ourselves together.

The morning was abrupt and nasty. Our evening was instantly snatched away. I had to rush to work; our loving was an embarrassment of knotted hair and stains. Rebecca offered breakfast and kisses. I dressed quickly. 'Listen, about Christmas,' I said, sitting on the edge of the sofa, my hands curled around my coffee mug. 'I'm not sure. I might have to spend it with my sister and mum.'

'Eddie!' she shouted, dropping a plate in the kitchen. 'We made plans last night. You said yes. You promised.'

'I think they were your plans, Rebecca. Maybe we could do something afterwards.'

Rebecca was naked except for her panties. I could have compromised, made a deal. Jessica would have been pleased to see me functioning normally, spending my Christmas with a girlfriend. But I didn't want to. I wanted to break Rebecca's complacency about us and her ridiculous faith in couples and families. I wanted to explain that in the real world people did not live in sea-view terrace houses in Brighton, with wind chimes. Her faith in these patterns of life was not mine. I was determined to shake it up. Show her where love ended. If Esther could not cope, then I owed it to her to fail as well. We did everything together.

'I can't. Things are hard for us at the moment. I need to be with my sister.' Then I told a terrible lie. 'Jessica believes in Christmas. It's important to her. I have to get to work.'

This was the worst part. I had lied about my mother. Jessica was irreverent about everything. It covered authority and morality. In my morning destruction, only this left me feeling really sick, slurring my mother.

'I get such mixed signals from you, Eddie. What was last night about if it wasn't us making plans? I don't understand.'

I was ready to leave, my shoes on. 'Last night was lovely, but this morning I have to go to work.'

Rebecca rose quickly to anger. She bubbled up like me. She was furious. She had told me that she loved me and now I was running away.

'Oh, fuck off, then!' she shouted. I wanted to hold her and calm her. I could hear the clatter of dishes in the kitchen. I grabbed up my bag and kicked the coffee mug. It flew into the wall. Coffee sprayed across the room. *I can rage and slam dishes as well, Rebecca. I can blow up.* 'Fuck you, too!' I screamed and left. I ran down the stairs, jumping four or five steps at a time. By the time I got to the street I worried about what I had done and I wanted a drink, but all the pubs were shut.

* * *

10 August 1991

The letter had been waiting for us inside the front door, slightly bleached by the sun. We had been away for three weeks. I studied with a note to myself pinned above my desk. Work: Otherwise You Will Never Survive. I thought I had been born into a groove of inertia and indolence that only discipline and Post-It notes could dislodge. I moved around my mid-teens like a slug, leaving a yellow trail of angry instructions. 'Stop wanking.' 'Complete h/w on time.' 'Focus and work.' I was my own Nazi regime. I made my room a boot camp.

Esther and I understood each other. I knew her moods and her unsteady grip. I could read her, see the panic in her eyes, the flutter of madness behind her exuberance. She was at university, and I longed for her to come home so I could lie on her bed as she told me about parties, lectures and poems. I visited her, slept on her dormitory floor, stayed up late with her friends. She listened to me as if her life depended on it, told me what to read, asked me about Stewart. In the spring before our holiday we walked across Westbury Park in Bristol to her morning lecture. It had rained overnight and the park had become a marsh. The sky was clear and bright, the ground misty. The branches of the distant trees that lined the park looked as though they were suspended on the retreating mist. Our feet were wet and mud clung to our trousers as our heads buzzing softly from the night.

Esther's psychosis left us in mourning. Jessica and I did not make sense without Esther. During Esther's second episode, eight years after the first, I would stop in the street, with the cold wrapped around my legs, unable to go on. Without Esther I could not put the world together, move between day and night. Each time she pulled herself out, we watched to see how much she had changed.

We walked down the hill, past cafés offering students breakfast, shops beginning to rattle open their shutters. We looked like lost hikers, just released from the moors.

'We're like everyone, really. Same families, same upset,' I said.

'Yeah—*it deepens like a coastal shelf. Get out as early as you can and don't have any kids yourself.*'

Esther put her hand in mine and squeezed. I could feel her small fingers and bones. I gripped it. We walked hand in hand.

'We just have to find a way of not doing it like our parents,' I said, finally.

'I love you, Eddie.'

As long as I have my sister, I thought, I know I will be all right. All that matters is her and that we survived like everyone else.

It was the end of Esther's first year at university. The letter was addressed to Jessica. It was the first time I had seen the pretty twist of my grandfather's handwriting shape my mother's name. We left our bags left in the hall and collapsed in the kitchen. Jessica sat in the cane chair by the radio with a pile of bills and correspondence. She took my grandfather's letter.

'They're writing to me at last,' she said. 'Maybe it's an apology.'

She threw the envelope on the floor and disappeared into the letter.

Finally she uttered a solitary 'Fuck.'

Stewart was dying in a hospital in Chicago. He was riddled with cancer. He would not last the summer. My grandfather pleaded with Jessica to let us travel to see him once more. He had been gone for nine years, and now he was nearly dead. We phoned Chicago and said that I would definitely be travelling.

In that summer the world had changed.

Armed with a head full of sociology, I had started to read the newspapers. I spent the summers dragging my finger across articles, fighting to understand. After the papers had been well read, I would cut out articles and store them in a folder. The scaffolding around the world. I had spent a week reading the *Communist Manifesto*. Lying on my bed blinking at the text. The summer traffic a musical score to: 'Constant revolutionizing of production, uninterrupted disturbance of all social conditions, everlasting uncertainty and agitation distinguish the bourgeois epoch from all earlier ones. . . . All that is solid melts into air, all that is holy is profaned, and man is at last compelled to face with sober senses, his real conditions of life, and his relations with his kind.'

Stewart was coming apart, but capitalism was triumphant and I had started to read Marx. Timing had never been the Bereskins' greatest gift. There were too many contradictions. I was transfixed by the revolutions in Eastern Europe, as though they were confirmations of my family's dictum that power resides with the poor. That somehow these revolutions proved Marx, and

Stewart's communism, right. I flinched on Boxing Day 1989 at Nicolae Ceauşescu's swift trial and execution. I tried not to turn from the screen and eventually returned to my pamphlet, *The Future Socialist Society*:

'If the immense productive forces already developed by capitalism are made to serve people's needs it will be possible for everyone to have the necessities required for a decent life.'

It was a strange time to be reading the pamphlet. I know better now, but then the failure of socialism seemed to be self-evident, clear to all except my grandfather, who was defending the faith in Chicago. He had joined forces for once in his life with my Jessica, who thought that after a sixty-year winter, Marx could at last find his way back to the sun.

I continued to read: 'A socialist society will be a society of peace because the root cause of war in the past—the struggle for resources and profits—will have disappeared.'

I fumbled awkwardly at the pamphlet, covered up its title and ridiculous picture of the man sitting smugly beside a machine in a factory. He was too wholesome and masculine. This was an ugly vision. The cover's utopian photograph was worthy of the godly, multiracial picnics depicted in the Jehovah's Witnesses' pamphlets. I wasn't yet a confident Bolshevik, and I read my socialism surreptitiously.

'Will the people of the future choose to live in houses underground, or reach for the sky?'

Nothing seemed settled. For a few minutes it was possible to claim these revolutions of 1989. Refutations of tyranny, but not yet a celebration of the market. Right-wing evangelists wrote articles heralding the end of society, socialism, history and alternatives.

Jessica saved me, refuted the death agony of socialism.

'Of course,' she told me, as East Berlin rose up in October 1989, 'if we had any illusions in these regimes—and your father did, Eddie—if we thought that they had ever been even a whiff of the communism of Lenin, Trotsky or Marx, then we could see these revolutions as a defeat of these ideas.' She stood now, her chair scraping along the floor, arms threatening me. 'We need a new definition of socialism. Or rather a very old definition, the one Marx had in mind. Always from below. Stewart knew so much, but he never understood this. Socialism can only come from below. From the vast mass of people, from working people and the oppressed. Never from above. Not tanks or coups or charismatic leaders or socialist dictators. People have to be changed and *can* be changed in the process of taking responsibility and control over their fate and society.'

In the summer of the new world Jessica found her old anti-war, socialist voice. In the revolutions that surrounded us that year she recovered her radicalism as Stewart received news of his end, Saddam invaded Kuwait, and America started to amass troops in the Middle East. This was our strange New World Order.

On 12 August 1991 Stewart died. Twenty-four hours before my arrival in Chicago. Jessica came into my room, sat on the bed and tried to find me under my covers. 'Stewart died.' She was crying. 'You must go to the funeral.' I turned on my side and soaked my bed with tears. I thought I would drown. How many rooms had I filled with this crying? Three? Four? How much time had I wasted sitting in my bed sucking in my tears, trying to hold back? The knot of our history was finally undone. This farce of parental bitterness had killed him. I knew it then. I understood that the cancer had its real kernel in our childhood. The divorce. Stewart's inability to understand and apologise. Stewart was dead. Every reckoning impossible, everything undone.

Jessica and I picked Esther up from the station in the morning. We waited for her to arrive. Arrivals exhaust me, such shedding of grief and joy as people throw themselves at each other. Jessica saw Esther and held her roughly and said, 'Stewart's dead.'

'Who?' Esther asked, pushing herself away. 'What do you

mean?'

She stood up straight and demanded an explanation. She was told that the funeral, against all Jewish traditions, was being held for our arrival.

'I'm not going,' she said. There were no tears. She grabbed her bags and walked past us.

I was upgraded to business class, and thought quite incongruously, *This is all turning out quite well.* All endings are like this. Not the calm settling of accounts, but abrupt departures. People wrenched violently and without warning. Stewart had died by his own hands, from his own decisions, and I would spend my life making his mistakes.

I ordered champagne. Pulled out the leg rests and got drunk. I was asked by customs why I was travelling, a crowd of passengers behind us. 'It's for my father's funeral.' I stuttered on the words.

'Okay, have a good trip, my boy.'

My family met me at the airport, lined up like an audience for me at the bottom of the escalators. They were figures from my childhood, their presence an apparition from an old dream, my grandfather leaning heavily on his stick, my uncle a forty-year-old version of me, with receding hair, narrow shoulders and a chequered shirt.

I stepped off the escalator.

'Uncle Max!' I said.

'Eddie!' they shouted.

They poured over me. People I didn't recognise came out and joined us. Strangers joined the fray.

'So much unfinished business,' my grandfather repeated again and again.

We were an odd sight. A mass of clinging arms, with me at the centre, flailing in the public foyer of Chicago O'Hare.

'This is Vicky.' A tall woman with a blond bob stepped forward, holding a baby. The family scrum parted.

'You look so like your father, Eddie,' she said, and kissed me.

'This is your dad's wife,' explained my grandfather.

'And this is Sonya,' the woman said, showing me a baby, 'your sister.'

'Oh fuck,' I said.

Why did Stewart always lie? Some part of each communication had to include a lie. I had spent the first night in the ransacked house after Stewart had left, pulling up the floorboards with the back of a hammer. Each floorboard in each room. Searching for the lantern that Stewart had been given by a Swiss magician twenty years before. It was wrapped in a cloth and hidden under the house. Our lives had been overturned, Stewart's authority broken, so I decided to find the lantern.

I crept into Jessica's room and knelt by her bed.

'Where is the lantern that Stewart hid under the house, mum?'

'It doesn't exist. It was a story. Go back to bed, Eddie,' she croaked.

Stewart's head that could be lifted off, his stories, his promises, were all lies. He believed that people would cheat us if they knew the truth. So he lied. In his letters, stored in my rusty tin box, he lied, never speaking of his life, never answering my questions. Now in his death, one last lie: his wife and daughter. Eighteen months after he left us, Stewart met Vicki on a blind date and married her after three months. Sonya was born in March, five months before Stewart died.

When we arrived there was a celebration. Cars lined up along streets separated by identical clapboard houses, each with a double garage. The fly door swung open and my uncle announced, 'Eddie's here.' My grandmother, Zoe Bereskin, opened her arms. 'Stewart, thank God you've come back!'

'It's Eddie, mom,' my uncle said.

'Stewart, we thought you were dead. Who's Eddie?' she repeated.

I knew my grandmother by post. She had sent us recipes and

socks since the early 1970s. Every month a yellow bubble-wrapped parcel arrived with socks and underwear for my father, recipes for my mother and knitting for us. Then letters. Twice a week letters came, read to us over breakfast. We ate to news of my grandfather's ailing health and deaths.

'Grandpa continues to get physical therapy twice a week for his accident and to consult too often (for my liking) with his lawyer in order to sort out the details of the accident. In the meantime, we don't have a car so we rely almost exclusively on your Uncle Max to chauffeur us around. It is a task Max does without complaint.

Rita Slomin died last week. We have known her and Martin for a lifetime. But that's how life goes, as one gets older, one's contemporaries die, leaving only a few of the old-timers to survey the new scene.'

And breaking, without pause, into instructions for recipes.

'Remember, Jessica, that you have to preheat the oven to bring out the egg whites. The cake can be served hot on its own or with custard, whipped cream, ice cream and blueberries (this is my favorite combination). Don't forget to dust the cake with powdered sugar. If it sticks to the pan after baking, you should try lining the pan with aluminum foil and grease well. Tell me how it turns out.

Know that I love you sweeties with all my heart.'

None of us doubted that she loved us. Her days—five thousand miles away—were spent searching Chicago market stalls for my father's undergarments, presents for us and food tips for Jessica. Our births triggered a love that was boundless, ridiculous for two children she rarely saw, children who would soon be completely out of her reach. The house was a monument to us, an act of resistance to the divorce and separation. Every corner, wall, sideboard, cabinet, bookshelf and table had framed photos of Esther and me. Sitting in the bright snow on the banks of Lake Michigan, smiling broadly in our school uniforms. Our images on a faded calendar. On the collage of family photos in the corridor, we were at the centre. Now, with guests filling the house, it seemed like a museum to lost children. Missing since 1981. Please report any sightings. We had died years ago, but were remembered in these photographs scattered across the house. Our smiles shone out, mocking our grandparents' belief that everything was all right, that these children were still alive and could still be loved.

I arrived in the morning and was rushed quickly to the cemetery, given an ill-fitting suit and yarmulke and squeezed into an old Buick.

'It is wrong for a parent to bury a child,' my grandfather said as he shifted the transmission into drive, then without a pause asked me, 'Have you been following the news, Boyo?'

Morris Bereskin remained committed to the end. To him the revolutions in Eastern Europe were a party test to see who would remain standing. My grandfather was the last old communist in the world, standing erect, stubborn and proud in downtown Chicago.

* * *

Morris Bereskin, 1991

The front door of the house was never used. There wasn't even a key for it, just a faded note tucked on the inside glass panel telling visitors to use the back door. The backyard was strewn with garbage cans, broken air conditioners and car parts. For months every year the household jetsam was covered in snow, not a faint dusting but great plunging metres of snow, and in those months the garbage can looked like a frozen victim from Chicago's Vesuvius, caught mid-gesture by the frosty lava of an Illinois winter.

It was summer. I had been in Chicago for a few days. The house was full. The festive atmosphere felt strange for the aftermath of a funeral. The fly door constantly opened and snapped shut. Neighbours and my grandfather's comrades arrived with meals: chicken soup, boiled chicken, chicken *schnitzel* and chicken salad sealed in Tupperware. I sat and ate. I was good for the part. I helped my grandmother in the kitchen and discussed the wording for my father's four-paragraph obituary in the *Chicago Free Press*.

My grandmother was the household maid, offering guests drinks and food, taking the men's orders.

'Zoe, can you bring us tea, please?' Morris yelled.

'Sweetie, can I get you anything while I'm in the kitchen?' she asked me.

The afternoons, two days after the funeral, had thinned out. Now we were alone except for a couple of my grandfather's friends.

'Look at this.' My grandfather unfolded a paper and read. '"The war, if we decide to fight one, will rebound badly. America, acting now as the global superpower, doesn't need to cast much more than a fleeting glimpse at the Soviet Union, a power that has waned remarkably in the last years." This is the future. America's war must be opposed.' He slapped his knees with the paper.

'Yeah, of course, Morris, but who's going to stop it?' his friend asked him.

'Zoe, where are those teas?' my grandfather called out again. 'I think we shouldn't immediately assume that Gorbachev will let them get away with it. I suspect he has something planned.'

'Jesus, Morris, why do you still expect something from that place? It's rotten. It'll go the same way as Eastern Europe. Gorbachev will be the next Ceauşescu,' chided his friend.

My grandfather paused. 'Perhaps, but Lenin didn't expect the revolution in January 1917. We never know exactly the turn history will take.'

He got up, moved to the hall, and shouted, 'For Chrissakes, Zoe, the tea. Where's the tea?'

There was the sound of something breaking in the kitchen.

'Oh, I don't know anymore, maybe it's up to this generation'—he pointed to me—'to solve the questions that failed us.' He sat down close to me and put his arm over my shoulder. I heard my grandmother cleaning the broken crockery in the kitchen. With Morris's arm around me I felt complicit in his yelling.

'Your grandfather was the most committed of all the Chicago communists,' his friend said, adjusting himself in his seat. 'I remember in the early 1950s, we came over to eat when Morris was out. We waited for him. It was cold. Zoe was cooking, so we sat in the kitchen. When he came in he was radiant. We asked him what had happened. He beamed at us and said, "I came home early from work and I said to myself, what would the party want me to do? So I delivered leaflets about our public meeting for two hours." Your grandfather was our inspiration. Always optimistic.'

Zoe came in. The tray rattled as she hit the doorframe, muttering a barely audible 'Oh dear' as she stumbled over to us.

'Jesus, what happened, mom?' my uncle asked.

How long have men been nagging you, grandmother? Freedom and communism in the lounge and serfdom in the kitchen.

The house had been lined with books. But as Moscow suffered more ignominious defeats, the books beat a hasty retreat. The shelves lined with Lenin, Marx and Engels were shuffled first from the lounge to the corridor, then to the chipboard shelving lining the stairwell to the basement, until, with Boris Yeltsin's rise to power that year, they found their final resting place in the damp rooms under the house. After Khrushchev's secret speech in 1956 telling the Communist Party of Stalin's crimes, Morris had boxed up Joseph Stalin's collected works, sealed the boxes and stacked them in the garage, where they remained. 'When I heard of Stalin's crimes,' Morris told me, 'it was as though a child had died.'

In 1968, when Soviet tanks rolled across Dubchek's spring, comrades raised doubts again, but he defended the intervention. Yet still his books continued their shuffle along the house. After the storm had passed in 1968 he took to reading in a torn armchair in the basement. For a month he returned from work, ate and descended the stairs: read, made notes and came up to sleep. A new shame, another impossible defence, had forced him underground. After a month he returned, declaring that he finally understood the decision of the Central Committee of the Communist Party of the Soviet Union to intervene in Czechoslovakia. To each new objection he would utter a barely comprehensible formula and then plunge himself into another distracting campaign.

'Comrades, the situation in Czechoslovakia was counterrevolutionary. If we had left Dubcek to himself it would have awakened nationalism across the region, in the Ukraine, in Czechoslovakia itself and across the Soviet Union. But this would only be the start. What was the alternative? Let the old wartime collaborationists and the fascists return? Let's not have any illusions about the non-revolutionary forces waiting in the wings. I have no doubt that the intervention is proof of the unshakable commitment to Marxism-Leninism and proletarian internationalism. The Soviet Union intervened not only to defend Czechoslovakia's socialism but also the international struggle.'

By the time of my arrival, his books had found their final, shameful home, and now colourful biographies of Gorbachev were piled high on the coffee table.

My grandfather arrived in Chicago in 1927 a young man, working in a market stall, a proud Jew with the sweet odour of the Russian Revolution still blowing across the world. He volunteered for the war as soon as the USSR was invaded in June 1941.

The liberation of Europe after the slaughter signalled the rosy dawn of a new world.

* * *

July 17, 1944
Dear Zoe,
It is difficult to grasp as yet the magnitude of present-day events. We are witnessing historical mass production, history moves on wings and tanks and jeeps, it is indeed mobile.

The road to Paris is being traversed by us relentlessly and with Russian verve. Nantes, Algiers, Versailles are no longer mere words gleamed from history books, they are real and alive. The spirit of the Renaissance, symbolic now of the renaissance of A44 and after, is pulsating with the blood of democratic Frenchmen, Americans, Canadians. Paris, where some of the greatest and most basic tenets of cultured, civilized man were forged in the fires of revolutionary struggle, is again destined to become the center of the conquering armies of the United Nations. Today it was within sound of our guns. Tomorrow in Paris Frenchmen and women will join us in clearing the Germans from France. What glorious chapters have so far been written by the French underground will be paled but not forgotten by the deeds of valor that the Parisians will achieve. Their joy and heart-rending happiness at being liberated is a lone justification for the sacrifices so far made.

Your regular accounts of Stewart's peregrinations give me a great amount of real, genuine enjoyment. He is a typical free junior citizen of a free world, raised under the guidance of intelligent parents. I am sure that any talents he may possess will be done full justice by us. It goes without saying that Stewart and you are the apples of my eye. Stewart is the tangible expression of the justness of our cause. We are fulfilling our responsibility to their generation. They will grow up in a society free from fascism and wars.

As ever,
Solidarity, peace and love
Morris

* * *

Chicago, 1991

There was something worse than the photographs of our childhood, the endless happy faces, our little, bestial smiles like spotlights, telling everyone who entered the unforgivable lie that we were still there. The smells were worse. I opened the door to the basement, to its smell of sawdust and damp. My hands gripped the doorframe as I staggered down the first two steps, turned and pulled the door shut behind me. I sat. We had lived here in 1979. We had stayed in the basement. A bed made up for Jessica and Stewart, and small singles for Esther and me. All in one room. The cobwebs cleared away, a bare bulb hanging in the centre of the room, which was dusty from my grandfather's books.

I remembered Esther and me squeezing through the laundry chute in the upstairs bathroom, landing in piles of household clothes in the basement below. Stuck between the bathroom and the basement, a child cut in half by the daytime world of the soapy bathroom and the underworld of dirty washing. My legs in bunched-up shorts waving in happy distress. Esther laughing and pushing me through the hole.

'Just let yourself go. It's all right, I've got you,' she said, holding my ankles. My muttered screams echoing to her through the basement.

'I don't think there's enough clothes for me to land on. Have you got me? Stop it, that tickles. I'm falling.'

I fell, Esther catching my sandals. I sunk into Zoe's washing and laughed, rolled myself up in the clothes that smelt like their hugs, Zoe's cheap perfume, Morris's Old Spice. I pulled away the shirts and cleared space for my head. I looked up. Esther was staring down at me.

'My turn!' she shouted, throwing herself into our secret underground.

I sat on the basement steps, leaning my head against the handrail. These scenes had been absorbed into the walls. Voices calling me, my sister's thin hands waving at me as she made her descent into the laundry. I stood slowly and walked down the stairs. The large room was still lined with books, my grandfather's armchair in the corner and nine blue metal trunks, each padlocked. The shipping labels were still on them. They had stayed here unopened since my father's arrival from London nine years before. Sealed shut, padlocked and hammer-closed. I tried to lift one, rattled a lock. I looked around the room for something to open them with.

I broke open the first chest with a hammer. The lock broke on my first blow. I swung the blue lid open. Folded neatly were rugs, lampshades, candlesticks and books. In the second chest were albums. Photos of us, locked away. Isaac's watch. The contents of our house in this Chicago suburb, hidden in a basement. The corpse of our old lives. The details of our home, meticulously packed by Stewart. In the third chest I found the plastic wallets with our pocket money. Full. The fourth chest had Stewart's recording reels stacked twenty high, each labelled. *Eddie's first words, 1969. Esther's school story, April 1974. Lennon and Yoko in bed, 1971. Eddie Kidd, 1979.*

I slumped to the floor, leant against the open chest. My hand brushed the fur carpet that had sat in Stewart's office like an island in the middle of the floor. I was exhausted. I wanted the riot of memories, each knocking around incoherently in my head, to quiet. I wanted even the joy of my time here with Esther to go. I wanted the memories over.

'Fuck this family,' I shouted.

Chapter Seven

The Living Dead

25 December 2002

It was hard to relax knowing that I would be facing trial in the new year. Taffy warned me during our weekly call on Christmas Eve: 'Be ready, comrade. We'll mount the best socialist defence possible, but the pigs tell us they have footage. If it comes to it we'll find somewhere for you to hide. But I'm optimistic.

'Now I know that I have long been considered ultra-left, over-optimistic, and over-confident. In fact, I would go as far as to say that miserablists positively loathe me. I'm just far too chirpy and love activism too much for people's taste. So I've learnt to be aware of that—and you need to be as well, Eddie. But even within our ranks there's a split between Bolsheviks who are looking for the coming explosion and Mensheviks who want to keep accommodating and compromising because they think this low level of struggle will continue indefinitely.

'It is too early to decide tactics at this stage, Eddie, short of the defence that we are currently mounting. Still, free thinking about tactics is of the essence, especially until we have more evidence about what the police are up to, and then we can change our approach in a more rounded, fulsome, open, clear way. Pardon the usual degree of over-optimism and speculative thinking.'

His gruff advice rattled the phone. He finally rang off with the words, 'I have to go, Eddie. The kids love Christmas. I hope you can wangle some sort of break from all the pressure you're under. Take great care of yourself. You are *so* vital to us all. Lastly I just want to say, comrade, that we'll make 2003 the year we stop the war and rip the fucking head off the global bourgeoisie.' He hung up, not wanting, I thought, for me to voice any doubts, to question our readiness for revolution. There were two wrongs at the end of that year. They criss-crossed each other in a web of global and personal confusion that I tried to climb out of and flatten down with my feet. The war, to me, was familiar: the promises of laser-guided missiles, precision bombing and democracy. The old lies. We had been here before. Blair was the new loud-hailer for the lies: 'WMDs are but one aspect of the new dangers we face. The Cold War has ended. The great ideological battle between communism and Western liberal democracy is over. The struggle for world hegemony by political ideology is gone.'

His certainty and pleading eyes, his self-righteousness, filled most of us with contempt. When he spoke, I stared at his thick hands on the desk in front of him and wondered if anyone had ever told him that he was stupid. He looked too large under his suit jacket, which twitched on his shoulders. This wanker, I thought, even has time to work out. He was about to crush Baghdad in his sweet appeals for compliance and democracy, and the liberal papers agonized: *Saddam is evil, but on the other hand, he was worse when we funded him.*

Our rumbling movement had started to be heard outside the circles of activists. Most of the anti-war groups were full of people who didn't know the words to the Internationale. A "fuck Blair" generation of school kids and tabloid readers. As Blair prepared his sermons for the new year's war, a million people were stapling cardboard placards together and writing up their own anti-war anger, like mine, like Taffy's and Jessica's, on the backs of cereal boxes. 'Stop Blair's illegal war.' 'Bush #1 terrorist.' 'Make tea, not war.' 'Jail Tony.'

But there was a second wrong. My sister. Her rapid-fire psychosis poured out of her in her hospital bed. She crouched in the middle of the mattress as though she was about to start a race. Her eyes were fixed as she tried to keep up with a reality that kept shifting in front of her. She shivered on her bed, holding onto herself—because she was coming apart, because she needed to stick herself together, to hold her limbs in their sockets.

She had always been the thin-boned bird I had found in the garden as a boy, fallen from its nest and too weak to fly back. It had been mauled by the neighbours' old cat, which had been too lazy to kill and eat it. I brought it in, cradled in my hands. 'Take that filthy thing into the backyard and wash your hands,' Stewart had shouted. Instead, Jessica emptied a box and folded up a dishcloth. The bird was so light that I had to keep looking at it to make sure it didn't disappear. I could feel its scaly feet clawing weakly on my hands. We put the box in the coal shed, in the corner by the window where it could soak in the spring sunlight. 'It looks like Esther,' I said. Jessica hugged me tightly. The bird was gone when I got back from school. Jessica told me that it had flown away.

I looked now at Esther's little see-through frame, her bones prodding at her hospital gown, and remembered that bird.

We visited her on Christmas day. Each time I pushed the stiff door open and entered the room, I was scared that she would finally have disappeared, that her thin, impossible skeleton would have collapsed. I held my mum's hand on the way back in the mini-cab. We looked like strange and silent lovers. I thought, *Maybe Esther won't come back this time*. Jessica, always more practical, spoke. 'I should have insisted that she got rid of the baby.'

'That's past, mum. She's going to have it.'

I hated visiting her, and I hated leaving. If we were not there to see her, to prove she existed, she would vanish. Her life was so faint that she would disappear if we closed our eyes for a minute or left the room. Only the small imprint of her feet would remain, just visible where she had been crouching on the bed, as proof that she had briefly been here, to remind us that if we had stayed with her, she would still be with us. I was angry with Rebecca for assuming that we could already make plans together, that the world was neat and could be organised simply by a force of will.

People, she thought, could choose to be happy and predictable. I hated her optimism, her unworldly bounce and aimless smiles.

* * *

1991

Stewart was washing dishes in his mobile home outside Chicago. The floor shook when he walked across it; the fake mantelpiece above the ornate fireplace rattled with each of his heavy steps. This particular path to the kitchenette at the back of the lounge made Stewart think that this place, his *bullshit home,* really was made of cardboard. His arms were full of dirty dishes from the meal of roast chicken and corn on the cob. He was thinking about the assignment tomorrow. His footsteps rocked the caravan as they always did. The room vibrated and from the corner of his eye he saw something slip on the mantelpiece and fall to the floor—the old colour photo of us. Eddie and Esther. It was almost too twisted, even before it fell, to make out the faces. He had not straightened it, had not even gone near it for some time. That part of the room had been contaminated. He took a wide, strange route around the fireplace, sticking hard to the wall left of the mantelpiece without realising what he was doing, just to avoid that curled-up photo. Now as he put the plates into the sink and ran the water, he thought about us.

He tried to distract himself, sunk his hands into the hot water, but it didn't help. He remembered how he held us long and hard in the mornings before we were packed up for the last time in the car. The way he squeezed us and how we held on. My arms around his neck, my warm tears smeared on his shirt. My need for him unlimited; our separation soon unlimited. He remembered how I struggled to catch my breath in his arms in the early evening glow of the sun as we held him goodbye before the car ride back to Jessica. I liked the feeling. Safe. An embrace that filled all the absence.

Stewart leaded on the sink, splashing water chaotically on the upturned and dirty plates. Suddenly he yelled, breathed in, and sobbed uncontrollably. His knees buckled and he crouched on the floor, sobbing. Vicki rushed into the room and saw Stewart on the kitchen floor, worried that his crying, his yelling like a wounded beast, would bring down the caravan's cardboard walls and wake their three-month-old daughter.

I thought I must have heard him crying that night, the same night that I hid my head under the covers and cried.

* * *

1 January 2003

The new year came. We knew that the war had been planned, that the invasion would take place before the paralysing heat of the summer descended. We predicted an Easter invasion. There would be a Pyrrhic victory and then the gates of hell would open. The occupation would signal a resistance that would not rest. Our rag-tag bunch of part-time intellectuals and street agitators were great diagnosticians. We condensed, explained and synthesized our politics on the high streets.

'The war they want to wage is a symptom,' we explained on street corners, 'not of American power and supremacy, but the ebbing of that power. America is over-stretched. It's hegemonic only in military strength. Its crisis compels the American ruling class to control oil resources and strategic territory round the world.'

As tanks and politicians positioned themselves in the new year, we fought their plans with analysis and protests. We sold papers and started conversations: 'The neo-conservatives represent a group of the American ruling class, principally among the oilmen, who see the end of the Cold War as a missed opportunity for American business...'

So we were oddly euphoric in January 2003. As arguments,

lobbies and protests spread, we began to think we could actually stop the war.

Jessica always surprised me. I sat on her sofa on New Year's Day. The road outside was quiet for once. I sat in the warm room with my shoes off, listening to the trickle of light rain on the roof and windows. We sat like this, screwed up, as little of our bodies protruding into the world as possible. I always got Jessica wrong. We had spent the morning at the hospital and the afternoon taking turns making each other pots of tea to punctuate our political conversation. I heard her humming in the kitchen as we shuffled through the old newspapers and holiday reading that had built up on the kitchen table.

'Your father was difficult, but for a while we were a good team. He liked me speaking. Sometimes he insisted that I speak. Stewart didn't have any of that macho disdain for a woman's success. We used to have such debates… there were those who argued that we needed spontaneity, but Stewart, everyone thought it was strange he was still in the Communist Party, Stewart argued for the hard grind of organisations and politics.'

The two of us clutched our tea, our glasses streaked with steam.

'But wasn't the level of political discussion higher, among students at least?' I said, sounding high-pitched and naive.

'Nonsense. Sitting in they could do, but thinking was another matter. There was, I suppose, more hope. There wasn't any notion that capitalism was inevitable. Capitalism seemed to be under attack from movements and ideas everywhere. And the workers took action. Nobody expected the miners to strike after almost half a century. They'd been complacent since they got defeated back in 1926. And then suddenly they went on strike in 1969, and it was effective! All over, teachers and civil servants were forming strong unions. It was extraordinary—our heroes had been all abroad, you know. The Viet Cong, the Black Panthers, Malcolm X, Muhammad Ali, DRUM, the Derry civil rights marchers. But suddenly it was all happening here in the UK. For six years, Eddie, I saw people fight and organise here. We only lost because the Stalinists and the Labour Party won leadership over our movements. Today they don't have that sort of influence. The Stalinists are dead and New Labour are war-mongers. There are other contenders to ensnare us, of course, but I am positive. So positive.'

I thought that I knew my mother. I imagined she had been eaten up by the past. Now I was not sure who she was. Each time I thought I understood her, she confounded me. Trying to fix Jessica in one spot was like building into sand.

I had been settled at the library for three years. I shunned training courses and kept to my four-day week. 'Denying the capitalist your labour,' Jessica commented, laughing. I wasn't, to my secret shame, the hard man of wage-labour. But I was still young enough to think that the new year would be different and that I could reinvent myself. The easy lure of my life in the library proved, for now, too much. I wheeled the trolley loaded with books, bent over like an old man with a walking frame. When I was on desk duty I wrote reading lists for the Read Against the War notice board: Robert Fisk, *The Great War for Civilisation*. John Rees, *The New Imperialism.* I sent emails to members of the Save Tooting Library Campaign.

Jessica never said as much, but I felt her disapproval. I could hear a faint hint of disdain every time she asked, 'How's the library, Eddie?' She thought that an activist should pack bourgeois society under his thumb; success would be proof of his contempt. She thought that we had to be informed about each strand of the world: political economy, philosophy, literature and science, like the best Bolsheviks. How could I not fail?

'What's happened to the girlfriend you mentioned?'

I was as startled by the question as Jessica was by the escape of it from her mouth. We stared at each other. Since Rebecca and I had argued I had left my phone off, turning it on only to get messages.

'Oh, we've gone our separate ways.'

'That's a pity.'

'Why?'

'Because you must get lonely.'

We are our parents, not in partial fractions but in complete sums. Each particle is filled by them, each reflex a copy. I am my father. Each of my actions is a repeat of his, behind black-rimmed glasses and the lens of a Rolleiflex. He set me up. Jessica's hands fidgeted with the newspaper on her lap, the two of us wishing that we had not exchanged this intimacy. If there was another question, another word, her son would probably cry and we would both hate that. Instead I got up and made us another cup of tea.

* * *

Stewart and Jessica, September 1967

They drove to Sheffield. The meeting was held in a lecture theatre at Sheffield University, the hall prepared with posters advertising their visit. Leon owned the headline; Jessica and Stewart appeared in brackets: 'Film-maker Stewart Bereskin introduces his short film *History Lesson*.' Leon had travelled on the train and was sitting at the front of the room, resting his feet on his guitar case. The room was already full, the thin benches packed. Jessica spoke first. She stood over her notes. The room was hot. People had lifted themselves onto the desks that ran along the room. One woman squatted on a windowsill, blowing smoke from her cigarette out of a window she kept ajar with her foot. The hum of whispered conversations continued even after Jessie had started to speak. She faltered on her introduction.

Stewart stood up and spoke over the muttering. 'Comrades, this is a political meeting, not a cabaret. Please keep quiet.'

Jessica continued. 'I get the impression that you want the

para-techniques and the songs.' She indicated the projector that was in front of her. 'So I'll keep this short. We are here because of the war. We are the children of war. But we need to do more than just oppose war. What happens when we have forced the US to withdraw? Celebrate? Already the war parties in the States—the Democrats and the Republicans—are facing their stiffest opposition from veterans and students who have been lied to for years...'

Jessica Joseph had been a radical before Stewart arrived. Her break from her family was an escape from their conservatism. Stewart and Jessica both fled in the same year: Stewart across North America from his father's controlling brand of communism and Jessica to London from her blue-lipped Tory household of English Jews. Jessica's parents were eccentric only in their interest in politics. Their children were expected to have opinions on everything: Darwin, Suez, ancient Rome. But for these Tory-Bolsheviks, the opinions had to fall into the right camp. Her family's line was harder than anything she found on the New Left when she finally got out.

The Joseph family was shaped like a gun, and Jessica was the trigger. She set them off and escaped. Reading was their religion. They read collectively, like slaves, in the sitting room, on those bloody hard sofas against cushions printed with English hunting scenes. Their legs were neatly crossed, their allocated readings unfolded on their laps like hymnals. They spent every Sunday for two years reading *en famille* Gibbon's six-volume *History of the Decline and Fall of the Roman Empire*. Their father the General sat over them, their mother, his adjunct, trying to love them but corralling them back when there was a break in discipline. Over dinner they would argue with their father dividing his children up like the chapters he had given them to read: 'Jessica, you take the role of Romulus Augustus just before he is overturned by Odoacer in 476'—then, skipping two millennia—'What are the Americans' interests in North Africa after Suez?'

As an unaligned socialist, Jessica organised a reading group of Marx's *Capital* in South East London. Stewart had asked her, when they first met, what she did in the evenings. She answered, 'Bookworming, comrade, like Karl Marx.'

Now she paused and breathed in deeply. 'But we need more than "Hey, hey, LBJ, how many kids have you killed today?" We need politics. We need to know how to sit in—but also how to think. We need to think about alternatives, imagine another politics—remember what the demonstrators sang in Paris?' Jessica picked up a sheet from her notes and read, '"Everything is ours, nothing is theirs. Everything they own was stolen. Nationalisation and workers' control and not a penny's compensation."'

Jessica made no concessions to the meeting. She wore an ironed blue shirt buttoned up to the neck and a long skirt. She looked like a suffragette, her hair tidy and combed. When she sat down, students clapped. Some cheered. Stewart whispered into her ear, 'You are a traitor to your class, comrade. I love you.'

Stewart spoke next. He had spent two months making the seven-minute film. He hired an editing suite at the Hornsey School of Art, found clips of historical footage: Chamberlain waving a piece of paper from the steps of an airplane; newsreel shots of the bombing in Vietnam; anti-war protests.

'Leon,' Stewart said. Leon got up and sat on the corner of the table facing the room, his guitar ready. Jessica couldn't help thinking: *he's going to fucking shoot us with his guitar*.

Stewart turned a switch on the projector. Nothing. He scrambled under the table for the plug. Still nothing. The room remained silent, then there was the slow hum of the fan. The reels, protruding from the top of the projector, started to rattle, then turn. The machine shook rhythmically in the middle of the room. Leon looked up. *History Lesson* flashed up, unsteady on the screen. Leon looked down to his guitar, fingered his first cord. An image came onto the screen: a parched and cratered field, nothing living. Each scene flickered briefly on the screen. The effect was impressive. The audience was transfixed by the images and Leon's rough cadences. Stewart's montage of war was beautiful and tragic. Where was the liberation? His American, communist hope? Could possibilities of another future be derived from the charred and screaming girl running naked towards the camera with her arms open? Stewart had failed at the one role on which he prided himself most: purveyor of revolutionary possibility. Leon's voice was loud and strident.

History lesson, it's time to remember
Time to remember the deeds of the great
Please pay attention, don't let your minds wander
Day dreams and playtime can wait.

* * *

August 1991

Behind my grandmother stood two of her old friends, both sighing and moaning. The rabbi struggled over Stewart's coffin to pronounce the Hebrew as the wind blew across the cemetery, pulling up our jackets and yarmulkes. I put my hand on my head to keep the skull-cap from flying off and felt the wind across my body. The men looked devoted, bent slightly, holding onto their heads in silent lamentation before God and death. As the last words of the Hebrew prayer sounded, the coffin was lowered into the grave. My grandmother's wailing rose and the women behind her echoed her distress in harmony. She grew louder as my father sank deeper into the ground. Then she was silent. The cemetery stood still. Everyone looked to my grandmother, the conductor of our grief. She turned, looked at me, and let out a shout.

'My son!'

She fainted, falling back on the woman behind her, who

collapsed on the woman behind *her*. The three women fell like dominos, letting out a descending wail as they reached the ground. I managed to wedge myself between them and the ground. The cemetery erupted in panic. I was pinned to the earth by the three substantial women. They were still but I struggled, trying to keep my yarmulke on, lying across a grave. The women seemed to press their weight against each other. I could not move. For a moment I gave up the struggle to free myself and lay still.

My grandmother thinks I am my father and that I am dead. She is trying to push me back into the ground. I stared at the sky and the trees around the walls of the cemetery. The sky was a cold blue, strange for August, the clouds torn and scattered by the wind. The moon shone full and icy in the daylight. I felt comfortable and warm under my human cover. The stone supported my back like a bed.

I thought that maybe I was dead. Maybe we all were. That the dead and the living had been mixed up and the day and night had merged. I could stand up and my father would be there at his own funeral—or I would fall into the ground and sink into his coffin. I would lie with him, squeezed against the wooden sides of his bed, like I had as a child. We would talk once more and settle some of the life that had been so broken. Pat it down, level it. Bring our hands across the earth and tell each other that it would be okay. We would lie like this, softly whispering to each other in his coffin. He would explain what had happened. I would tell him how much I had missed him, how angry I was. He would stroke my head, his hand cold because he was already dead, and tell me that he was sorry and that he loved me. That everything would be all right. When this was done I could get up, kiss his clammy cheek and see him smile, run my finger for the last time along his creased brow. I would step out of his grave and see the moon fade from the sunlit sky, and all the living would take their places and all the dead would stay in theirs. No more would my world be confused between night and day, living and dead.

My grandmother was resuscitated. Mourners in ill-fitting black suits helped the women off me and led them back to the cars.

* * *

2 January 2003

When did I know that I loved her? It was almost two months after we had started seeing each other. We weren't talking and I missed her. I was rid of her, free to work in the evenings, to drink with my friends, to flirt. I could not sleep. After the third night I woke and ached. I turned in my bed, sleeping for an hour, waking again, cursing the night, wishing I could hear the birds, that there would be a sign of the morning. In the day I stared at my phone until it was wet from my palms. As night approached I turned the phone off, because I couldn't bear that it did not ring. I spent the next night fretting, turning in my sheets, staring at the silent phone, resisting the temptation to turn it on. Finally, sitting up naked in the bed with my dim bedside light illuminating an open book I could not read, I turned on the phone and waited for the sound of a missed call or a message. Nothing. I passed the night waiting. Now, I thought, I loved her. This glorious love had me desperate and sleepless.

This was the only way I could comprehend how I felt for Rebecca, in the quantity of suffering I envisaged if we were to separate. That night, when she didn't phone, I thought that if we were to break up today, Tuesday, I would feel sick. I would not be able to sleep for three days, until Monday. Then for the following five days, until next Friday, I would still feel ill whenever I thought about her, but already I would have started to recover my sleep. In the following months she would start to fade as my life became cluttered again by temporarily forgotten anxieties. I would still be struck by sadness during a meal or as I got into bed, but even this would fade. This was, I thought, the only way I could understand love: as the suffering it would cause. This was the only way I could recognise that I was in love now.

I don't think we are built to love, not more than once or twice. We don't learn the knack. I thought about my mother and knew that she could not cope with loving again. I could see her more clearly, her constant activity, the hum of the radio always in the background of my childhood. When she slept, I could hear the babble of voices in her room, the low mumbling of people on her bedside table. Even when she read, the radio was there crowding the room. She needed this mess of soft noise to deaden the pain. I wondered whether the thoroughfare of lovers after Stewart was an attempt to chase away doubt and regret. I saw her, frail now, snapping at us like a hurt animal. Perhaps love should be rationed only to the first people who come into our lives. There should be a pact not to die. I wondered whether any good had come of my love. Did I enjoy loving my parents? Was my sister helped by my love? Was I any better for beginning to love Rebecca? We love too much. I wanted none of it.

* * *

August 1991

My father fought death until the end. He took on the cancer with his fists. He gripped it in his hands and tried to stop its unravelling. When he was finally hospitalized, he still fought, waving his young daughter away. He did not want to be taunted by life, by reasons not to die. He knew I was coming and tried to hold on, but he kept slipping. Finally, when the cancer pinned him down, he sat up in his bed, his father staring at him from the corridor. He shouted for thirty seconds. 'Oh my God, I'm going to die, I'm going to die. Leave me alone, please leave me alone for five minutes. I am very tired. I am going to die. Fuck, shit, fuck, fuck.' He fell back dead. My father's last words were *fuck* and *shit*. What better epitaph for his life? Fuck and shit to life.

* * *

January 2003

There was a basic truth to Mark's obsession with a younger woman. Fifteen years separated Mark and Giuliana. Mark was strong and fit and, in his effusive and careless way, attractive. But Giuliana was striking, her face intriguing. You wanted to linger on it, to discover the deep hollows around her eyes and study her dimpled chin. Her beauty reminded me of Rebecca's and forced me to ask the question: how much of what we are inside is because of the way we look outside? Like the rich, I thought, she had done nothing to be mysterious and intense, to arouse respect and curiosity. I felt sorry for Giuliana that the random ensemble of bone and flesh could so determine her fortunes. It had been the reason for her relationships, why she never had space to breathe between lovers. There was always a quick jostling to the front as men elbowed each other aside to woo her and show off. Giuliana was the queen and we were her players. Giuliana's cruel beauty was the reason she had never been single and the reason Mark had gone mad.

In my desperate attempt to explain this to Mark, I even quoted Ben Jonson to him:

And punish that unhappy crime of nature,
Which you miscall my beauty: flay my face,
Or poison it with ointments, for seducing
Your blood to this rebellion. Rub these hands,
With what may cause an eating leprosy,
E'en to my bones and marrow: anything,
That may disfavour me...

As Mark felt his decay at forty-six, he counted his decades and weighed up his plans and ambitions and compared them with what he had expected to achieve twenty years before. As he aged he seemed to need the affirmation of Giuliana's taut, impervious body. His obsession with her youth was a never-ending fiction. Youth begets youth. Our desire for further plunging and undulating youth only deepens the older we get. I told him to cleanse himself with Woody Allen. 'First it's the women ten years younger, then fifteen years younger, then it's your wife's daughter. Mark, you better watch out,' I said. 'We can't delay our own demise by hitching up with nymphets.' Mark didn't answer, as though he was really considering a child bride, as if I'd given him the idea that he'd been searching for. *Fuck*, I thought, *I should just keep my bloody mouth shut.*

* * *

December 1991

After the funeral I thought I would meet Stewart in London. I thought I would run into him in the street and suggest a coffee. He became present suddenly in my life. I saw his red, slightly pocked face, his large and fleshy ears in the distance on the way to work, in shops on the weekend, his hair catching the light and turning dark red. He appeared to me in dreams. He was dead, but now always just out of sight. He was not cremated, so he could, I thought, technically still come back. Buried, but whole. My complete father still bent over, underground. The first winter of his death was bad in Chicago. Four feet of snow fell on the city in November, then more in December. Cars went into heated garages and roads disappeared overnight. Tunnels had to be dug through entire neighbourhoods. I received letters from my grandfather, his usually strident voice muffled by the snow and grief.

December 16, 1991

Dear Eddie,

Today, Monday, Chicago—this city of 2.5 million—is digging out of a horrible snowstorm. On Friday evening at 5 pm it struck. And for thirty hours, dear grandson, winds of sixty miles an hour lashed the city and all of Southern Illinois. Almost twenty inches of snow fell, easily the worst snowstorm for a hundred years. People were stranded everywhere. At hotels. At airports. In their cars. At hospitals. I was driven around the city by friends in an emergency four-wheel-drive truck and so I saw some of the strange happenings... people on skis in the center of the city, people in snowshoes tramping over snowdrifts twelve feet high with groceries or essentials like medicine. Of course, some idiots were also out in their snowsuits on Saturday night—at the height of the storm—lugging cases of beer home on sleds. The National Guard was using personnel carriers to take essential workers to hospitals and old folks' homes. The Chicago Police Department authorized snowmobiles to operate on the streets for emergency purposes all day Saturday.

For the last two weeks the temperature has gone down to minus forty degrees. Our electricity bill will be 25% higher than normal. But there is a kind of carnival atmosphere in the city. Many people are helping their neighbors.

We have had to leave Stewart for a few weeks because of the snowfall and the cold. Grandma hasn't been able to leave the house. I am going to end my Monday snow letter with an expression of love... we all miss you very much.

Solidarity, peace and love,

Your grandfather.

The winter was now my enemy, sealing up the ground, freezing the cemetery. I worried for my father's comfort. Frozen in his box, unable to push off the lid and scoop away the loose soil. His temporary rest, testified by my sightings in South London, had now been hard-frozen in the deep winter that caught Illinois in 1991. I only concluded that he was finally dead from my grandfather's weather reports that year.

* * *

December 1991

We packed ourselves into the Peugeot Estate and drove to Yorkshire. We bounced on the seats like kids and took turns choosing the music. Even after the divorce there was a clutter of men. The certainty of strange voices downstairs and in the bedroom. We had not had time to be together. Jessica rushed to cover her life with more chaos. Now we had a month together. Clothes fell out of our cupboard, dishes filled the sink and we stayed up late.

The Peugeot broke down. We sat listening to the sound of trucks revving at the service station outside. Drivers sat at scattered plastic tables under lights that shone too brightly. Jessica was suddenly in tears. 'Fucking hell. I have spent all my life driving shit cars. Second-hand wrecks. I never have any money.'

The narrative of our lives was solved. The arguments between Stewart and Jessica had been about their cars: the Wartberg, the Fiat 500, the Renault 19. There had been cold winters in the backseats of old cars, waiting hopelessly as the engine failed to start. My slowness at school had been caused by the petrol fumes I inhaled as I push-started an old banger. I hammered my fist on the table. 'Those bloody second-hand cars,' I repeated.

Jessica put her hands over her face. No money. No AA membership. Life a series of breakdowns.

'Is there anything I can do?' A burly man who looked a bit like Rambo came over to the table.

'You could fix our car,' Esther said.

Jessica slid her hands down her face, wiped her cheeks. 'Our car has broken down.'

Esther and Jessica sat in the car. I stood in the sleet with Rambo.

The car was fixed, except for the headlights. As we left the motorway the darkness enveloped the car. I walked in front of the Peugeot flashing a torchlight across the road. I looked like a funeral director. We got drunk the first night to celebrate our arrival—our survival. We were together and wanted nothing else. Esther was radiant. She told us, 'You know, there isn't a day that goes by when I'm not terrified that I am going to fall ill again.' She cried. For four years we had not discussed her illness. We let it hang there, neither entirely forgotten nor completely present, but Esther had still been in its grip. Four years later she fell ill again.

Chapter Eight

New Dawns

3 January 2003

Rebecca left a message on my phone. I had been telling myself, as though I was repeating a religious mantra, that I didn't want to hear from her, that it was better that she hadn't called. I did this enough in the days since our row, so solidly, with such stalwart will, that I had begun to believe it. I did not normally believe my lies; I prided myself on honesty. My pact with my fucking honesty became a habit of never believing anything that crossed my mind. I turned on the phone late on New Year's Eve and heard Rebecca. I almost lost my balance and sat down, my stomach turning.

'Where are you, Eddie? I've been trying to phone you for days. I keep getting your voicemail. Listen, I really need to speak with you. It's important, really important. Something's happened and I must see you. Please, Eddie, turn the phone on.'

The automated American woman told me there were two more messages.

Rebecca spoke again, an hour after the first call.

'It's me again. As I can't get you, I wanted to tell you that I'm pregnant. I'm pregnant and drunk, which I shouldn't be. I don't know how many weeks. I am in crisis and I need to speak. For fuck's sake, please answer, Eddie.'

The message finished. Another message, two minutes later.

'Eddie, I wanted to say happy new year.' There was a long pause, filled with her heavy breathing and loud music and laughter. 'I want to wish both of us happy new year.' Why had she said 'both of us'?

* * *

December 31, 1999

It was Millennium Eve. The world was meant to shudder to a halt. The Millennium Bug would bring down late capitalism. What two hundred years of anti-capitalist protests and revolutions had failed to achieve, the date change to 2000 would. When I met Mark it was hours before the Millennium Bug was due to strike. We met already drunk and walked to the park. Groups of people swayed and walked together in drunken unison towards the end of the world and the fireworks display on Tooting Bec Common. The evening was mild and my jacket was open. Mark was wearing cords, the centre crease and pocket pleats ironed perfectly, a tweed jacket and a deep red paisley patterned scarf. He looked like Sherlock Holmes walking under the moonlight in late-nineteenth-century London, with me, his bow-legged informer, chasing after his giant steps. The park was wet and our feet sank into the grass. I had brought a bottle of sparkling wine. Mark had brought champagne. We were taking long swigs from my bottle and saving his for midnight and the Apocalypse. Alicia was coming later, but we would have been better off without her. Mark would be distracted. He would put on that voice he used with her—part-child, part-cartoon—and it would be "sweetie" everything. *Sweetie, will you hold the champagne while I swing Eddie around? Sweetie, are you okay? You seem subdued, sweetie.* I hated all that crap. I just wanted Mark.

'I think we're on the verge of something big,' I said, looking at the slushy crowd, all of them like us, drunk and festive.

'The problem, comrade Eddie, is we *always* think we're on the verge of something big. I'm not sure. Maybe actually, for once, we should be honest and say we are on the verge of something very, very small. Small is okay; small is honest.'

'You're missing it, Mark.' I coaxed. 'You're so big. You see over the head of the world. From down here, I tell you, there is a shift.' Mark laughed loud and hit me in the middle of my back. I jolted forward.

'If you say "crisis" and "turning point" every day you'll be proved right eventually, but no one will be listening to you anymore.'

I jumped up and down on the spot in mock anger. 'You are such a bloody pessimist.'

'Come here and make up.' Mark scooped me up. I quickly looked around to make sure that there weren't any anti-Semites or homophobes in the audience. No one saw us; no one cared. I loved London. The city was socialist. An impenetrable fortress of communal living. A hippy heaven that inhaled the world and exhaled prejudice and hate. I saw in the crowd blissful harmony and disinterest. Mark put me down. I was bobbing and drifting in my early drunken euphoria, feeling exaggerated love for everyone.

Alicia was walking towards us. I shouted and waved. I was a Titan. I knew I could lift anyone up to my mood before the coming spectacular end, the great turn, the crisis. Everything would work out perfectly in the new millennium. Esther would stay strong. Jessica, too. She was still fit, not too old. I could fix the world. I could even lift Alicia and carry her off.

'Alicia!' I cried and gave her a kiss. 'You look lovely. We all look lovely and soon we're going to see the fireworks.' Alicia just smiled. Mark leant down and cupped her face with his large hands. 'Sweetie, so pleased you're here.'

What had I wanted from the new millennium? I wanted the spirit of Seattle and anti-capitalism to ripple out across the world. I wanted ever-widening layers of young militants to discuss the real Marxist tradition. I wanted to end the triumph of capitalism and to finish with New Labour. I wanted to bury the retreat of the revolutionary left. I thought that in this century, in the next decade, I would finally affiliate to a party; the greatest prophets, I was sure, are those who organise for the future today. I couldn't do this alone. I needed more than my campaigns and reading. I had to sign up.

The new century was about to be celebrated in the cloud-clogged skies above Tooting. It would be our own gunpowder plot against globalisation and war, our blood-red and black revolution. In my drunken utopia that night, a few minutes before the fuse was lit, I really thought the people around me signalled Phase One in the festival of the oppressed. The revolution was going to start with a fireworks display on a steep knell in Tooting, South West London.

I realised then that I was a little ahead of the game. I thought life was long and history short. I tended to see every civic gathering as the possible start of socialist revolution, not the ebb and flow of a parliamentary system. I agreed with my comrades' prognosis that we would be living either fascism or socialist revolution in fifteen years—and though we may have been exaggerating, that night, as the jumbled countdown to the millennium started, I was hopeful for socialism.

Half the crowd had already reached the future, while the other half was still five seconds from it. Contrary to our normal instincts, Alicia, Mark and I were in the second division, chasing down those who were already cheering and popping champagne in the new century a few metres from us. *Five, four, three...* Our arms linked like Morris dancers. We looked at those rushing forward, even more hopeful than us, with anxiety and surprise. Mark's voice was louder than mine.

'They got to the twenty-first century before us!' I shouted, as the first fireworks hissed up and disappeared into the low clouds.

Alicia said, 'Even at a firework display revolutionaries can't get it right.'

Mark pulled the cork out of the champagne bottle. Alicia took the first gulp. I swigged second and a man who had just joined us took the third mouthful.

I don't know why I shouted BUNDLE. It must have come out of the same normally dormant instinct that made me shout at the police three years later. I screamed BUNDLE loud enough for all the men in the surrounding crowd to turn around. Even amidst the rejoicing they heard me as if I had blown a note on a dog whistle to a pack of hounds. The 'bundle' has a long pedigree for men of a certain age and class. It was a single word that summarised male socialisation in British state schools in the 1980s. When screamed in school corridors up and down the country, it signalled a suicidal stampede. The rules of the bundle were simple and brutal. One person, normally a popular bully, would throw himself on a hapless friend and that person would crumble and fall to the ground. As his victim fell, the bully would shout BUNDLE. The word would trigger a rush to the small heap lying in the corridor and a series of wild and frenzied leaps as boys, one after the other, threw themselves on the human mass until there was a pile of flinching, stationary bodies on the floor.

At school I had special responsibilities. Man-Kit didn't speak much English; he had recently come from Hong Kong. I escorted him during his first weeks at school, explaining the system, gesticulating the rules in a sort of rudimentary sign language for him. It was his induction into the strange customs of Northern European boyhood. He stared aghast the first time he saw boys whizzing through the air from both ends of the corridor, crashing and exploding into each other like kamikaze pilots determined to kill themselves even without their airplanes. In those days if we'd had a few sticks of dynamite at school we would have launched the jihad in 1984. Our own army of boy-bombers, ready to do anything on a single command. Man-Kit stared at the pile of boys, the muffled tears of those suffocating at the bottom just audible. He turned to me and said his first full sentence in English: 'Why they do that then?'

Why they do that then? I couldn't answer the question twenty years before and I didn't know why I issued the cry on the first morning of the new millennium. But I screamed BUNDLE and threw myself at Mark. I looked like a child clambering onto his father's back. Then Mark made a mistake: he obliged. If he had remained standing the game would have been off. Instead, he carefully sunk into himself, ending up on the ground like a coiled snake. Our new friend, who'd commandeered the champagne, handed the bottle to Alicia and joined my ridiculous call to arms. 'BUNDLE!' he cried. Then large, booted men flung themselves on us, all uttering the same word as though they had just remembered their way back to the Promised Land, their long, pent-up odyssey in the hostile wasteland of adulthood finally over. I could hear the wind howling and breaking around their bodies as they picked up speed in their low-altitude, wingless flight towards us.

We lay on each other in our mound, too drunk to feel inhibited. Slowly the layers of men started to peel off until there were just three of us in our own private pile on the marshy ground. Finally Mark stood up, unfolding his hulking frame limb by limb. When he was fully and painfully upright he rubbed his side and said, 'Next time can we just have a group hug?'

I had fractured four of Mark's ribs. For two months he couldn't walk, breathe or demonstrate. I nursed him in guilt, with politics and apologies. 'Stop fucking apologising,' he said at the end of the first month, holding his damaged side as he shuffled painfully along the kitchen floor. 'It was an accident.' So my new century started with a failure to communicate. I had wanted to tell Mark that I loved him and instead I had shouted BUNDLE. I had pulled him to the ground and broken his ribs. More than ever I needed a revolution to cleanse me of the muck and prejudice of ages. To help me replace bundle with love.

* * *

4 January 2003

I spent the day in hospital. Esther told me that she was dead. She said that the screaming in the corridor came from others who had just died and were refusing to accept it. The nurses who came to her room with smiles and pills did not know that they were also dead. The medicine she swallowed without resistance was, she told me, to keep the demons away. Upstairs there was a permanent flat wailing, Esther said, from those who weren't helped by the pills. She cried and whispered to me, craning forward so I could see the tendons in her neck, that her fear was that soon the pills she took would not keep the flesh-eating demons away and she would be transferred upstairs. What could I say? That she was wrong? That it was not really like that? Would she listen? She wasn't getting better, I thought.

'I don't trust Jessica. I think she works upstairs,' Esther had said when I arrived.

I left Esther and caught a bus to Jessica's. I let myself in. She was sitting in her reading chair, one leg tucked under her.

She asked as I came in. 'How's Esther?'

'Shit,' I said. 'She thinks you're a demon.'

My mother looked like an imposter, like some old woman. Her arms were pale and stringy. I looked away. I couldn't cope with Jessica's old age. Her physical decay was too much for me. Her beauty had dropped off her like loose clothes. As a boy I had often fallen asleep wishing that I would die before she would. I wanted the same thing now.

'Maybe she's improving, if she thinks I'm the devil.'

'A demon,' I said, correcting her. 'She still has enough sanity to know that Blair's the devil.'

I perched on the arm of the chair.

'I didn't want this,' Jessica said.

'I know.'

'No, what I mean is, I didn't want to be a mother again. To fall in love with a child. I don't want to take the risk. I did it with Esther and you, but I don't think I have the energy to risk the pain again,' Jessica said.

For years everyone thought Jessica was strong. She wore leather jackets and tight clothes that hugged her figure. She swore in the car, slammed her fists on the horn. Our mother was a rebel. She taught us to break rules, but she was not tough. I was learning how weak she really was. She could not stand our pain. The more she suffered from Esther's sickness, the more she insulted the world. She goaded me just so we could fight. The fighting distracted her.

I had introduced her to Rebecca. The night after, she commented, 'One thing I really don't like about Rebecca, and you have to watch out for this, is the cross.' I was impressed she had even seen it tucked into Rebecca's cleavage, hidden behind her high-buttoned shirt.

'It was a present from her mother. I don't think she's religious.'

'Oh, crap, I can't stand people like that. Why doesn't she have the fucking guts to throw it away? God, these weak people. I am surrounded by such pathetic people.'

I was practiced with my mother, but I fell into the same traps. I raised my voice, spluttering, 'Listen, it's complex. Perhaps she was religious and she isn't now. But to be honest, I don't care.' I could feel my head filling with blood.

'You're making excuses. I can't bear those people. You say she's active in the anti-war movement. Well, how does she square it? I find it hard to believe how you can call yourself a socialist while making alliances with all those imams. It's called opportunism,' Jessica shouted.

I wondered what would be left of her in five years' time? Her bitterness was a cover for her suffering. Her make-believe regrets and her love for us were killing her. I did not challenge her. I was afraid of her wrath and tears. Who would be left, I asked myself, when her own death came? Our life is just the continual folding over of what has already happened to us, so each time we think that we have moved on we see our childhoods staring back at us. For my mother the past was all there was, and her head was crowded by the voices of her spent life.

October 24, 1984
Dearest Eddie,
Your appreciated letter of September 10 just arrived yesterday. Thank you for it. It took two full weeks to arrive even though you used two 31-cent stamps—almost twice the required amount. Our American system delays things, but usually only by two or three days.

In a brief way, this note is basically being sent to acknowledge your most recent one. It is, don't you believe, not only courteous to get a quick reply but satisfactory to know that your thoughts and feelings (on paper at least) have arrived safely.

Now that you are older, 'your own man,' perhaps you will visit. This brings me, Eddie, to the essential plank in this letter, the foundation. It is this: America compared to England. Now that you are sixteen, you can make a choice. Compared to the UK, North America—that is, essentially, Canada and the United States—really is a better place to live and work, from my point of view. And I would dearly like you to share in this viewpoint by experiencing firsthand what this continent has to offer you. There is less snobbism here and therefore, there is more opportunity; the class system, that is the delineation between workers, the middle class, the management class, the bosses, and the owners, is much less defined here. It isn't heaven in America, but it isn't the hell, the clash, the greyness of argumentative Britain. People in North America, fortunately, do not 'know their place,' as they do in England. And this means, Eddie, that if you have the imagination, the heart, and the soul to expand your horizons in America, you are not limited in any endeavor you may choose.

America does not have streets paved with gold, nor are we free from the daily struggles of worker and boss which life anywhere on earth entails; the main thing, though, is that it is just much easier to live here than it is in England. We don't have all the same crap about the Queen and her goddamn family that leaches off the public purse in your country. We don't have

Margaret Thatcher (though admittedly Ronald Reagan isn't much better). But we don't have upper-class snobs and all that B.S. (bullshit).

It would have been nice to have received even one postcard from you while you were working in Iceland, as you mentioned in your previous letter, if for no other reason than STAMPS. I save stamps and would have been happy to get one from that out-of-the-way and largely unknown country. Are you planning to return this year? By the way, did you know there is a big Icelandic population in Illinois? When you visit, you might care to have a look at what we've got. Do you speak the language? ...a little?

Although Grandpa still 'works,' that is, he tries to sell real estate, last year he didn't sell a single thing. He and Grandma survive solely on their American government pension. If you include the fact that they also support Max, who at 40 years of age continues to live off his parents at home, then you can get a pretty good picture of what life is like at 14 Sunburst Crescent. It is not exactly the breadline or the soup kitchen, but it is not easy.

As far as my own plans are concerned, I have none... at least none that are firm. I expect to continue to be here at least for a year, but beyond that, I do not know. The economy in the United States is on a downturn and is suffering because of so-called free trade, which was introduced by the Republicans.(Did you hear what that idiot Reagan said last month? It was his idea of a joke: 'I've signed legislation to outlaw Russia forever. We begin bombing in five minutes.')

Please try to write again and more regularly.

Solidarity, peace and love,

Stewart

P.S. I had a strange dream last night, Eddie. Do you remember the day we visited the stunt man Eddie Kidd? How we almost lost our lives in his upturned car? I woke up laughing from the dream. You, me and Eddie Kidd having a drink and laughing together. I miss you Boyo.

* * *

5 January 2003

I was inundated with phone calls and messages. I was going down, so everyone was kind to me. My scrappy peace was disturbed by Taffy's telephone call. He threw legal jargon at me, testing out a new defence. 'Listen, comrade,' came his gravelly voice, 'the police will try to make out that you are part of a fucking conspiracy—it's the way they think. So what we have to do is paint you as Mr Responsible. You will be the representative of the public revolt against the lies and war. We will present you as everyone. This way we make the trial an indictment of Blair and Bush. Everything they stand for, and everything we're against. This trial will pitch our movement against their war machine—we will become the prosecution and you our chief witness.'

'The trial of the century?' I said 'I'm not sure I like the sound of that, Taffy.'

Why could Taffy not mount a modest and appropriate justification for my actions? If life could proceed in small measures, Taffy had to shun them for great ones. Eddying vistas, dizzy heights. I was the same. I spent my life splashing around in the sandy shallows, but I always needed to see the world from the deep blue depths. My trial, like our entire project, had to be the exposure of global capitalism. Now I just wanted to get off.

'Rubbish,' said Taffy to my complaints. 'It's the best chance, otherwise they'll have you, and you'll have to disappear or serve your term.'

I didn't question Taffy's ebullience for fear of the usual rebuttal. 'The point is, Eddie, I worry about your survival. You are important, accepted, respected, inspiring to the mass of the young. Don't be modest. A fighter who inspires is what Lenin was to hundreds of millions. The time has come. Being a sect is over. It's time for all of us to accept that we must become mass tribunes of the people. Our biggest fight is against fatalism and impotence. Eddie, we are the *global* wealth-producing class. We can seize all power. It is imperative that Lenin's message is restated now. Don't let the bastards grind you down! *We must survive*—for the world, we *have* to! And we can *win*. Think about it, comrade, and a have a bloody good New Year.'

He hung up, sounding ecstatic at his drunken theorizing. My mafia boss and socialist lawyer.

When I phoned Rebecca a few days after her messages, I was no clearer about what to do. I kept my phone off and spoke to Jessica and Esther on public phones. I contemplated every future. I could make a sharp break, refuse to see Rebecca and deny the child. I could leave—take Taffy's advice early. Abandon my charges and Rebecca. But I was defeated by the logistics. If I left, on what money would I live? I spent two days on fruitless reflection. Since when has time ever resolved a dilemma? What could forty-eight hours do? But I decided that, for now, I couldn't run, not because of the case or Rebecca but because of Esther. I thought that as she was falling, finally tumbling, I might be able to push her back, at least for now. I could be her emergency brake.

So I phoned Rebecca.

'Eddie, where have you been? Can we meet? Please? When are you free?'

We arranged to see each after my shift at the library on 6 January.

I spent my library hours hatching all sorts of absurdities. I was excited about seeing her. I remembered how beautiful she was, how we made love the last time. I thought that we could have the baby, live together and be happy. I saw images of us, like an advert for a mortgage, walking along the seafront in

Brighton, complete and indebted. The three of us. Eddie, finally respectable. My dilemmas resolved by pop-up common sense.

I didn't have any illusions about my life. Singledom had given me little except the resolution not to be single. A life shaped by loneliness and lustfulness, scorning the trap of children and the nuclear family during the day and masturbating at night.

Like every generation of activists I believed that capitalism was going to be replaced by revolutionary upheaval or go down to common ruin. I thought this was going to happen in my life time and that we could—that we were *compelled* to—spurn all ephemeral commitments to growing older. I remembered the urgency in my father's voice, his forgotten plate jumping to his staccato hammering on the table as he told us, 'This is all nothing. In fifty years—less—our society will be transformed. Our families and dinner tables will be the oddities of an antique society studied by the new world. All that is fixed, everything that we can see and feel—the grain of wood on this table, the institutions, schools, beliefs—will all have been blown away. Nothing is fixed, Eddie. You and Esther will be the pioneers of this new world. Remember, kids: "All fixed, fast-frozen relations, with their train of ancient and venerable prejudices and opinions, are swept away, all new-formed ones become antiquated before they can ossify. All that is solid melts into air, all that is holy is profaned, and man is at last compelled to face with sober senses his real condition of life and his relations with his kind."'

He finished his table lecture so worked up, so convinced by his own eloquence, that he leapt up like the revolutionary storm imminent in his mind's eye. He held our heads in his bowled hands and sealed the speech with a full-stop kiss. At the dinner table he was more prophet to us than scientific socialist. 'Never believe anything you're told at school,' he would say every morning, packing us off like four-foot disciples. Now planetary collapse was the new urgency to my father's prophecy. Maybe he was right, but what short lives we lead. My father had helped breathe into my sister an awful restlessness, when she needed to know that what we held onto today would be there tomorrow. I saw the end of the world each day, tomorrow, next month. What arrogance to think that history and revolution would open up in our few years of life.

I received notification that my next court appearance would be on 10 February.

* * *

6 January 2003

I didn't really understand what Rebecca's message had meant. I was distracted, my knee vibrating under the table. The café was a collection, it seemed to me on that day, of young adults bored with their jobs and themselves and their children. Men trying to fake an interest in their families, playing with their phones and newspapers. This was a conspiracy for us: over-gymed parents hating each other and their children. The men wearing tight T-shirts and white trainers, the women in capri trousers and pink shirts. The high pitch of children crying made me sweat, sick at this prophecy of our future.

I believed that my understanding of children was profound. We fuck them up, sure, but they are egocentric brats to start with. Socialists suffer with our belief that communism is the authentic outgrowth of our social being and capitalism a distortion of it. I argued the opposite: that because we are narcissistic cannon-balls, society needed to civilise us. Communism, I would say with red-faced insistence at meetings, was the highest form of civilisation that could tame us, turn us from ourselves, calm the angry tantrums the capitalist market only encouraged.

The meeting was my attempt to act like a serious prospective father, to discuss how 'we' would manage our lives as parents. A woman bumped into me with her young daughter clinging to her. I looked angry. 'Well, I am so sorry,' she said sarcastically.

'I want the kid and I want you, Eddie.' Rebecca fidgeted with her fingers.

'I'm not sure how I feel about children,' I said pathetically, too cowardly to say what I thought, scared that I would lose her.

'This isn't planned, but when would we ever plan for children?' She paused and looked around. 'It doesn't have to be like this, Eddie.'

I felt ugly opposite her. With her life in turmoil, sleepless half-moons under her eyes, she was still beautiful. And I was such a fucking cliché of a man. But I could see reflected in her eyes the three of us: a bohemian couple who went on demonstrations, talked about politics, forgot our washing up but loved our slightly neglected daughter. I was jolted back by the clamour of cups and shouting.

'Eddie, I love you,' she said quietly.

'Well, if we did try to make it work, I might be in prison,' I said.

We had drunk two coffees each. My head was spinning.

'Then we will come and visit you until you're out. It sounds quite romantic.'

'There is nothing romantic about children. They're hard work. They are what you become.'

She had her hands on the table.

'Why are you so bloody negative all the time, Eddie? It's a strange trait for a revolutionary.'

I heard my mother's 'Be positive' tagged onto the end of every phone call. She believed positivity was sometimes enough to overturn the establishment. Her positive post-fix was learnt from Stewart. Our movements, our will and our organisations could make the difference. For me this was 'be-positive' determinism. Simple will does not change the world, and revolutionaries do not make revolutions. But where had I learnt to be so miserable?

We left the café. I held Rebecca's hand and we turned our faces up to the January sun. I could feel her hair brushing my neck. We stood for a second transfixed by the light, absorbing its heat.

'I'm coming to the court with you, of course. I photocopied the leaflet and have given some of them out. So there will be a few of us, shouting "Free the Downing Street Tickler."'

From here, from my high perch, I can see everything. There were only two occasions when I felt positive about her pregnancy, two moments. The first occurred in the café with Rebecca that day. I don't know how this thought had barged through the din of couples and babies that had been drawn to us that afternoon, but in came this image of a child, already about four, between Rebecca and me, and a finger painting stuck with a magnet to the fridge. The second time was as I made my way along the Strand to court weeks later, the sky spitting against my face, and I thought about how I would play games of hide-and-seek with my child. I would not be like my father.

* * *

9 January 2003

We were back together. We made love all day and spoke about children's names. In those sealed moments, our phones off and the doors on our other lives closed, we could be anything we wanted: a proper couple in love, lolling lazily in bed in early January, joyously separated from the world. I wondered whether we were cramming in our promises before the smog seeped under the front door of Rebecca's flat and blinded us again.

Rebecca was speaking about her childhood. 'I used to get very scared. I was scared of the supernatural. I had an overactive imagination, especially ghosts. My mum used to get irritated with me; she should just have come to sleep with me. I remember being so scared and calling to her through the night. It was the worst fear, that sort of fear. In order to survive I developed a prayer. My mother's recommendation. She would say: "Ask God to keep you safe." She would read to me about Daniel and the lions' den, Bible stories. So this is how the prayer goes: "Dear Lord Jesus, please keep me safe and not scared and not for my eyes or ears to play tricks on me or for me to see any horrible things or hear any horrible things. Or to think any horrible things, or for me to be scared at all." I was covering all the bases. I think I probably fuelled the fear because I was fascinated by all things ghostly. There is also the theory that I'm slightly psychic and that I am picking up on things and that is why I get scared. I think my interest in the supernatural is an interest in fantasy. Something else than the mundane.'

'Are you a low-level psychic, then?' I asked.

'I really like make-believe, like magic. I like the idea of the subtle. Things that hover around us that we only glimpse occasionally. Why do you think that is? Do you think it is because I am very bored?'

'I don't know. Are you bored?'

'I don't know. Am I so bored with ordinary life that I have to live somewhere fantastical? I don't know. I think dancing and music are magic.'

'Can you make some magic now?'

'I don't need to now, because I'm not feeling bored.'

'Do I bore you?'

'No, not at all. You are my magic.'

'That sounds corny. Tell me about the future, if you're psychic.'

'Children. Two. Two little free spirits, maybe three. No, I am the third. They've brought out my free spirit. I imagine a house in Brighton. You are sitting in the lounge and reading and you're commenting on what you are reading. I'm listening, less for the significance of what you are saying, but just to hear your voice. The significance of you speaking. I'm in another room playing with the kids. They're drawing. Lots of colour. No, we're messing around on the piano. Nice smells from the kitchen. Maybe I'm cooking. No. That's too gendered. *You're* in the kitchen cooking.

Throwing out your voice. You're saying, "You won't believe what happened today. You know that guy?" And I'm saying "Wow, that's interesting," but I'm not really paying any attention. The house is full of noise and it's the evening and I am not the one making the noise. I'm just in the middle of it, enjoying it. You and the kids. A space infused with noise and love and family that I am at the centre of. But the thing is, it's never going to be like that—is it?'

'Why not?'

'Maybe it's not going to happen like that because I'm just not that kind of person. I take up a lot of space and make a lot of noise. I tell stories.'

'What are you wearing?'

'I'm wearing a long skirt and bare feet.'

'Incense? The supernatural?'

'No. I'm a mother. I have children. I have you. I will have no need of magic anymore. Just you, the kids and my music.'

* * *

10 January 2003

I fought to do what I had never done before: to trust Rebecca and let her in. I decided to show her the family jewel: Esther, holed up in hospital, our anorexic bird with her big belly, her shoulders, like wings, hunched up high with her head resting on her raised knees. If the walls were dimpled and soft and if straps hung off her encased body, the scene would be complete. We were almost there. The fucking asylum, almost built.

She knew I had come into the room, but she didn't turn. My little bird-sister was crying. I sat behind her on the bed and put my hand on her shoulder and adjusted her nightdress. Esther didn't move, just looked out the window at the sky. A dirty blanket of cloud covered the entire window. I thought maybe I could accelerate Esther's recovery, part her psychosis, if we could just travel to the Mediterranean. Everything would be better if I could only turn on the sun. She continued to sniff and cry.

I moved closer to her and put my arms around her. 'I know,' I said, 'it's incredibly hard.'

'You don't know, Eddie. You have no idea,' Esther said with a lucidity that surprised me.

'It's a figure of speech,' I said, moving away from her. 'It must be incredibly frustrating.'

'Frustrating?'

'Well—' I began.

'Frustrating? You make it sound like a failed business deal. It is not frustrating. I am lost.' She turned around on the bed and stared at me. 'Why are you wearing those shoes?'

I look down at my white sports shoes. The contrast was dramatic against my black cords and padded hoodie.

'I don't know. I always do. They're comfortable. I like them.'

'They look terrible. You look like Stewart.'

Esther moved up from the foot of the bed and lay on the raised mattress. Her head sank into the pillow.

'I can see you but I can't reach you,' came her muffled voice.

'It's the drugs,' I said.

I hadn't told her Rebecca was coming, and now I didn't know why I'd suggested it. Esther's sickness had always been our secret. Each time she was ill she was hidden away, not allowed to enter life. Jessica and I became her jailors, discussing who could see her. Who would understand? Who would drive her further into the psychosis? I was bringing Rebecca for myself, and it was selfish. I moved to the windows. A group of nurses huddled in a small circle in a concrete courtyard below, smoking.

'I was thinking about what you said when I last came,' I said, turning back into the room. 'I don't think it matters if you smoke.'

'What?'

'I mean if you crave a cigarette and it helps stop the panic.'

'I get scared. Nothing makes sense, everything moves around

in the room.'

'Then you can have a cigarette,' I said. I thought I knew what the illness meant. Esther had been uprooted from the world; nothing held her down anymore. Nothing had meaning. The world was crowded incomprehensibly with objects and events. My white shoes. The nurses' wide grins. Her own thoughts. I thought that the drugs would re-cerebralise her, de-alienate her, give her a chance to return to the bed, to the table, the floors, us. Fix her memories into a temporary order again. Esther would be able to escape her disorder and mayhem and come back to a world of ordered mayhem and war where we were all mad together.

'I can't believe you're encouraging me to smoke when I'm pregnant, Eddie,' Esther said.

'I'm not. I just think when you're sick it's a minor misdemeanour, and it might help the panic and fear.'

'Have you got any cigarettes?'

'No.'

'Go and get me some, please.'

'Do you think it's a good idea?'

'It was *your* idea.'

I picked up my coat from the chair and walked through the door, and then hesitated. 'I also want to introduce you to someone. A friend.'

'Girlfriend?'

'Sort of.'

'A sort of girlfriend? Maybe she can have a cigarette with us.'

I left the room with my hands in my pockets, checking for change. I might have succeeded in persuading Esther to take up smoking. Now she would be sick and have an addiction that would deform the baby. Why had I mentioned smoking? Because I'd inherited my family's urgency about life. We had to survive pre-revolutionary society in any way we could. If inhaling nicotine or abusing alcohol were necessary, then so be it. I wanted Esther better and I didn't care about the cost. I wanted her back. I wanted to pull her up from the bottom of the sea, where she stared up at our faces, refracted and twisted by the water.

As I walked out of the hospital into the brittle, cold winter, I thought that maybe the cigarettes and Rebecca would ease Esther's suffering, give her something more than my presence and useless words. It would be something concrete, like arresting Tony Blair and stopping the war. Maybe I should organise a demonstration against her psychosis.

When we came back in, Esther was sitting up in bed with makeup on. I hadn't seen her done up like this in years. Esther's cheeks were red; her glasses were on the bedside table. Even in sickness she had painted her face for Eddie's coming-out party with a female friend. When we were properly inside the room, she adjusted herself in the bed like a real patient, puffing up the pillow, readying herself for guests. She smiled, her lips glossed. *She's done all of this for me.*

She suddenly looked confused. 'Eddie? Eddie? I didn't know you were coming today.'

'But I went out to get cigarettes and meet Rebecca—I've only been gone ten minutes.'

Esther was silent. She didn't understand. She fell back into the pillow with a dejected look. Rebecca unzipped her coat and stood at the foot of the bed, smiling. *Esther, say something, someone say something.* But we were all silent. For days I had practiced what I was going to say: 'This is Rebecca, who is a special friend. I have been very keen for you to meet her for some time.' Why did I need to use euphemisms that sounded like I was introducing a geopolitical relationship? 'I wanted her to meet you even if these are difficult circumstances.' I thought it might be easier to make these introductions under the cover of Esther's psychosis. Maybe she would forget that it had even happened and not tell Jessica. I had unilaterally jettisoned our careful vetting procedure and admitted a stranger into our family secret.

Rebecca had said, 'Are you sure, Eddie, that you want to do this? Is it the right time?' I said, 'I want everyone to meet you. Even if they're sick. Esther is very important to me.'

'Oh, Eddie,' Esther said in a faint whisper. 'I thought it was the doctor.'

'You put on makeup for the doctor?' I asked.

'Of course. I always do. Doctors deserve respect.'

'It depends if they're any good.' This was the first thing Rebecca said. 'I'm Rebecca, Eddie's friend.'

Esther stared unblinking at Rebecca. There was an interminable pause before anyone spoke again.

'Can you take me to the toilet?' Esther finally said.

'Yes, I'll take you,' I said.

'I don't want you. I want her.' Esther started to move out of the bed.

She had changed her nightdress and was wearing one I hadn't seen before. It had huge doves flying against a field of oversized daffodils. She put an arm through Rebecca's and they walked out of the room as if they had been doing this for years. Rebecca winked at me before the heavy door swung closed and left me alone in the room. I heard Esther call out, 'Eddie, we'll meet you downstairs. Bring the cigarettes and my shoes.'

I gathered up our coats and put the cigarettes in my pocket. I looked for Esther's shoes under her bed. I opened the small cupboard next to the window. There was a pile of Esther's detritus: used tissues, discarded sweet packets, scraps of paper that she had written on, then thrown away. There were also two half-eaten bars of Sesame Seed Snaps. I stopped, trying to remember where I'd seen these before. Stewart. Stewart used to give them to us. I held one of the small, sticky bars in my hand, broke off a piece and put it in my mouth. The memories filled out.

Stewart turned to us on the plane, peering through the seats in front of us, where he sat with Jessica. 'Kiddos, I've got a special present for each of you.' He squeezed an arm through, his fist loosely clenched. 'Esther first. Open your hand.' Esther obeyed. 'Now close your eyes.' Esther furrowed up her brow, locking her eyes closed. Stewart dropped the clammy bar into Esther's outstretched hand. She immediately opened her eyes. 'Daddy!' she exclaimed loudly. I finished my sesame bar in two mouthfuls. Esther savoured hers across the entire breadth of the Atlantic.

I held the candy in my hand, with Esther's careful teeth marks across one corner. Maybe, I thought, I had eaten three of these bars since the flight to Chicago in 1979. I was three Sesame Seed Snaps away from Stewart. Four from the time we secretly shared one in his office, the three of us kneeling on the floor in secret collusion, breaking our pre-dinner fast. Five away from the time when I stole one from Esther's candy stash in her bedroom. We could travel on sesame seed bars—back to when Esther was well and Stewart alive.

I pulled myself up from the floor and put a hand on the bed to steady myself as the blood rushed into my head. Esther was with me when everything was being made. No one knew my world except Esther. I realised that without her I would always be alone. We were each other's foundations. I knew that the terrifying and fragile edifice of life would crumble if Esther didn't get better. I needed to buy some more sesame bars. I gave up the search for Esther's shoes and left the room with Rebecca's and Esther's coats over my arm.

I found the courtyard on the ground floor. Staff and patients smoked and spoke to each other quietly, seeking shelter from the drizzle under the high windows overlooking the concrete garden. It felt like a speakeasy full of sick people, contraband cigarettes traded by uniformed nurses to the terminally ill, who held themselves up by clinging to their mobile glucose drips. Esther, shivering in her psychedelic nightgown, and Rebecca, with her non-matching clothes, looked at home. They were huddled together under an overhanging window ledge, sharing a single cigarette.

Esther, slightly bent over, still had her arm in Rebecca's. The illness had turned her into an old woman: into Jessica. She shuffled around the linoleum floors of the hospital without raising her feet and walked leaning against the wall. I thought about how Esther always lost her modesty when she was sick. How she would have pulled up her nightdress in the toilet with Rebecca in the room, perhaps still attached to her arm. I cringed. I shouldn't have let Rebecca come.

'Coats,' I said loudly, approaching them with fake bonhomie. I draped Esther's coat over her shoulders and saw her wet feet on the concrete floor. I stood close to Esther, so we formed a crescent. I held out the cigarette packet.

'We begged one from a nurse,' Rebecca said, indicating the group of uniformed staff. 'Esther was telling me about you.'

'I hope not,' I said.

'Why? You've got nothing to hide,' Esther said sharply.

'What was said?'

'She was saying that I had to look after you,' Rebecca said.

'I said that I love you very much and that you are a good brother,' Esther said flatly.

'I can see that.' Rebecca pulled deeply on the cigarette.

'You look like a proper smoker,' I said.

'I was.' Rebecca smiled and passed the cigarette back to Esther. 'Your sister wants to read something she's written.'

Esther opened her hand and unfolded a piece of paper. 'I don't want to read it, can you?' She thrust the worn sheet towards Rebecca.

'Do you want me to read it aloud?'

Esther nodded.

'It's called "Secrets."' Rebecca said, her voice stuttering slightly on the title.

Every week he told us a new secret:
"We are going to live forever."
"I can remove my head."
"I love you more than all the little girls and boys."
I wrote mine down
IN CAPITALS on the back of sweet papers
The smell of sesame seed bars and Opal Fruits
And his promises.

I hid them in my books
And read them when I was lost.
With broken promises
The past has made my future.

Rebecca finished the poem and held the paper in her hand.

'Fuck,' I said.

'Why did you say fuck?' Esther asked.

'I don't know. It's very good. Very good. I'm just remembering those secrets.'

The poem was bleak and true. It felt like a series of blows: as relentless, I thought, as this winter and Esther's recurrent sickness. Our happy subversive Fridays when Stewart would whisper a secret to each of us as we giggled and twisted in excitement, swearing an oath to hold the secret in silence forever. Stewart wanted to keep it between us; he knew that it would make us closer to him. I committed my Friday secrets to memory; Esther stored hers on scraps of paper in her diary like a multi-coloured mosaic. But Esther was wrong. It was not the past determining the future, but the goddamn psychotic, sick present poisoning the past. Our glorious, funny, dead past. Our Friday secrets. The present was ploughing over, in deep waves of earth and rock, the past *and* the future. That is why I had said *Fuck*.

'I like Rebecca, Eddie,' Esther said taking the poem back from Rebecca's outstretched hand. 'I think you need to be careful not to fuck up.'

Rebecca laughed loudly. Esther smiled. 'Do you hear that, Eddie? Your sister's orders: Don't fuck up.'

Esther took Rebecca's hand. 'I hope that in time you'll become one of our family. As strange as we are.'

* * *

11 January 2003

I sat between two strangers, waiting for my order at the New Abacus.

'I know I'm going to be seeing him in two months' time. That's why I'm moving closer, for practical reasons, but also for him.' She was talking quickly to her male friend opposite. 'We're not twenty-one anymore. I'm too old for that. It's not a question of whether we'll be together in a year. It's just been so long since I was in a relationship. I don't know what to do.'

Under my hands was the blue paper placemat menu, which listed uninvitingly the roasted, fried and grilled goods that would arrive greasy and ugly. The repetitive beat of a drum machine came from a speaker over my head. A short, heavily lipsticked woman with a tight white and orange T-shirt was trying to sit down. The man opposite her handed her a note.

'Sam lives there. You know I went to college with her. She's a social worker. She lives with Liz, who I went abroad with. So there's a good potential social circle. It's not that we'll be together in a year.' For a moment I felt comforted listening to someone else's life. I suppose her own fears and justifications pulled me away from mine and reminded me that I wasn't alone.

I finished my food and left, and so did any feelings of solidarity and comfort. I thought it would make me feel better being at the café, but then I was back in the flat worrying again. I wrote a memo to myself and pinned it to my bedroom door: 'If you don't cool it you'll fuck up.'

We both said 'I love you' and I was never sure I meant it, and then I would spend the rest of the day trying to take it back. *All that is spoken is true.* I hoped that it was not true, because rarely had something given me so little joy. I was fed up and tired. The only thing I'd ever been was a sloppy part-time revolutionary. Rebecca told me I looked at her with hate. When one argument was resolved I created another, I got down on my hands and knees and created another. 'I'm not going to sleep with you again unless you come.'

Because we had parted well this morning, I wished now that it was over. If it was all over now, everything would be all right at last. Nothing was enough. I could not read enough (and what I read I didn't understand) and I couldn't talk correctly (and what she said was never enough). Three weeks ago she had said, 'Eddie, I think you're the kindest man I've known. Eddie, I think I love you.' For days she hadn't repeated those words. Because she didn't mean it? Or because she had forgotten how she felt? *Rebecca, what did you say? Can you tell me how you feel?* I couldn't nag her for her feelings.

When we met she put her arms around my shoulders and kissed me, and I could see that she was pushing herself up and down as if she didn't want to stay. So I started to put pressure on her shoulders, forcing her to stand still in the embrace. Sometimes, to force her to do this, I wedged my feet on either side of hers. Occasionally when we made love she didn't make a sound. Then I would fail. Sometimes she laughed when I was rubbing or flicking or sucking her nipples. If I was between her legs and she laughed I hated her. Sometimes, when I was kissing her breasts and she laughed lovingly, or was quiet lovingly, I thought, *I'm going to bite off her nipple. Rip it off with my teeth.*

Each time we met I felt that I had to re-win her affection. So I struggled endlessly with heroic stories to impress her, and I always failed. She hadn't repeated those words for days.

13 January 2003

'I'm going to tell you about my morning full of desire for you. I wanted to make love to you. I woke up feeling so horny. I was going to get up and make myself a coffee, then read.'

'You're mad. That is nineteenth-century. Why didn't you masturbate?'

'I did. That's what I'm trying to tell you. I imagined you were holding me from behind, with your arm wrapped around my waist and your hand between my legs. I've been waiting to tell you.'

'That's very exciting.'

'Nine o'clock this morning. You know I'm a morning person. It was like a burning fire. I couldn't read my book.'

I had finally put aside my dogmas and agreed to allow Rebecca to do a tarot reading for me. She pulled the cards out of her bag and became serious. 'So, how shall we do this?'

'I'm following your lead.'

'Okay. First I'm going to clean and shuffle the cards.'

Rebecca swept imaginary dust off the table and started laying out the cards seven at a time.

'Why rows of seven?'

'Because seven is a magical number. It clears old energy. The way tarot works is that the cards represent archetypal energy. When we touch the cards we put our energy into them—'

'What do you mean by energy?'

'Like a frequency that is set to a pitch. A musical note. A mother has a certain note. *Bong*. Imagine it in terms of sound. We *are* certain sounds and those sounds lie in our consciousness and tune into the sounds of the cards. But they're not sounds. I'm only using a metaphor because it's easier for me to understand. It's energy.'

'How did you learn all of this?'

'I did a course. There's a whole theory behind it. I don't know whether it's true. Tarot holds within it an important philosophy of life, and the more you understand the symbols and pictures of the cards, the more you understand the meaning of life.'

'Jesus. Fuck.'

'Okay, okay, now you cut the cards and choose three. Use your left hand—it stimulates the unconscious, emotional side of your brain. Are you getting it, sweetheart?'

I handed the first card to her. She flipped it over in the middle of the table and a stern woman in red robes holding a scale looked back at us.

'Two more,' Rebecca urged, and placed these on either side of the woman. She stared at the cards in silence. 'I'm waiting for them to speak to me.'

'Why would they speak to you and not me?'

'Because I am a channel. A portal.'

'You are my portal.'

Rebecca arranged the cards around the table. 'Shame.'

'Why did you say shame?'

'Because it doesn't look all good, but that's life, sweetie. It's important to be aware of the bad as well. The main card in this spread is the card of Justice. It's a major arcana.'

'What's a major arcana?

'The major arcana represent psycho-spiritual shifts. Like becoming a mother.'

'What about war?'

'War is an outside event, but war may provoke an internal event. It's a relationship.'

'The dialectic.'

'People create wars and wars create people.'

'Is this your social theory of tarot?'

'Yes. Justice means keeping the balance—being judged for what you do. The feeling I'm getting from this spread is that justice will be done. For me, it means you have to make a decision—bringing your intellect and emotions together to make a just choice.'

'Because it's psycho-spiritual, it has nothing to do with my case?'

'Yes, it has to do with everything. But here's the thing: the external manifestation of being judged before a court of law is also linked to an internal process going on in you. Of judging yourself.'

'Well, I can't leave it all to the magistrate to decide if I'm guilty, can I?'

'The content of judgement is different.'

'This is beginning to sound too intellectual. I thought you were going to give me a feel-good New Age reading.'

'But, sweetie, there is an internal balance that needs to happen. The external trial is ridiculous. You were enacting justice against the war, don't you think?'

'So there's a whole other trial going on. I see.'

'Yes, it's about you leading a just life.'

'Fuck.'

'What is that word for clergy, priests, kings?'

'The ruling class?'

'Yes, the establishment. The red robe symbolises the establishment holding the sword of cold intellect. In her other hand she's holding the scales. The card is telling you to balance the external and internal manifestations of justice.'

'What's the relationship between the external and internal?'

'It's all about form. The question is manifesting itself in terms of the trial. But it's fake. The real trial is the internal process. Eddie's insides.'

'Isn't there anything about my love for you?'

Rebecca moved to the card on the right. It had a boy holding a cup with a fish jumping out of it. 'The Page of Cups. The cup is emotion, and the page represents a person—a child, sensitive and weepy, emotionally immature. Or it could represent a new journey within an emotional relationship.'

'So I am an overbearing, emotional child?'

'No, but that energy is very strong in you.'

'This is getting too close to the bone.'

'The child in you has led you to this point. The next card—where you are moving into—is the Seven of Cups. A card of illusion and emotional addiction. There is a man facing away from us, looking at a cloud. Impossible desire. On the cloud are seven cups. One contains jewels, one a castle, a ghost, a woman's face. This is your desire for the unattainable. It always makes you unhappy, an unattainable goal.'

'Is it your face coming out of the cup?'

'No, she's got straight hair. Perhaps it's an unrecognisable me—you'll never be happy with me because your view of me is an illusion. I will disillusion you.'

'I want this to be light, sweetheart.'

'But *you're* not light. If I can sum up the reading: there is an internal process trying to find justice and balance. You need to be careful to bring your feelings and rationality together. Otherwise you'll always be striving for what cannot be achieved—putting something on a pedestal and in the next breath knocking it down.'

'Say that again.'

'It's self-perpetuating. A feeling that life is never going to give you what you want. You don't see people in their humanness. It's a beautiful sunny day and you imagine grey, so life can never give you what you need.'

'Sweetheart, I'm feeling suicidal.'

'Shit, I forgot to do a card. The card of the unconscious.'

'Drawn with your left hand.'

'It's the magician.' Rebecca placed it below the other cards.

'Oh, shit, that doesn't sound good.'

'It's a card of power that brings things into the real world. One hand of the magician is pointing up to heaven, the other to earth. He takes heavenly magic and turns it into something real on earth. His tools are the wand, sword, cup and pentacle. It's the card of making magic in life.'

'Proper magic? You mean abracadabra magic?'

'No, psycho-spiritual magic in our lives. It's metaphorical. Making things manifest.'

'Is it my activism?'

'No, Eddie, not everything is about your bloody activism. It's processes going on inside you.'

'So you're saying I need to move beyond the external?'

'Maybe you have a power in your activism that you don't want to apply to your own life. It's an internal process. Unfortunately, it's not light, if that's what you were after. I'm tired now and frankly I'm feeling a bit frustrated.'

'Doesn't it make you feel closer to me?'

'I don't know. It's complex, there are so many layers. I feel tired. You don't want to accept the truth of it.'

'I am very impressed at how well you know me.'

'Does that scare you?'

'Yes.'

* * *

14 January 2003

I asked Rebecca about her lovers and about the sex she had with them. 'So tell me,' I said, 'how many men have you had, Rebecca?'

'Had? That sounds as if I've eaten them.'

'You know what I mean. Had, passed through, slept with. Come on, remember our pact of honesty!'

'It was your pact, Eddie. I've had sixteen. You're the sixteenth. Sweet sixteen.'

'Tell me,' I said, 'about the sex. How was it? What were the men like?'

'Do you really want to know? Most of them aren't important now.'

'Tell me about the important ones, then.'

For more than an hour I interrogated Rebecca (her word) about the sex. When had she first had it? What time? What place? What sensations had she felt? Then I asked her if she'd loved them.

'Yes, I did, two or three, but only sometimes. Listen, Eddie, I've had plenty of sex and it was—A she paused— "it is, sometimes, very good.'

I asked how large the men were, keeping my voice flat and my face straight so I didn't betray how much my questions were hurting me.

'In my experience, which is not extensive,' she said, laughing and nudging me with her foot, 'you're about average.'

But there was one man she wouldn't speak about. Michael. She told me his name so I could hate him. 'I don't want to talk about him. Okay, Eddie? Why are you doing this? You do understand that it is none of your business.'

I didn't speak to her for the rest of the evening. I hate her for having loved before and for the sex she'd had.

When I went to bed I thought about these men. Rebecca in ecstasy. A man, Michael, his face buried in her. Using his tongue, more gently, more lovingly, more erotically than mine. I imagined him calling out her name as she came in ecstasy on top of him. 'Rebecca, my darling.' Maybe she even cried for him and said 'I love you.'

Can you really do these things twice? Can you really feel these things twice? I felt sickened by Rebecca's duplicity.

Rebecca said that you need to be strong to be weak sometimes. To admit that you've been wrong. Then to apologise for it and, most of all, to be the first person to say, *I have missed you. I love you.* But I didn't speak because I always wanted to pre-empt her. Her doubt. Her waning love. Her criticism. So I said nothing, and pride kept us apart.

Chapter Nine

Endgame

17 January 2003

When I met Rebecca she had just had a scan. The 'child' was a bundle of cells, barely detectable at this early stage, a smudge on the shiny photograph. I thought, *if it's a girl I will call it Jessica, Esther or Karl Marx.* I had spent the morning at the dentist. I saw pieces of food clinging to his dental tools. The dentist shouted at his assistant when his hands were in my mouth. Did he think I couldn't hear because my mouth was open? 'What are you doing? Have you had any training?' Then he wiped his hands on his trousers and held up a pair of tweezers, 'This is your nerve!'

I held Rebecca tightly. Tighter, I noticed, than she held me. We went back to my flat. I had promised to cook.

'What's wrong, Eddie? Is it the tooth?' It wasn't. I put my arm over her shoulder and caught her hair. 'Watch it, Eddie. Be careful.'

I pulled her against my chest. I held her neck firmly and tensed my arm. I was furious with her. Why did I have to volunteer all the affection? Why didn't she tell me how much she missed me? Because she hadn't? I held her angrily. When we got to the flat she asked how I could live like this. 'Well, it's clean enough.'

We embraced again and this time I hated my elbows that stuck out while I held her, thin and hairless, like sticks protruding into the room. I hated the way my hands stumbled when I tried to caress her. My fingers caught in her clothes. We clumsily removed our clothes and I pressed her to my kisses, reaching down to feel her wet vagina.

She removed my finger. 'Don't, Eddie. It's sore.' So I used my tongue. She was slow in coming; I lost my erection and tried desperately to get it again, tugging violently at my penis. She tried to reach for it. 'What's wrong?'

'Nothing,' I said, and pulled her again to me.

I had never known how important power was. It shifted between us constantly. When she said that she was 'falling for me,' I felt a rush of adrenaline. I was careful not to return her words, although I wanted to. I walked proudly that day. But last night she didn't speak to me, and I craved to hear her say it. How could she sleep? I got up, suddenly knocking her. 'Is it your tooth, Eddie?' she asked.

'You know what hurts me more than my tooth? It sickens me, Rebecca, that we are two activists and we can't communicate. We can't tell each other how we feel.'

'My poor Eddic. What's wrong?' she said.

So I pretended I was comforted and I didn't sleep.

When I slept I had two dreams. The first was about Stewart again, dying of cancer, and how in his last week he refused to see anyone. He had turned his friends and family away, then with his last strength uttered a chorus of 'fucks,' collapsed back and died. He didn't pass quietly into the night. I woke.

When I got back to sleep I dreamt that I had climbed to the roof of my block. I had washed and shaved. I was wearing a suit I had bought for a family wedding. I noticed as I pushed myself free of the building that I was wearing the shoes Jessica found for me, and I cried out for her. As I jumped I glimpsed the blue sky, which darkened as I fell into the street, as though I was really falling through an ocean. As my descent quickened I could see the sky unfolding endlessly into the distance. I could breathe the air freely like the first breath. As I fell the tangled noise of cars and voices faded and I could hear, as it passed, the cries of the sky. A triangle of birds sang to me as they flew across my path, flying up and up, using the currents of air like stairs. As I fell further I could see their journey across the thousands of colours of the sky. Then just before I hit the road, they soared again upwards and I knew that I didn't want to die.

When I woke Rebecca was in the kitchen. I shouted to her, 'I had a dream that I was trying to kill myself.'

'Well, don't,' she said, 'at least not until I've given you coffee and told you how much I love you.'

Later, when I was alone in the flat, I asked myself one of the self-obsessed questions that have an ugly habit of preoccupying me: *How will I feel in ten years' time if I am who I am now?* We always hope that time will transform us. That in the future, ten years from now, we won't recognise ourselves. Against this I declared, THIS IS ME. I'm sitting outside in the winter sun. The uncut lawn looks like a meadow and the windows from the flat above are staring at me. 'Put your lights on, you prat,' is shouted from the road. Tomorrow doesn't, for these seconds, seem terrible, with the day behind me and the slight sense of relief I now have that I am about to write down my thoughts.

I have just spoken to Rebecca on the phone. I will see her again tomorrow. Rebecca has revealed me.

I said to her, 'I remember my mother telling me that we always love ourselves more than anyone else. Well, that's nonsense. I have so much hate for myself.'

Rebecca said, 'I feel that sometimes you are trying to thump me. You remind me of my father. How can someone with so little self-respect give anything to anyone else?'

'We're dealing with bits and pieces,' I countered. 'We speak through this haze and sometimes we can see each other. It's for those things that we struggle. To maximise the bits.'

Then Rebecca was quiet again. After a pause, 'But I'm tired of people who thump me. I'm fed up of people wanting something from me that I can't give. That I'm not.'

After another pause I asked her, 'What's wrong, Rebecca?'

'I'm okay. I'm just tired. No one told me that the pregnancy would make me sick in the morning *and* tired all day.'

'The kid's obviously going to be hyperactive. I would like to be there, but I suppose you don't want to be held at the moment,' I said.

'I would like a hug. I would like you to hug me.'

And five minutes later the conversation petered out with 'lots of love' and 'the same to you.'

I left the flat after the phone call and went out.

I wished I carried a gun so that I could shoot anyone who humiliated me. I'd bring it out from inside my jacket and shoot. Whenever I'm laughed at for the way my legs bend outwards or when I make a mistake and I can see someone smile. Or when I don't hear what I want. Without a pause, without a sentence, without a word, I would shoot them. How much of this is even about Rebecca?

* * *

'Eddie Kidd: Three Years after the Accident,' *Daily Mirror*, 14 August 1999

THE last time I interviewed Eddie Kidd he was King of the World.

Today the ebony-haired Adonis whose name was once synonymous with leather suits, sex and mean machines spends his days in a wheelchair looking out at a world he can no longer be part of.

Three years on, the world still doesn't quite understand what happened that sultry summer's day in 1996 when a routine fifty-foot jump turned into tragedy.

But Eddie does—and he is finally ready to take responsibility for his tragic fate.

'I was out of my head on cocaine the night before the crash,' says the man who today sits broken and brain-damaged in the wheelchair that has become his prison.

'It was my fault. I should never have jumped that day. I wasn't right in the head. But I thought I'd get away with it. I thought I was invincible.'

It's taken Eddie three years to admit what happened on that terrible day. Three years of piecing together the tragic jigsaw that saw him go from daredevil stuntman to cripple in a few horrifying seconds.

These days Eddie gets tired very easily. But still, as he poses for photos, he insists we lift him to his feet. 'I want people to see me standing,' he says, clinging to a wooden fence in the grounds of the nursing home. 'Because I *am* getting better.' Two years ago Eddie predicted that come the millennium he would be fit enough to jump over one of the Pyramids. His bikes are still waiting in his garage, but the man who once jumped the Great Wall of China knows that won't be possible now.

'But I'll never give up,' he says, defiantly. 'I used to think life was like the movies. I thought that just wanting to get back on my feet would make it happen. But real life isn't like the movies, is it?' he says quietly. As I leave his room he adds, 'By the way, remember to tell the people I'm happy—well, as happy as I can be under the circumstances.'

* * *

22 January 2003

There was a mirror that stood above the bed in Rebecca's room. It was slightly buckled at the top and the reflection is always distorted. When I stood in front of it I was changed. I looked, somehow, more muscular. It pulled down my neck, shrank my head and bunched up my thin limbs. I didn't look too bad.

I could hear her speaking in the lounge. The words bounced against the walls of the flat, slipping under the door to reach me. I lay on the bed. I didn't want to hear anything. Rebecca's voice was raised in excited cadences.

I tried not to listen. Instead I thought about my boss at the library, who towered over everyone. His grey hair parted in the middle, flopping over his eyes, and he was always jerking his head to clear it. Today he had worn a corduroy suit and a shirt undone to his chest. In the staff meeting he had removed his jacket and rolled up the sleeves. The muscles in his arms rippled when he punched the air; his wrists were thick and strong. 'Let's go around the room and see what everyone's thinking. You first, Eddie.'

I had stuttered, 'I— I think we need to look again at our book stock.'

'We've just been doing that. Has anyone got something to say?'

From the bed I stared at my feet. My toes were stubby and short; the gaps between them make my feet look like they had never walked. I heard snippets from next door, Rebecca speaking: 'I travelled to Bristol for the BBC conference. It was the normal muddle of themes.' Her voice rose to a new pitch again, 'But don't listen to me, I'm a cynical has-been.'

I cut her out again and slid my hands under my bum, squeezed my buttocks. They were fleshy and soft. The woman at the gym had told Rebecca this week, 'You have an amazingly athletic body.' I think that there is nothing about the way I look that I like. If I could shrink my hips, pull my legs together, broaden my chest. If I could concentrate and sound intelligent. If I could be more like that man in the undulating mirror. If I could just like myself a little.

'Okay, that's fine. We'll speak tomorrow and go through those tapes. Love, of course, to everyone.'

I heard the phone go down. I wanted to die. To be inhaled by the bed. I counted the seconds.

'Darling, where are you?' she cried.

'Coming,' I replied. I jumped off the bed, yanked my penis down, stared briefly at the curve of my legs and leant forward to the wall. I brought my head sharply against it. The door shook.

My head throbbed.

'What was that?' she said.

'Nothing,' I replied, standing. I brought a hand up to my head to calm its thudding.

Later I stood naked in the bath, listening to the fan heater rattling in the corner of the room and the water dripping off me. My shoulders were hunched slightly forward; my head felt oversized and too heavy on my neck; my back ached. *How much of him am I?* I thought. *If I could strip away my childhood what would I be? What would have happened to Esther?* Without Stewart's schizophrenic love, without the belt and cinnamon toast? The fan heater coughed and spluttered and a warm current of air caressed me. I realised that nothing would be the same.

* * *

3 February 2003

When I saw her standing there in the black jacket with the gold lettering, the slightly washed-out cords and black roll-neck, I realised that I had been with her when she bought those clothes. I remembered her picking out those shoes, with the silly pink flowers and the worn marks already where her toes sit. We had bought them together in London. It was a bright, sunny day. December, but more like October. We held onto each other, paced up and down the high street buying shoes, waiting for our bus and trying to find somewhere to eat. I remembered those men in the restaurant we spoke to, red-faced and drunk so that we had to strain to understand them. They were only interested in Rebecca.

I had been with her each time she wore those shoes, each time she'd slipped into them in the flat and thrown them off in the bedroom. She looked now like a photograph of the time we had spent together. Evidence that we, these two dark-clothed souls, had been happy enough that day to buy shoes with pink flowers.

Watching her stand in front of me clothed in the memorabilia of our relationship, I thought, *what if we did break up?* I started to cry.

* * *

February 2003

Mark had decided to leave Alicia after passionately kissing Giuliana on the weekend. There was something honourable in his morality. Nothing had happened except heavy petting on the sofa with Giuliana. 'So you've kissed her. Now stop being silly and stay with Alicia,' I said. But Mark couldn't stop himself, and I wanted to see this through to its chaotic end. 'The kissing was so passionate and meaningful, so intense. It was beautiful,' he said.

'Did you have sex?' I asked.

'No!' Mark answered adamantly. 'It was more beautiful than that.' The real shift came because of the sperm test. He'd had to make sure that he could have children. The text came:

`I am fine. The sperm test was good! I came home and told Alicia the news and she gave me a big hug. I celebrated by riding to Giuliana's for an hour as she was at home yesterday afternoon. Need to talk.`

I was inundated with messages. He couldn't speak, so he texted me surreptitiously. Under the table, in bed, on the toilet.

`I met up with Giuliana last night for an hour, almost led me to being found out but I just survived by the skin of my teeth and it was nerve wracking. I told her that I wanted to see her more and that I intend to split with Alicia, possibly in the next two weeks. We didn't have more time to discuss things unfortunately, very frustrating. I want to meet up but I don't think it will be possible. Remember to bring the posters for flyposting.`

He had sex with Alicia and then texted Giuliana. I didn't understand. He had a healthy and normal sperm count, told Alicia, but celebrated with Giuliana. I admired his Tolstoyan complexity but hated his duplicity. I sympathised with Alicia but encouraged Mark to start preparing for the split.

`I would add that I think sometimes it is OK to leave relationships that are not working, or if you want something else. You just need to weigh up carefully. Why would A want kids at 55? It would exhaust her.`

* * *

4 February 2003

I spent the next few days with the brakes on, pushed back in the seat, trying to stop the week from careering forward. But I still wanted everything done: the morning to be inhaled in a moment and the day gone. Life rushed into the future before the present had been consummated. The magnitude of Friday and my looming court appearance grew. I had already become the prison's political chaplain, giving advice and running campaigns, reading in my bunk after lights out. Prison would be my return to school, free of responsibility to run my life. I would escape from Rebecca yet be the perfect father and lover, permanently present in my absence. All my failures of adulthood absolved.

My fear was not prison, but rather the public performance before I got there. The anti-war groups had mobilised a campaign for the Downing Street Tickler, who my comrades thought was an anarchist. Taffy didn't help. His daily calls before the Friday appearance made me feel as though he was my promoter before a fight.

'Comrade,' he gargled down the phone, as though we were in 1930s New York and planning a dock strike. 'Have you thought about what you are going to say on Friday? It is important. Either you will be acquitted or the case kicked out. In each scenario you will need to speak. Are you ready? I have been thinking about what you need to say. It doesn't matter if you are sent down or not, you can make the same speech. You need to start with the global anti-capitalist movement from Seattle in 1999, then growing to include international or large regional demonstrations numbering in the tens of thousands. Then three hundred thousand at Genoa, reviving Italy's left from the suicidal stupidity of the seventies.

'Then move on, Eddie, to the anti-war movement. So this already active global minority of mainly young radical workers and students took our line as soon as Bush and Blair used 9/11 to launch a blitzkrieg against the tiny, incredibly poor state of Afghanistan—voila, the global anti-war movement was born. Your last point should be about numbers, comrade. Now you have to be honest, Eddie, that this is yet to develop into workers' mass strike action. But the global impact of Stop the War is immeasurably powerful and deep.

'Lastly, Eddie, you should indicate the US and UK ruling classes' shock at the scale of the anti-war movement. Mention that *New York Times* article, I have it here, yes, "the huge anti-war protests are a reminder that there are two superpowers. The USA and world public opinion."'

His voice sounded more ridiculous to me each day, as though he was talking to me from the bottom of the sea.

'Remember your uppercut, Eddie, come around the magistrate on your toes. Hit him quickly with your left and then your right. Practice in front of the mirror. Don't leave anything to chance, get him under the nose. Knock his wig off.'

Some people are not born in the right epoch. The dulled, eye-worn days cloud the horizons. Colour comes only from our imaginations and history lessons. Taffy was like this. He did not belong to this moment of democratic calm. He craved disjuncture and paroxysm. When he found none he exaggerated and raged. Each beginning, for Taffy, was the endgame, every defeat a beginning. So my trial symbolised the cosmos, and his defence the universe's last chance. Taffy needed the frenzy of revolution; instead he had me.

I spent Thursday night, like he said, in front of the mirror with the opening lines of two speeches.

Speech number one: 'I have been convicted defending our right to protest. Nothing will deter us…'

Then, pulling a more joyous face, stretching out a fake smile.

Speech number two: 'Victory against these bogus charges belongs to us all…'

Each sounded pompous. I gave up and tried to sleep.

* * *

10 February 2003

I walked the Strand like a gangplank. The morning drizzled. The dirt-white sky reflected the pavement. The city looked suicidal. The Thames was a referee separating the two sides of London from locking together in battle; it prevented the city from crowding even more people and ugly grey buildings across its stretching arm. I turned my phone to vibrate and held it in my hand. I could see a crowd outside the court as I turned into Bow Street. On either side of the pavement were police vans. As I got closer I saw the ranks of riot shields and helmets.

Friday morning is the best morning of the week; the prospect of a night without the threat of work makes the morning easy. The crowd stamped their feet to keep warm and sounded as though they had gathered for a celebration. Some were jeering merrily at the police: 'What a waste of money!' I came up stiffly, my grey woollen hat pulled over my ears, almost covering my eyes, my coat collar wrapped around my neck. I looked like Taffy's prize fighter, a hard man without a face.

'It's the Tickler!' someone shouted.

There were cheers and I lowered my collar and yanked off my hat.

'You dirty anarchist, causing such a disturbance.' Mark was wearing the suit he had worn the night I was arrested. He put an arm over my shoulder and spoke more softly. 'How are you feeling, comrade?'

We moved into the vaulted court, where more people were waiting.

It was nice to have Mark's arm around me.

'All these people,' he said loud enough for everyone to hear, 'are here to make bloody sure that you are sent down.'

There was a shout of approval. A clerk of the court stood in the middle of the hall. No one could hear him; he flapped his arms for a few seconds and left. I saw the red-cheeked faces coming in from the cold. I kept Mark close to me. Taffy pushed his way through. He wore a blue shirt, rolled up to his forearms, and a badly knotted tie strangling his neck.

'Right, comrade,' he growled. He acknowledged Mark as a fellow conspirator and solicitor. 'It looks good. It turns out the pigs haven't given me the tapes, so they can't present them as evidence. I think they're fucked.'

My name sounded over the white loud-hailers perched in the corner of the reception. 'Mr Bereskin, make your way to Court Number 3.'

There were two security guards at the door. The queue of protestors started to push against the guards. The court clerk was sternly telling Taffy, who had identified himself to the court as my representative, to calm the group down or the case would be deferred. Taffy crossed the hall. He lifted his chin and spoke in his great demo voice: 'A minute, friends, the court tells me that they need quiet and calm for the justice system to work. Only fifty of us will fit into the court, so I ask the rest of you to guard the anti-war barricades outside and make sure the police behave themselves while we defend our right to protest inside.'

We filed into the court. I moved to the front of the court, Taffy by my side. I turned around and saw a line of faces staring out, muted by the glass panel that sealed them away from us. I raised a fist into the air and heard a muffled cheer. I saw Jessica and Rebecca.

Love is love. But love is never over. I loved Rebecca and hated myself for it. I felt as though I was going to crumple up and fold in two. I held onto the bench and steadied myself. I rested another hand on the table in front of me. *Fuck, fuck, fuck,* I muttered. Even in the middle of the court, the noise of the room echoing around me, I felt suddenly broken. I cursed myself again under my breath, reliving the moments when we first met. Her urging me on as I shouted at the police: 'Just do it!' Her waiting for me after I was released. My excitement at seeing her, our careless flirting, the easy anticipation of our dates, the intensity of our sex. What a fool I was, I thought. How could that end up as this? I craved to hold her, here, this moment. I turned and stared into the faces behind the wall of glass, not focusing on any of them.

Taffy prodded me, pulling me back to the surface. 'Comrade, come back from the dead. All pigs are stupid and I love you.'

I had not understood why everyone was so pleased. The crowd trapped in the glass box looked ridiculous, but I was proud. They were experienced internationalists. The generation of Seattle. Our T-shirts read 'Rage Against the G8' and 'Don't Attack Iraq' and we talked about anti-capitalism as if it would start the worldwide revolution. We knew 15 February would be unlike any other day. We were pulling back on the same catapult; we waited and organised for the middle of February.

The magistrate came out irritated that his court had been occupied, its normal atmosphere of calm and servitude dishevelled. He wanted us out. Taffy looked like a barbarian conqueror sitting on the wooded bench, official crests embossing each surface. The magistrate stared at him over his glasses and signalled to the prosecutor to stand. The buzz of chatting from behind the glass partition continued.

'If there is any more noise I will clear the court.' The magistrate hammered his desk. Taffy, brimming with contempt, laughed through his nose.

The prosecutor spoke. 'Sir, after serious consideration, the case against Mr Bereskin, charged under Sections 2(1) and 5 of the Public Order Act of 1986 and after serious discussion, weighing the vital issues confronting the Metropolitan Police and their activities and priorities, and considering the seriousness of these offences and the clear breach of the Public Order Act by Mr Bereskin on 31 October, as well as the expenses that these violations have already cost, my client is, given the above, deciding to revisit the charges pending agreement, sir, on the continuation of this case.'

The thin man gave a little curtsy, smiling at his mouthful of incoherence.

'Wanker,' Taffy whispered to me. 'They're dropping the charges and he said you're in the wrong.'

The magistrate nodded. 'Very good. That pretty much wraps this one up.'

Taffy dragged his tie down his shirt. His shoulders bunched up and his fist clenched. He jumped up.

'Sir!' he exclaimed. Everyone looked at him. 'For the clarity of the court,' he continued, 'may I summarise what my colleague has just told us?'

'If you really think it is necessary,' said the judge.

'Yes, sir, I do. In the case of the Metropolitan Police against my client, Eddie Bereskin, charged under Sections 2(1) and 5 of the Public Order Act of 1986, all charges have been dropped. There are no grounds for asserting the 'seriousness of these offences' since no conviction, no prosecution, no crime, in fact *nothing* was committed. This case has been a travesty and a waste of time.

Yours and ours, sir.

'But we won. Eddie won. Our campaign won. You see, sir, what the legal system of this country does not understand is that there are people, great masses of people, who are seriously disposed to fighting to the death to win. To defend the right to protest. To stop an illegal war. We survived more than three months barricaded into this theatre of the absurd because we fought with a permanently ready-switched hand-drill to shatter the booted legs that attempted to smash apart our rights. The Metropolitan Police need to be damn sure that we can do it again.'

How did Taffy speak for so long on a single breath? His great chest was swollen like an inflated balloon as he slowly let out the pressured air. I knew he was a speechmaker, but I wanted to get out.

'Blair needs to know that we are on the offensive now. We are absolutely, relentlessly committed to preventing this war. We will do it. The bloodbath they are proposing in the Middle East will not happen. We'll see to that, sir.'

The air fully escaped, Taffy sat down, shrunken back now to his normal volume. Loud cheers escaped the glass wall.

'I said *quiet* in my court,' the magistrate repeated. 'This case will not be pursued, if that is what you mean, but this does not negate that the charges were serious. Any breach of the Act is taken seriously, and if at another date further evidence comes to light, then these charges can be, in a manner of speaking, resuscitated.'

Through his teeth Taffy muttered, 'They even try to take away our victories.'

I felt like a spectator.

'Does Mr Bereskin want to address the court?' the magistrate mumbled.

I didn't respond. Taffy elbowed me hard. I stood up.

I remembered the first line of my valedictory speech, but as I was about to speak, I thought of Stewart. A whole memory suddenly surfaced. We were leaving for Chicago in July 1979 and the mini-cab sped through the city's streets, the morning sun bouncing bright off car windscreens and bonnets, making the deserted city a utopia of light. Stewart was speaking to the driver as we crossed the Strand: 'You could always drop me here.' Warm air from the open window caressed me. I sat with Esther and Jessica in the back. 'I'm not travelling with them,' boomed my father, who lifted every conversation with volume and intonation. 'I'll be making my way back right afterward. I work here,' he said, pointing to Bush House as we crossed the river and passed Aldwych. 'You could drop me at work now. Hell no! I'll take them to the airport like I planned.' He was lying. Stewart told us that mini-cab drivers burgled the empty homes of their passengers, that this man might steal my pocket money and Isaac's watch. My father thought this aging, sweet-faced cab driver, who had struggled with our bags from the house and arranged them meticulously in the boot, was a thief. Stewart suspected everyone: judges, wives, children and the proletariat.

'Comrade. Comrade.' Taffy urged me to speak.

'I would like to say that I am not guilty. That the Downing Street Tickler has not committed a crime. But neither have those who are still waiting to be heard.'

Taffy was nodding his head furiously. He whispered to me, 'Mention the right to protest.'

'We were exercising our legitimate right to protest.' I heard dulled exclamations. 'No one, in court or government, will stop us from protesting. All attempts to stop people standing up in history have failed. Today they have failed again.' Again cheers.

'Mention the war. The war,' Taffy continued *sotto voce*.

'These are not normal days. We face an illegal war, one that is being organised not far from here. We did not stop the bombing of Afghanistan. But we can prevent the bloodshed in Iraq.'

A few cries of 'No War!' came from behind the glass wall.

The magistrate was playing with his glasses. I could see a slight smirk on his face.

Taffy elbowed me again. 'Talk about the demo.'

'We know that the Saddam Hussein regime is a brutal dictatorship, but that does not permit this attack and invasion. We will not rest until we stop their war—and we can do just that on 15 February. The day when all of us, everywhere, will be mobilising to prevent the war.'

I was going to continue, but the magistrate leant toward his microphone. 'Do you feel better now that you've got that off your chest?'

'Fucker,' Taffy said behind his hand. I was still standing.

'No sir,' I said. 'We haven't even started.'

There was another cheer, longer this time, and rattling on the glass screen.

The magistrate shouted, his face now puffed and angry, 'Clear the court.'

It seemed that Rebecca had already been making plans. Where we were going to live, how we would manage on my salary at the library and her work. She had organised a weekend for us in Brighton; we would stay with her mother. She was beautiful with the white-blue February sky against her black hair and her pale clean skin. She had been created for these winter days. She had a flush of pregnant exuberance that made me feel unhealthy and ugly next to her. On the day of the court case Rebecca had cheered from the back, and when I came through, ordered out of the court by the magistrate, she rushed up to me.

'Excellent result, Mr Tickler,' she said, more confident than me. Rebecca kissed me matter-of-factly on the lips, long and heavy. It was a proprietorial punctuation mark as though we had been together for years. She was saying, *I am Eddie's comrade-lover*. Then she went, not waiting for confirmation or for me to make a sudden public announcement: *Here is Rebecca, comrades. We are having a child together.* Rebecca left and in her place, as though they were the same person, was Jessica with her coat draped over one arm.

'You followed my advice, Eddie. Good. I'm going to see Esther and I'll call you later.'

'That's my mum,' I muttered to Taffy again as she elbowed her way through the crowd.

'Yeah, I've got one of those. Good that she was behind you. Mine used to come to all my appearances but she's too ill now. She hates the pigs and the Labour Party—all my family hate the Labour Party. Never been supporters. Too cap-doffing for the militant elements of the British working class.'

We were almost outside and I wanted Taffy to shut up for a moment and listen to me.

I said, 'My mum has been an activist since the 1960s. She's done everything. Best militant I know. I think she's post-revolutionary, if you know what I mean. We all need the revolution to clear us of all the bullshit of capitalism, but she's already been cleansed. She loved us so much as kids. She protected us from the world and from my dad. She's also a genius. I think she knows Karl Marx personally.'

'Yeah,' Taffy said half-thinking, blinking out the sunshine. 'All mums are revolutionary.'

I felt a strange moment of panic that I wasn't going down. I would have to cope on my own, left only with my panic-filled love for Rebecca. The fights hadn't really started in earnest, but I knew they would. Before we really understood each other, there would be a year-long baptism of upset, separations and reunions.

We pushed our way through the police in the lobby; people in the crowd patted my back like I was a politician. I thought that the anti-war movement was a fraction stronger now than it had been two hours before. The momentum towards 15 February was building inextricably. But it was not to these things that I turned, but to her. Always to her. I repeated in my mind how it had gone, my short speech. Jessica's advice: 'Eddie, if you're going to speak in court tomorrow, keep it short. The art of public speaking is brevity.' Foreign troops were massing again in the Middle East and all I could think of was how I had looked to Rebecca.

I felt the snap of cold air as I emerged fully from the building. Stewart was always calculating; he made plans based on mistrust of everyone. She loves me, so she will betray me; he is going to cheat me, so I will lie; I am in love, so I must protect myself. Everything my communist father did was built on a scheme, a great mountain of pre-empting. My mind ticked to the metronome Stewart had set. I reacted like him because I had copied him. When I lost him I knew I would lose everyone. So I always had to prepare to leave. I had to pre-empt life.

'We did it, comrade!' growled Taffy once we were away from the police, stamping off the cold. 'We're a good team. You should get nicked again.'

* * *

10 February 2003
Dear Sir
NOTICE OF DISCONTINUANCE
DEFENDANT: YOURSELF
OPERATIONAL REFERENCE NO. 01CX3327302
I am writing to inform you that I have today sent a notice to the Clerk to the Justices, under section 23 (3) of the Prosecution of Offences Act of 1985, discontinuing the following charge against you;

Violent Disorder.

On 31 October 2002 at Whitehall SW1 while present together with two or more other persons, you did use or threaten unlawful violence and your conduct taken together with that of the those other persons present was such as would cause a person of reasonable firmness present at the scene to fear for his personal safety, contrary to Sections 2 (1) and 5 of the Public

Order Act of 1986.

The effect of this notice is that you no longer need to attend court in respect of this charge and that any bail conditions imposed in relation to this cease to apply.

The decision to discontinue this charge has been taken because there is not enough evidence to provide a realistic prospect of conviction but please note it is anticipated further evidence may become available in the near future, as a result of which the prosecution may well start again.

CAUTION: This notice only applies to the charges specified in it, and does not have any effect in relation to any others that may be pending or other proceedings against you. If you are legally represented you should contact your solicitor immediately.

Yours faithfully,

Staggart
Senior Crown Prosecutor
Southwark Trial Unit

* * *

11 February 2003

Lifted by my temporary victory, I had agreed to spend a night in Brighton with Rebecca's mother. This was the last weekend before the demonstration. These were good days for us. I thought I was indestructible. We were going to stop the war. Esther was stronger than she had been for months, and if she wasn't better now, I knew she was going to recover. She would build herself up again and stand tall and happy. I was also clear of the case. It had finished with me feeling that my life fitted together. I was now a well-rounded activist who had carried out his attack on the police with a certain panache. And for these short days, before the trip to Brighton, I also thought that I was in love and that I would now instantly be propelled into a proper life, complete and necessary. Fatherhood, family and politics.

There is logical love and there is illogical love. The last is without warrant; it defies reason. I call this the *Jason and the Seven Argonauts* syndrome. I remember being turned over in bed when he came raging upstairs. He shouted like a hog as he hit me, but even then I thought most of this was for show. The force of his grunting didn't match the force of the belt against me. But for Esther it was different. In her thin frame that stretched out over the bed, he saw Jessica. Stewart, his blotchy face, twinkling above us in the solar system, *Hello dad, Stu, comrade. I love you.* I still wanted him even as I heard his grunts from Esther's room and her screams. *Love me, hold me, Stu, tell me a story and butter us together like sandwiches on your bed.*

I sat on his lap for *Jason and the Argonauts* that night. Esther didn't. It was her little 'fuck off'; this was her logical love. But I wanted him and I held his secret. An Eddie the Kid love special: beat me up and I'll love you forever.

At the beginning of February 2003 I thought Rebecca was my logical love. It followed our dates, the political discussions, our lovemaking and our still-bright future. We were two slightly alternative and averagely screwed-up people. Not bad for a part-time librarian. I swung my feet on the bed in the spare room of her mother's flat in Brighton, decorated with a patchwork bedspread, two neat bedside tables, a large paper globe with a dim bulb and a thick carpet. I kicked my shoes off and dug my feet into the carpet. The room was clean and I wanted to be naked in it, to roll around with Rebecca on the bed. I could hear the clatter of plates and laughter downstairs. I walked to the window and looked at the sea.

The evening had been easy. I was relaxed. We laughed as though we had known each other for years. Her mother, Judith, was young and she sat next to Rebecca, the two of them nudging each other through the meal like sisters. Her mother said 'fuck' a lot, like me. I think that's how we connected. She talked about her work as a legal secretary: 'All workplaces are fucked, but at least there are only three of us. The solicitor is senile—he's always been absent-minded and stupid. I do everything, the tea, accounts and the law. It's fucked. I spend most of the week fending off landlords. My boss just sits on the cases. This week I had to counsel an old man who has two court cases pending. One to enforce payment of his benefits and the second to contest a Possession Order. It's fucked. My life is about constantly obtaining documents and witness statements. But the chance of winning either case is decidedly fifty-fifty. If my boss wasn't senile he would be stopping the eviction of tenants from a block in Hove. The landlord wants to turn a hundred rooms into fifty studio flats and sell them at half a million pounds each to the usual middle-class yuppies. Fucking hell.'

Judith told me that occasionally on the weekends she smoked a joint and walked on the beach collecting driftwood. She spoke to her daughter every night, 'to keep in touch,' as though Rebecca had emigrated to Australia, not moved an hour up the M23. As she cleaned the table she joked, 'I don't have any illusions about men and I don't expect you're any better. But ignore me, I'm a bit pissed.'

I laughed. Rebecca let out a long 'Muuuuuum.'

'I'm not a real man. I was brought up by my mother and sister. I consider myself an honorary woman.'

'Those ones are the worst sort, they don't know what they are. Insecure. Fucked!' she shouted from the kitchen.

'I'm not fucked,' I pleaded.

Rebecca rolled her eyes at me. 'Please, mum, Eddie's our guest. Don't let him see what we're really like or he'll run away.'

For all of her mother's 'fucks,' I was put in the spare room. 'That's where the double bed is, silly,' Rebecca had replied to my whispered protests.

'It's to stop us fucking,' I replied.

I lay on the bed and had decided to tell Rebecca that I loved her when she came upstairs.

'Sweetie,' Rebecca kissed my neck. 'You were sleeping. Can you hear the sea?' She walked to the window.

'I can't hear anything,' I complained.

'Yes you can. Listen.' She patted the air with her hand, telling me to be quiet. I heard traffic.

'That's the road.'

'You're such a Londoner. You hear nature and you think it's cars.'

Rebecca came back to the bed, pulling her top off. She hit the paper globe, which swung heavily, throwing its dim beam from side to side. She knelt at the foot of the bed in her white shapeless vest. She pulled it up slightly, exposing the bottom of one breast, and then ran her hands over her stomach. There was still no sign of the pregnancy. She puffed herself out and smiled. I looked at her, shadows swaying evenly across her body as she moved in and out of the light. I felt a shiver of excitement that she was my lover. She fell down on her arms and crawled up the bed, over my body. I heard her mother pull the light-cord in the bathroom and start the fan.

I couldn't concentrate.

Once Lenin had won the argument in the Central Committee for an uprising against the Kerensky government in September 1917, the only question that remained was when it would be carried out. This was not a small point. The Bolsheviks, though now the majority in the Soviets, knew that in this period of great upheaval popular opinion would change quickly. If the mood for mass action was missed or not properly led, it could become dispersed and defeated by the forces of reaction.

Trotsky said that if General Kornilov's attempted coup in August against Kerensky had been successful, if the Bolsheviks hadn't defended the Provisional Government, fascism would have been a Russian invention and not an Italian one. But without decisive leadership from revolutionaries, the same readiness for resolute action could be turned to the advantage of other parties of the left: the Social Revolutionaries, the Mensheviks.

Rebecca was now hovering over me, holding herself up.

So the Bolsheviks had to act, but they needed to make an audacious offensive appear defensive, as though they were defending the authority of Soviet power, as though they had no choice. The Bolsheviks needed to move now or not at all. To seize power, consolidate their majority. The pretext was the defence of the Soviets. The aim was the revolutionary overthrow of Kerensky.

Rebecca was still over me, smiling, teasing me with her hair.

'I love you,' I said.

'Hah,' she replied and fell on me laughing. 'My mother says that I'm not a very reliable person to love. But who cares?'

I tensed. My face flushed red and I swallowed hard. I couldn't look at her, so I pulled her close to me and put my arm around her head. My throat felt dry and I could feel my heart thumping. I squeezed her neck harder.

I needed to make this look defensive.

'Eddie, that hurts.' I pulled my arm towards me. I heard her choke. She emitted a muffled cry. I let go and sat up.

'Eddie,' she said and turned towards me. The white vest covered one breast. I kept swallowing. She tried to touch me again. I turned slightly and quickly thrust my clenched hand into her face. I felt her nose and lip against my fist. The force threw her back. I leant forward and hit her again, harder.

She cried out softly. The fan in the toilet was still whirling. Rebecca now lay curled up on the bed, holding a pillow over her face, a circle of blood traced around her mouth. She was crying. I pulled on my shoes, leaving my socks on the floor. Where had I left my wallet? I needed to get out.

Before he went to prison for rape Mike Tyson was every boy's hero. He tried to kill his opponents. Smash them, break their bones, finish them. Tyson's anger, his tight jabs, his short, compact body, built only to hold up his muscle-power, were a source of great excitement.

Stewart, my big-headed father with his bird neck and communism, loved boxing.

'Eddie, don't forget to watch the Tyson/Bruno fight on 25 February. I don't have much faith in the Brit, Boyo. Tyson is unstoppable. I wouldn't like us to be caught in his way. Anyway Boyo I love you, keep your defenses up, practice that left hook. Solidarity, peace and love.'

But by the late 1980s Tyson was already a wavering star, his fights more messy. His thirty-second knockouts were now stretched out. Our muscle king with his killer punch was being fought into the late rounds. But I still loved him and dreamt of having the same power, in the playground, at home.

I wanted to hit Rebecca again. Lean over and pound her again, simply for the primordial thrill of smashing her face. It was easy. I hated her.

So now Tyson relied on his fumbling pre-fight rants. He was nasty. The fighters sat against a white promotional banner advertising the fights. The fake glare of the spotlights had Tyson fluttering his eyelids to focus, as though he was trying to flirt.

'What's your strategy for this fight, Mike?' a journalist asked.

I thought about Mike now, while Rebecca quietly sobbed, as I got up from the bed and looked for my socks.

'It's simple. I want to finish him. I'll hook him under the nose, like this.' He jabbed his fist in the air, pulling it under an imaginary nose. 'Hit him like this and knock his nose into his brain. I'll try to catch him right on the tip of his nose, to punch the bone into the brain. That's my strategy.'

The journalist and cameramen laughed nervously. His promoter guffawed.

I pulled my shoes on, stumbling on one leg. I hit the lampshade, opened the door and left.

I ran up the dark street and turned in the direction of the train station. I knew I was too late for the last train back to London, but I kept running. The road was lit by fallen bowls of light from overhead street lamps. I saw the moon, bright and whole. I kept running. If I ran fast enough I would erase what had happened, move far enough from Rebecca to unfold my violence, pull back the blows and straighten out the moment. Stewart's name was not tattooed on my forehead. I was, if I kept running, a clean piece of paper; each fold of life would not come up with his name. I was Eddie, darting in and out of the fallen circles of light, free, undoing with each stride what I had done, what had been done to me.

I took a taxi back to London and sat in the front next to the driver, resolutely ignoring the ticking meter. My head swelled and pounded. I needed to leave when I got home, pack a bag and disappear again. Pick grapes in France and un-Eddie myself. I spent my adult life like an expectant mother, a bag always packed to run away. Ready to leave and start again. The car came into the city, swung onto the Brighton Road, through Croydon and Mitcham to Tooting. Groups of people were leaving pubs, talking too loudly and zigzagging across the road. Red lights stopped us on empty streets. I got out and paid with my credit card, automatically calculating the time it would take to repay the journey in library hours. Three part-time days.

I packed a bag but didn't leave; instead I turned the flat over for signs of her. I went to my books and pulled out the card she had given me that was keeping my place in the Percy Bysshe Shelley book she'd also given me. *Eddie, I am proud of you. Thank you for giving me so much hope and for the big struggle. Love, R.*

I threw it onto the floor. The Post-It stuck to my fridge signed 'R' and *Remember our night*! that I had found after she'd gone in the morning, days after we first met. Then the small gifts already exchanged in our short life together. The chrome kettle that squatted on my stove to save room in my small kitchen, she said, a practical present that made us both laugh. I put it in the middle of the room with the others. Then the book of Shelley's poetry.

Rise like Lions after slumber
In unvanquishable number—
Shake your chains to earth like dew,
Which in sleep had fallen on you—
Ye are many—they are few.

She had written a dedication inside the cover—not one line but a full page. She knew this was going to happen; taunting me, she had written one full page of sweetness which ended:

'To the most fabulous and beautiful person... I want you to have this, because it has inspired me. Please read it and know that you have my heart and passion now and in the future... R.'

I went to my music and pulled out the CD that she had mixed for me, with the sleeve notes to be read, she said, as I listened to each song.

READ THESE PAGES WITH THIS CD.

Track 1. *Stand and Deliver.* This is another song I played to you on our journey to Oxford. I had to sing the words to you so you could hear them. They are dramatic, over the top and '80s and soooo fun to be dramatic to. Until I saw you be '80s dramatic to them... you totally outdid me—all I could do was watch... When it comes to '80s dramatic I realise and accept (begrudgingly) that I have to step aside and leave it to you, Eddie—I cannot compete with your brilliant '80s dramatic!!

Track 2. *Move with Me.* I played this song to you just after I had instructed you to walk into the room with nothing on and an erection. I was wearing my blue dress with the buttons down, exposing my cleavage, and we masturbated together... I played the song because you make me feel as sexy as this song.

Track 3. Aaarh! I don't have the version you played—but nevertheless—*Hallelujah*. The song we danced to on the pavement in Highgate when you told me, "Kissing is cheating." There were moments in that dance where we were the only two people in the world, all overwhelmed with feelings of love, and you said to me that you were feeling like you wanted things you don't normally want… it was a sense of the possibility of happiness in love that you/we had stopped thinking possible. Do you remember?

Track 4. *I Want to Know What Love Is*. "I want to know what love is. I want you to show me. I want to feel what love is. I know you can show me." Eddie, Eddie, Eddie… you have shown me what love is.

Track 5. On our way to the train station, to go to the public meeting, and I'm playing you *Twist and Shout*. You are encouraging me to sing at the top of my voice to them—which is something I do willingly, happily—something I've never done with anyone. And you sing out to Piano Man, which I have not included in the selection (space constraints). Which leads me to one of my most cherished memories—the arm writing-guessing proposal on the train… If I stare at my right inner arm for long enough I can still see the faint outline of the words…

Track 6. *Rolling Stone*. So we're sitting outside eating lunch and Dylan comes on—and you think back to a time when you were unhappy and this song came on and you thought you were like the rolling stone and this worried you: "on your own, no direction home, a complete unknown, just like a rolling stone." I think to myself and say here (coyly)… let me be your home.

Track 7. *I'll Stand By You*. Okay, I debated about whether to include this song! I am a sucker for dramatic emotional love songs—and this is one of my all-time favourites.

> While it is corny and overplayed, the lyrics are significant and express so much of what I want to let you know I feel for you. It is a beautiful song and while all the other songs express our precious memories, this one expresses my hopes and dreams for our future. So cringe if you must, but listen to the words. From me to you! "When the night falls on you/ and you don't know what to do/ Nothing you confess/ could make me love you less."

There was now a pile of her in the room. I threw it all into a plastic bag and took it downstairs to the bin. I hadn't changed the sheets since she last stayed. I pulled them off the bed and left them by the door. The sun was coming up now. I undressed and curled up in the sheetless bed.

Chapter Ten

The Dialectic

August 1997

Esther phoned me. She had been well for a few years. She was ridiculously happy now, and we forgot that she was often not. She lifted us all.

'Eddie, I just wanted to say that I found something out today. Jessica was married before Stewart, for two years.' Her tone was oddly ebullient.

'What? Who told you?'

'She had a child. The man was older than her. They got married when she found out she was pregnant.'

I sat on the sofa in my shared lounge, a finger shutting my right ear, the phone pressed hard against the side of my head.

'She signed a visitors' book with her married name, so I asked a few questions. I think her husband was French.' She was breathless.

Even though the news had shocked her, it had not dented her exuberance. She sounded excited.

Each year, another subject buried. Our childhood had been a recent addition. Jessica shouted, 'Don't exaggerate; you had a perfectly normal childhood. You were probably spoilt. Anyway I don't want to talk about it. What is the point of this solipsism anyway?' That finished it. So Esther and I remembered together, in secret, away from our mother. Soon there would be nothing that we were allowed to talk about. Jessica never spoke of our childhood, or of hers, or of any time before Esther and I had been born. Topics for discussion shrunk every year. Two decades of silence. 'I am allowed to have secrets, and I don't think what happened before you two came along is any of your business.' But no life can be lived in silence.

'Charges dropped against Eddie Bereskin,' *Socialist Worker*, 11 February 2003

Peace activist wins!

The news has just come through that the police have dropped all charges against Eddie Bereskin, one of the main victims of the police arrests on the peaceful Halloween protest organised by the Stop the War Coalition in October 2002.

Seven people faced charges following the protest. The most serious charge Eddie faced was violent disorder. This carries a maximum sentence of five years. There are still some six people facing charges, although it is believed that these are all of a minor character.

Eddie's campaign received widespread support from across the movement, and was publicly endorsed by Lindsey German of the Stop the War Coalition and the Labour MPs George Galloway and Jeremy Corbyn. The activity of the defence campaign ensured that the police could not just sneak the case through unobserved and contributed materially to Eddie's eventual victory.

To all those who helped, many thanks!

* * *

13 February 2003

There is an absurd amount of water in this city. Why don't the clouds part for a few days? Why can't they even tantalise us with the lie that the sky is actually blue, that it reflects the open, hopeful, cloudless ocean? Instead the city has been stitched closed, sealed by a thick impenetrable layer of dirty grey. The city needs therapy. There are even daffodils in the shops, bunches of them tied together with eager elastic bands, their pathetic heads ready to shed their petals in a desperate bid to out-stretch one other. They are the most appropriate flower in this sunless land.

In February hope is hard in London—it is as though I am taking a wild, unforgivable bet against ridiculous odds. We have to stop the war, to turn back their springtime invasion, but we also have to confront the country's late-winter lethargy. Our weather system long ago lined up with the government. 'Let loose the clouds. Open up the skies. Let it rain!'—these are the battle cries of the British ruling class. We face one of the oldest, most wizened and experienced ruling classes of the northern hemisphere—and their guard-dog and faithful ally Captain Drizzle. Curse this country.

Did Stuart have to leave? He could have served his sentence for battery and theft and then repaired himself and died in London. Instead he fled, his fingers still scuffed from ripping up the house and us. He went, but he could've stayed, reconciled himself to his violence, apologised. Found God. Decided he needed redemption. Because anything would have been better than his disappearance… except, maybe, his presence.

Rebecca said we could meet. Not in the cafe, in the park. I sat on the toilet today, trying after my first coffee of the morning to shit, pushing my arse deep into the pan. I rested my feet on an upturned bin, a trick Rebecca had taught me. 'It helps the bowels by curving the body to ease the movement. You should know this, Eddie,' she'd said. 'You told me the Bereskins were experts in shitting.' 'How the hell would I know turning up a bin would help?' I said, laughing.

When I was done I cried. It was the smell of our faeces when we went to the toilet that made Esther and me feel as though we were violating one of Stewart's sacred laws: to call him to clean our bottoms, to remove the clinging, stubborn shit from our hairless fleshy assholes. Our little voices filled the house in the mornings (for me) and the hours after school (for Esther): 'Come and see me!' The smell yesterday in the toilet brought it back. I knew, even when I was nine, that it was strange, pretending to be Eddie the Kidd in his caravan, swinging my legs as I sat on the toilet calling Stewart because he wanted to know we still needed him. Answering our call, wetting the toilet paper, walking between the bathroom sink and the toilet was his ritual of love and insecurity.

I made the decision to meet Rebecca. I had been in a frenzy of cleaning her away, wiping down surfaces for traces of her fingertips. Pulling her out of my flat was what I had always done. I ran away from what I had done. My world was cast into violent opposites. I missed her; I had to leave. I loved her; I had to go. My life was spent in constant flight, in permanent transition from ever trying. I had to destroy the possibility of our being together, because it had already been destroyed twenty-one years ago, when the world exploded in a cataclysm of broken hearts and incomprehension.

I had set up my life so that each fibre which held me in one place could be easily broken. I could leave my library job, if I chose, at the end of the week. The flat had a three-month renewable lease so I could get out quickly. Even my politics: I was the egg-throwing anarchist who turned up to meetings every fortnight. I was part-time in my life. Never straining enough, never completely committed. I could always wager a bet on my life, because it never meant much to me. I was always going to be reinvented, turned around. I *could* still train to be a doctor. I *could* move to Marseille. I *could* commit myself to the revolution properly, completely. I could even love Rebecca without violence, without hesitation. *Tomorrow*.

I wanted to meet Rebecca because I needed to apologise. I wanted to stop running. I wanted to hold her and tell her to laugh at me, tell her that she could love me and that I would not be like my father, I was not Eddie anymore. I wanted to have the baby. I wasn't going to prison and I wanted her to have the child—a little Rebecca, who would demonstrate with us and shout in high-pitch for me in the night. I wanted to try.

The meeting had been arranged by text message. I might have

clamoured for our reunion against everything I had ever done, but I was still a fucking coward:

Text 1: `really need to see you, E`

Text 2: `fuck off, R`

Text 3: `I don't pretend apologies are enough. What I did was unforgivable.`

Text 4: `u r a bastard. Never want 2 c u again.`

Text 5: `I can be different. I will be. I want to tell you. I love you Rebecca. Please.`

Four hours passed before she replied.

Text 6: `okay. Just 2 show what u've done.`

I pulled up my collar, tied my scarf around my neck, flattened my hair and ran through my lines, each time sounding more like the cliché of the violent man. *I will change. I will be different. It won't happen again.*

The park should have been closed and the gates locked. There was only me walking slowly, clutching my clothes tight around me. I saw two runners in Lycra, plugged into their music. The trees stuck out of the ground, bare and twisted like knotted arms and fingers. One tree had broken out in blossom and I began to worry that the frost would soon kill the pink flowers clinging densely to the branches. A few birds sung and hopped between the flowers. I took it as a positive sign.

I sat on the bench near the entrance to the park, where I could survey everyone who entered. I would see her before she could see me. I sat, stood, sat again. The boards of the bench were stiff. I waited, practising as though I was going before the magistrate again: 'I do not want to apologise, Rebecca, because I can't. What I did cannot be taken back. Nor do I think I can be reformed in a simple act of will that I can just turn on. But I want you to know that I am going to start the long process of fixing myself up. Because I love you and I want us to be together.' It sounded trite. The birds tweeted inanely in the dying blossoms. Were they laughing at me? I needed to get it right.

Even though I saw only the top of her head bobbing along the concrete horizon, I knew it was her. She appeared in quick inches rising up, as if she was being pulled out of the ground until her height had been completely extended. She was wearing her long puffer coat. Her hair was tied back, black curls escaping the band and colonising her face. Then the anomaly: the sunglasses as black as her hair. Her eyes were completely blacked out. She continued to bob up and down as she walked towards me. Her glasses were all I could see. All I cared about. What had I thought? I smashed my hand into her face and made her bleed. Did I think that she would sleep it off, wake up in the morning with forgiveness and no markings? I hated myself. I wished I wasn't here to witness this grown, proud, beautiful woman hiding her bruised face under a pair of glasses. She looked like Jessica. Like fucking Jackie Kennedy.

I stood up and turned toward her, still holding my coat closed. Ten metres from me she stopped. Rebecca was scared; she didn't want to approach me. She looked around to see if there was anyone else in the park. A witness to this duel, someone to protect her from me. Her eyeless face was a blotch of white and black marked against the cold sky.

I saw Jessica again. She'd picked us up the day after the fight in dark glasses with a determined, clipped 'Hello sweetie.' I saw her first in the blurred window standing outside the classroom door. I knew it was her, even in the sunglasses. I knew why she was wearing them. She stood next to the headmistress, beckoning to me. I collected my pens, brushed the pile of wood shavings from my pencil sharpener into my hand and slid the contents into my pencil case. I was nervous. I closed my messy exercise book, packed together my drawings and scraped the orange plastic chair back from the table. My mother had come to get us and I didn't want to go.

Stewart had driven us to school, more jovial than normal, his tone and enthusiasm a tonic for the night. He gave us great kisses in the morning when he came down. Esther was eating her cereal slowly, the book open. He bounded in and held her in his arms. 'Hello, sweetheart, what are you reading?' Esther was irritated at being disturbed. I saw her smile, her head now pressed against his shoulder. She didn't answer, but closed the book, her finger keeping her place.

'Where's mum?' Esther asked when Stewart was in the kitchen. 'She's gone early to school to finish some grading. I'm taking you in today.' I could hear the cupboard above the sink open, Stewart reaching in for the bottle of cod liver oil. The rattle of cutlery as he rummaged for a spoon. He called us into the kitchen for our morning ritual. Esther got down slowly. I was more obedient and hurried in, eager and stupid for the glutinous poison we had to swallow every morning to our father's gentle reprimands. 'Until Esther invents a potion to make us live forever—so we can be together forever—we will have to settle for fish oils. Sorry, sweetie-pies, but I want you to be strong, to survive capitalism. The struggle requires longevity and the ability to swallow bitter-tasting remedies. I love you both.' Like this, with the same words every morning, we would obey. We would grow up with healthy bones, ready for the transition to socialism.

Esther's good mood was gone; she dragged herself into the kitchen. Stewart was on his knees, holding the bottle. He looked distracted. I was the first in the queue in a chequered shirt buttoned up to my neck, maroon cords and sandals that made me look like a miniature Jesus. Our washing was suspended from the high ceiling and the kitchen smelt of our clean clothes. Stewart's face was marked with torn pieces of toilet paper stained red from his morning shave. Stewart could always be identified: his voice always bellowing and his face badly shaved.

'Do we have to take it today?' Esther's appeal was pathetic. Reluctant though we were, we rarely dared to challenge our routine. Stewart crouched on the floor, a bottle in one hand and the spoon in the other. He shook his head to clear his thoughts, frowned and considered Esther's request. He smiled, his forehead folded up. He placed the bottle and spoon on the ground and opened up his arms. I ran in. Esther, realising what she had succeeded in doing, followed me into Stewart's embrace. He put his head between ours and brought us together tightly, his face bristling and chafing our cheeks. He didn't say anything. The three of us caught in an early morning hug, the sun, flooding in from the window, warming our bodies, our hearts racing because we had won the right not to be poisoned again.

'Of course you don't have to take it. I won't tell anyone if you don't. We'll take it again tomorrow.'

There was no tomorrow. We never took cod liver oil again and we were never held tightly in Stewart's arms in the kitchen again. We drove to school bouncing on the seats. Stewart forced us to sing with the windows of the car down:

In the town where I was born
Lived a man who sailed to sea,
And he told us of his life
In the land of submarines
So we sailed on to the sun
Till we found the sea of green
And we lived beneath the waves
In our yellow submarine.

'Sing loud, kiddos, to wake up all these dull Brits!'

He took us into school. Esther ran back to the classroom. 'What about a kiss for me, kiddo?' he shouted as she ran off. She stopped, swivelled on her heels and ran back. Her bunches, neat and symmetrical, her thin face and round glasses made her look old. She was happy to be at school, to kiss Stewart, for the morning to have been like this.

I cried. He came to the door of the class. Did I think he was coming in? That he would play, paint, add up and spend the day with me? Perched too large on the plastic chairs, his legs taller than the small table where the children worked? When he bent to kiss me, I remembered suddenly that I would be without him and that he would return to Jessica, the fight and last night. Back to being grown up, where adults screamed and hit each other. He was going and would not come back. I cried. The teacher stood by the door patting the heads of her four-foot-high pupils as they filed into the classroom. Stewart was on his knees holding me.

'I don't want you to go, daddy,' I snorted.

'Boyo, I'll see you in a few hours,' he said.

'I don't want to go to school today. I want to stay with you.' I was crying heavily.

The teacher disapproved. 'What is all this, Eddie? Come on now.' My histrionics were unacceptable. Stewart, normally charming on parents' evening, glared at the woman. 'My son is upset. He will go in when we are ready.'

'I love you, daddy,' I said pathetically.

Stewart stood and pushed me gently toward the door. 'I love you too, Boyo, and I will see you tonight.'

The door was closed. Stewart stood outside the class peering at me through the glass panels of the door. I undid my jacket and took my box of crayons to the table. My head hung low. I couldn't do anything; I couldn't stop the fighting. I couldn't stop Stewart from leaving me today or Jessica from picking us up like a glamorous extra from *Dallas* with her sunglasses on. I couldn't stop the catastrophe. Our divorce.

Rebecca and I still stood, separated by the bench, wondering who would draw first. Who would pull out the first sentence? Shoot.

'Can we sit?' I said at last.

'No. We can speak from here,' she said.

We fell silent again. A runner passed, breathing heavily, the synthetic buzzing of her headphones filling the air. Rebecca pushed her glasses up her nose. I sat on the arm of the bench. She didn't move, and I felt encouraged. It was three days since Brighton. The day after, I had stayed in bed in the dark, my flat quiet and my head strangely clear. I didn't read. I lay silent, thinking, regretting the night and her absence.

'How are your bowel movements?' I asked, not knowing how the sentence had come out.

'What?' she replied.

'I was wondering whether you have been shitting okay?'

'Fine,' she answered sharply.

'Great. Regular? Every morning? Or twice a day?' I said, really wanting to know.

'I don't want to talk about my fucking bowel movements. I don't want to talk to you. What did you want to say?'

Why didn't she use my name? Why didn't she mention my name?

'What do you want to say?' she repeated.

I shifted on the arm of the bench. I didn't want to say anything; I just wanted to hold her. I didn't want to risk being offended again for nothing.

'I know I can't apologise. I hate what I've done and I can't take it back.' For all my resolving, my courageous resolutions to stare at her, to look into her face, I stared at the ground. I lost my place. 'I miss you. I hated you because I was scared. Because my dad hit my mum. Because I don't know how to love.' I hated the sound of my words. It was saccharine, apologetic drivel. I sounded self-justifying. I wanted violent punishment. To have my act exonerated in pain. I want Rebecca to hit me; I wanted to be punished and then freed. I saw a worm wriggling pathetically on the concrete under the bench, its pink dirty skin against the rough path. I lost my thread again. 'I think I was constipated,' I said. 'I mean I hadn't been to the toilet for a couple of days. It always affects my moods.' Rebecca let out a shrill laugh that echoed across the park. The birds in the blossom tree stopped tweeting. 'You did *that* because you hadn't been to the toilet? You're sick. You make me sick.'

'No, I don't mean it was because I was constipated. Of course not. I'm not making excuses. I don't blame anything except myself. Not my father. Not my childhood. I did it. I hit you.'

Rebecca sat down on the bench, her hands in her pockets. She didn't turn to me but stared out into the park. In profile I could see that her eye was still discoloured and moist. I couldn't look at her anymore.

More runners. A couple, chatting to each other. They were dressed up with such precision, so neat, their socks pulled up over skin-tight leggings. The man wore hot pants. Wires joined different parts of their bodies. The woman asked, 'Would you suck his cock? You wouldn't?' The man didn't answer. 'You would?' she cried. 'You dirty bastard!' They didn't notice us.

'I know you can't try me out again. But I want you to have the child and I will be a good father. I will support you.' My words seemed pathetic to me. Hopeless. I mumbled.

Rebecca straightened herself on the bench and pushed back her shoulders. I struggled to hear her when she spoke. She looked at the trees and the empty common in front of her. 'Last night it was the end of the world. I was with my mother, and this time it was going to come in the form of a wave. A tsunami. We were in Brighton and the wave was coming and we had to crouch down on the floor like this—' she bent up, lowered her head and back and pulled up her legs— 'and we felt this big wave crashing over us. We had to hang on. We knew it was the end of the world. There'd been a frenzy of preparation. Then the wave went over us and we survived. Me and my mum survived. We had been given a second chance.' She paused. Her voice grew louder, more confident. 'Then I spoke to you on the phone and you were upset about something and I was trying to tell you that we'd just survived the end of the world. I wanted to tell you but you didn't get it: Whatever you're worrying about, it doesn't matter because we survived the end of the world. My mother and me survived and you're being so petty.'

She stopped. I felt chastened by the dream, but as usual I didn't know why. Was there redemption in the apocalyptic wave? Was I petty? Had Rebecca and I survived? Or had she survived me? Was it our second chance? Our possibility to escape the crashing wave?

'There is no child, Eddie,' she said.

My mouth dried up. 'What?' I stuttered.

'It was easy. Easier than I thought it would be. I stayed in Brighton and had a termination. I cut you out.'

The park was deserted again. I wanted to be interrupted. For someone to walk past us, for a noise, something. But there was not a note, not even the sound of the wind breaking on the trees, not a sound from the deluded birds playing hide-and-seek in the blossoms, pretending it was spring—nothing. Not a single sound to punctuate Rebecca's last sentences. There was nothing on this dying earth to help me.

'The woman at the clinic asked me if I was sure. It took about half an hour, and then I bled. I didn't even cry. I was with my mother. There is no child, Eddie.'

I thought that I was now standing on the pivot on which my life would forever turn. The moment of shock and awe, of calamity, that would not be silenced slowly by a gradual forgetting. The memory of Brighton and that night was all that there would be; it was the new core out of which my life would spring. I thought as I sat against the bare planks of the bench that what I had done would always be done. It could never be erased or taken back. My life would now always be that night.

My life would be the bedroom with its thick pile carpet and the heavy swing of the paper globe throwing its shaft of light on to the bed and flashing the world into bright, white relief. I would sit permanently in the darkened auditorium against the walls in her mother's house, watching the pool of light falling on us. I was sitting now on the bed. Rebecca still smiling, my face still. All I would hear was the cry, until the globe swung back and Rebecca was lying in a ball clutching her face. I would sit with my fists clenched, my face tight and tensed, as the tube of light fell off our bodies and the bed. I would see us, fixed in this absurd and permanent tableau, the glare of light revealing our old pose. Rebecca still smiling, her mouth slightly open, my face still, and then the relentless, merciless fall of the light, the metronome-swing of the lampshade again across our bodies. Darkness for a second, then her cry. The light creeps up the bed again. Blood is running slowly through her fingers. Each time the same, each time more, swinging endlessly over the same memory. Time is marked by repetition, not the forward crack of fresh life. I would always live here. On this bench, in her words, in that night three days ago that I made. 'I cut you out.' I had made Brighton my fork in the road.

The depopulated park was strange now. How could it be so bare? Was there a crowd of people bunched up at the gate waiting for us to finish? The air was cold and motionless. How could we be sitting here, still silent? I shook away the stale self-pitying, my morbid and self-fulfilling nostalgia. I felt we could refuse to be lodged in the past. I wanted to tell Rebecca this, but instead I said, 'Did the termination affect your bowel movements?'

I had hit her twice properly in the face to make sure that I hurt her. I had wanted to break her face, crush her nose. To destroy something. I had wanted to do this more than anything else at that moment. It felt instinctive. My violence, primordial, satisfied a real urge. I'd wanted to smash her face like I'd longed for an ice cream as a child, like I sometimes wanted sex. I was humiliated, and I also wanted to hit her for the sheer bodily pleasure of the violence.

Before, when we slept together, our bodies crossed in an uncomfortable embrace, dry sperm on my chest, a smear of it on her leg. We had brought each other to happy climaxes, joking in the bright room in the middle of the day. It felt subversive to be naked when we should have been working. Afterward we had fallen into an afternoon sleep, curtains clumsily closed, a strip of white daylight forcing its way through.

'I want to ME when we get home,' Rebecca had said, laughing, when we met.

'Is that short for Masturbate Eddie?' I said.

'Good, very funny, but it means Move Equipment. I need to clear the room of my recording equipment, but you're giving me ideas,' she had responded.

'I want to MRFF,' I said, squeezing her hand.

'I'm not indulging you, Eddie.'

'Masturbate Rebecca's Free Fanny,' I whispered.

We did, and then we slept, insolent and cocky. She woke after an hour. I dragged myself up from my heavy sleep. I wanted to be alone, and turned away from her angrily. If I could grow my hands one hundred times, I thought, I could crush her in them. Grind her into a ball of dough in the palm of my hand. We fell asleep again.

Now Rebecca pulled out her phone and started tapping on the keys. I thought that maybe she was going to phone someone, or detonate a bomb that had been wrapped around her limbs under her coat. She continued to text. I couldn't think of anything else to say; the pregnancy was gone. Rebecca was motionless except for a finger scurrying across the small keypad. She stopped; I heard my phone buzz in my pocket. I didn't connect the two actions. I left my phone unanswered. She started typing again, shorter this time, the phone buzzed again. I stood up to straighten my pocket and pulled the phone out. I opened the first message, Rebecca's last:

`read your message please.`

Then I opened her first message:

`I don't want to see you again. What you did to me as a lover, you did to me as a friend. I hope` you find a way out, Eddie. R

Rebecca still didn't move. So I texted her back, still standing. My fingers were cold and stiff, nervously pressing on the keys, hitting the wrong letters. I was aware of her sitting, poised to go. I texted:

True, what I did cannot be changed. But what I'm doing now I have never done. I am not running, making excuses, blaming. I can be different. I can show you. Please.

I pressed send. There was an interminable pause as the message was transported invisibly to her. I heard her phone beep. She lifted her hand and read the message. Then she typed briefly. My phone vibrated.

no Eddie. It's too late.

But still she stayed, not moving, not typing. Maybe she wanted to be persuaded that I could really be different. My hands shook as I texted again.

please Rebecca march with me on 15 February. Like we did on Halloween.

I sent it across the two metres that separated us. I heard the familiar signal from her phone, her hand lifted from her lap. She read and paused. I texted again, my thick fingers stumbling over the keys, deleting words, retyping.

We could demonstrate together, start again. I won't get arrested or tickle the police.

I sent it. She read again. Desperate to keep her still on the bench, I typed again.

I have a theory about your dreams: they are a sign of the build-up to war. Your subconscious rebelling against destruction. Please march with me.

Then another, before this one was even fully sent.

Rebecca, don't go. Stay. I miss you, I won't comment again on your bowel movements. I will never hit you.

Her phone buzzed. My hands were shaking from the cold. More messages. I had to send more messages. Her phone was vibrating and beeping in a frenzy.

imagine us on 15 February. Against war together, Rebecca and Eddie.

Now, there were only seconds between the phones buzzing, my messages arriving, her glancing at the screen. I thought, *if I can keep sending them she will stay*. Each message was a small rope tying her to the bench, making it harder to walk away. The phone beeped, her finger hitting 'open,' the message flashing up on the screen. I wrote in a cold fury.

Please 15 February. We still have time. You found me in this war and I can change on that day, when we stop it.

The phone was wet in my grip; my fingers slid on the keys. I dried my hands quickly on my trousers. My phone buzzed. I opened the message.

stop it Eddie. I am leaving.

Rebecca stood up in profile; all I could see was black, her hair and coat done up to her neck, almost touching the ground. She turned toward me and spoke.

'We managed to break the illusion in the end,' she said.

'What do you mean?'

'Do you remember the reading? The illusions in the Seven of Cups. We've broken the illusions, but through the destructive power of the Tower. I had hoped for the gradual positive transformation of the Death card. Slow change. Together we could have slowly shed the skin of illusions. Your life is the Tower, Eddie. Swift and violent.'

She stuffed the phone in a pocket, turned to her right and walked away. Dumbly, I tried to text again.

please Rebecca.

I shouted to her when she was near the gate. REBECCA. My

words hung in the air, louder than I wanted, silencing everything else except her soft steps away from me. She kept walking through the gate and then, like she had arrived, she shrank slowly and gently into the concrete horizon.

* * *

14 February 2003

Jessica was expansive. I hadn't seen her like this for a while; she even spoke generously of Stewart. 'He was a difficult man. I blame his freelance work. He had a very good work ethic, he worked incredibly hard. But the effect of so many knockbacks, work planned and then rejected, it was devastating. There was something awful about the way the men treated Zoe. She was a wonderful woman but they rubbished her, put her down. I always wanted him to help bring you and Esther up, even when we weren't together. But he was so angry, so bitter.'

I repeated the story of Stewart's funeral. The family house in Chicago that was a shrine to us, each surface lined with photos from our childhood. Like a museum to grandchildren.

'Don't, Eddie, it's too painful,' Jessica said.

I replied, too eagerly, 'Of all the things we must learn from Stewart, the most important is never—no matter the reason—to be bitter. Bitterness is the cruellest emotion.' The cruelty to children is done twice, once in childhood and then when we are adults, to our own children.

Jessica shut me up again, her eyes ablaze, fixed on an idea. 'Enough of your misery, Eddie. You think too much about the past and you don't think dialectically. From quantitative incremental and gradual change to qualitative change. Heating water degree by degree is quantitative, but at a hundred degrees the stable liquid turns to steam. Stewart wasn't always bitter. He didn't have to end up that way. We want to change the world but we discover, bit by bit, that we are changed by it. But it works the other way too. The dialectic is optimistic. Because struggle is dialectical. And so is life.

'Today we think we can see how everything in the past moved. We imagine that if we look closely enough we can see everyone's contemplation. But what good is that, Eddie? Sometimes you should just forget the last thirty years and then open one eye and look around. When you've done this you'll have the bits and pieces that we had to manage on. I mean, it didn't have to happen. Stewart's bitterness. Our lives are not a jigsaw puzzle for us to complete. If you look around with one eye closed you'll see more clearly.

'Please just stop with your desperate reminiscences. Your version of history feels like a story from Homer—life by predetermined bitterness. Life is the leap. The contradiction. The interruption of gradualness. Life is possibility and choice. You must turn your history into a guide to action, not contemplation. Just understand the dialectic, Eddie, and *live*.'

* * *

15 February 2003

By mid-February winter had begun to wane. The sun shone. Flowers came up, taunting us with the hope of spring, like the flags of a pathetic army. Then spring broke off and winter snapped back, killing the flowery promise. People pulled on their coats and scarves again and swore at the weather that could not make up its mind, hated the dashed hope and doubted that the sky would ever break.

Each street was full, every tributary, from the Strand just across the river along Charing Cross Road, Tottenham Court Road, Bloomsbury and Euston. Small streets fed larger ones. Tube stations were closed. When trains ran, they were crowded. Coaches stretched from Euston Square to King's Cross. It was cold, the sky light blue. I didn't recognise anyone as I searched the crowd outside the Goodge Street tube station for our delegation. No one. An old man, unshaven, wearing a suit jacket and red braces, nudged me. 'My daughter's demonstrating in Glasgow. Couldn't come down, too far for her. I just got a text from her, thousands up there as well, she said.' He smiled at me and stepped off the pavement.

Jessica was meeting me. I heard a samba band playing, carving its way into the crowd. I recognised the band leader hammering on a snare-drum, wearing plastic strap-on breasts and a ballerina's tutu.

I said to the man, 'Can you believe these numbers?'

'Amazing. They have to listen now,' he chimed. He lifted his phone in the air to photograph the bobbing heads of the crowd.

In the office block opposite me I saw people leaning out of their windows, not, for a moment, understanding London. The face of a young woman turned toward me, incredulous, open-mouthed. I screamed, 'There is nothing like the power of the people. The power of the people, oh yeah.' A few people joined in, until hundreds of us sang. I felt like a sixties hippie with my jean-jacket done up, its white fake-shearling collar around my neck, my dark-rimmed John Lennon glasses. I threw my fist into the air and jumped up. I saw a small group holding a homemade banner: *Zimbabwean asylum seekers against the war. Jambanja now.*

I spotted Mark in his suit and cashmere coat and shouted to him. He came over and squeezed my cheek. 'Not bad, comrade. We can organise a good demonstration. Do you think they're all from Tooting?'

I felt my phone vibrate in my inside pocket. I didn't recognise the number.

'Hello,' I shouted.

'Eddie? Eddie?'

'Who is it?' I covered my exposed ear and pushed the phone tightly against my head.

'Eddie,' I heard again. 'It's Jessica.'

I crouched down so I was in the forest of legs and children. I could hear.

'Sweetheart,' she said, sounding more like Stewart than herself. 'I can't come to the march. Esther's had the baby. I'm at the hospital.'

'Oh fuck,' I said.

I could see two children, a boy and a girl, singing together, trying to keep up with the slogans shouted above them. The girl was older and she held the boy's hand. They danced and skipped together on the spot. They thought that they were alone, hidden in the subterranean bracken and knotted branches of the crowd.

'She's fine, sweetie. The baby's okay. They gave her an epidural and she'll be okay. The baby is, well, almost cute.'

When I looked again the children had gone.

'Eddie, are you there?'

'Yes. Should I come over?'

'No bloody way. One member of our family has to be on the demonstration. What's it like?'

'Brilliant. Tell Esther we're going to stop the war and that I love her.'

'She's going to be fine, you know. It will still be a while, but she will be fine. But for now, sweetie, march.' She hung up.

I could hear Stewart in her voice. It made her words sound like an embrace, a soft order.

I stayed crouched on the ground and put the phone away. I covered my face with my hands and cried. My sobs were lost in the noise around me. Tears poured through my fingers and down my arms and onto the ground. I yelled as though I was being dragged into the tarmac. I couldn't hold myself together anymore. I couldn't pretend anymore. I was going to dissolve, fall onto the ground and leave only my worn jacket and jeans and a pool of tears. I wanted to see those children again.

I wanted to remove all the children here, to remove them from us and find them a place where every day would be like this one.

Then I felt ridiculous that I was crying. I had cried too long, it was now indulgent. Stupid. I dried my eyes on my jacket sleeves, sniffed and wiped away my snot. I took a giant breath before I stood up again and faced the demo.

The crowd started to move forward. Mark had found the Tooting anti-war banner and pulled me toward it. My eyes stung in the light. I saw Alicia holding the hand of a young man. I smiled to myself and didn't tell Mark. We moved past the Goodge Street tube, no one sure if our route was the right one. We stopped, every street, corner, alley and doorway gridlocked by our bodies.

'Get on my shoulders if you want a look.' Mark knelt down. I climbed up. I rose above the march, tilting and tipping until Mark found his balance.

In the distance I could only see more heads. When I looked behind me I saw protestors all the way to the junction where Tottenham Court Road meets Euston Road. The city was improbable. London, from Mark's shoulders, was a million coloured dots. An impressionist's painting, an undulating sea of dismembered heads. We were still and I turned back to face the way we were trying to march.

I saw the children again, closer now, riding on their parents' shoulders. They were holding hands and singing again.

'Sergeant Higgins' march is a sentimental march and when you see them pass, smile, smile, smile.'

Stewart was carrying Esther and trying to see where the march was going, why it had stopped. He was longing, Jessica knew, to run along the pavement and start a chant or lead a charge into police lines.

'Kiddos,' he said to Esther, craning up his head, 'why don't you try to shout one of the slogans from the demos?'

Eddie sat on Jessica's shoulders in his favourite patched demo jeans and lined denim jacket.

'Just let the kids sing what they want, Stu,' Jessica said,

unstable under the weight of her son.

'Sweetie, we need to train them to be class fighters. To know the slogans of our movement.'

Esther bounced up and down on Stewart's shoulders, then held his unshaven chin and ran her fingers up his face to his lined forehead.

'Then we'll shout,' Esther said, suddenly exuberant. 'Land, peace and bread.' She began to shout: 'LAND, PEACE AND BREAD!'

Eddie saw his parents looking quickly at each other, Stewart's eyes wide and excited. He winked at Jessica.

'You've taught her well, darling,' he said, laughing.

Eddie held Esther's hand and they shouted together. 'LAND for the peasants, PEACE for the soldiers and BREAD for the workers!'

'You look beautiful, sweetheart,' Stewart said to Jessica, his words just audible over the children's shouts.

Finally we started moving again. Mark was no longer sure of his step as he tried to edge forward, holding my legs against his coat. I saw the children but couldn't hear anymore what they were shouting. They stretched upwards on their parents' shoulders. I was suddenly raised up. As I kept rising all I could see were the children, their voices dimmed by the distance but their hands still linked: the boy carrying the soft flesh of early childhood on his arms, his sister lean, her bones traced through her pale skin, and all I saw before Mark lowered me to the ground were their fists in the air pushing at the daytime moon, at the sky and the world.

Postscript

Is all my life that night with Rebecca, when I thought I was hammering down fate with my fists? I wore my family like an epic tragedy, a cheap sequel of my father's past: child of Bereskin sharing his father's madness and violence like I carried his bad posture. I thought my path was determined, hard-frozen into life. I followed this path, maniacal at times, sabotaging any chance of independent action.

I survived by running away. I earned my redemption on the road. I started by teaching English at the modern school in a clumsy concrete building with noisy air-conditioning on Mao Tse-Tung Avenue, between the battered and torn houses and shops, the smell of the port—rotting fish and tanker fuel—blowing through the city in warm gusts.

Staring out at my first class under the bright banner 'English Taught Here': 'When Gandhi was leaving the UK after his first visit, a journalist asked him, "What do you think of British civilisation?" "I think it would be a good idea," Gandhi replied.' No one laughed except me. I howled with the effort and planned a new journey. I would teach until the end of the season and leave again, head north. Beira, then Harare, Lusaka. Up I went, sending postcards and letters as though computers hadn't been invented, promising to come home in time for Esther's birthday. Yet I kept going. I kept disappearing.

Chasing another job in another school, I took the train to the coast. I lay on the dirty, damp sheets on my cabin bed, the windows nailed closed to keep in the chilled air from the air conditioner that had broken down years ago. I slept with the door open to feel the passing breeze from the windows along the carriage. I almost didn't exist on that train, invisible and unknown to the world. It had been three years since I left: Esther better, the child recently born and Jessica's trench coat folded away for the summer. The train moved slowly on the tracks as we haggled for lunch and dinner from the railside hawkers.

When I arrived I lived in the terraced houses of the old town where I could hear the sea, the façade of the city broken. I was in a local school, making do on a salary that was paid every three months. Each time I thought of Rebecca I threw another experience at the memory—sweated sand and salt to dig the school latrine with my class or taught late into the nights. Only then, many months in, was I more than a *mzungu*.

I fought and worked against memory until I couldn't anymore. I lasted four years. I discovered that I had a gift for travel; exile and escape, it seemed, was something I could do.

I thought that I could make a transformation in another civilisation. But wherever I was I thought of the same women. To the people you love distance is a formality; your mind draws them constantly back. This was my journey back to myself.

When I returned Esther was strong, her child already at school. Her efforts to come out of the old sickness had worked up a muscle in her of immense, taut strength so she could climb out of every deep valley. She fell again, but kept rising. I leaned on my strong sister, like I had always done. Jessica was already the militant grandmother who insisted on socialism and reading. I stayed with Esther and occasionally at night I read my niece to sleep. She had one father and two mothers. The Bereskins understood the dialectic.

For now I am alone, quarantined with books, my sister's child, Jessica and our politics. I am a revolutionary who believes in absolution, the clearing away of history and legacies. I was only as determined as we all are, as I chose to be, Jessica said. The haze cleared and allowed us a proper glimpse of ourselves. This is what we are fighting for, to clear the haze, to see again. Sometimes I can even imagine, in my mind's eye, Stewart smiling at us.

Eddie Bereskin, 2012

Acknowledgements

The great Guyanese writer and revolutionary, Walter Rodney, wrote in the preface to his masterpiece *How Europe Underdeveloped Africa* that the habit of authors to claim 'all short-comings' in acknowledgements of this kind, was nothing more than 'sheer bourgeois subjectivism.' Remedying such 'mistakes,' he went on, is always a collective responsibility. I am not sure that I can implicate those who have helped me with this story; perhaps if I had more assiduously followed the advice and copious criticism of friends who read earlier drafts, then the project would have been more successful (and never published).

We often have a lazy habit when reading fiction of seeing the author in every scene and his voice and troubles in each chapter. This is particularly true in a story like *Eddie the Kid* that mixes real and made-up events, but the 'tangle' of these elements in this book has created something entirely fictional. Though I may have disturbed the still waters with my own life, it has been from the ripples arching away from me that I have written.

I owe many thanks: Colin Fancy encouraged and inspired me with his own work and supported my writing with advice and criticism. Kim Wale read several drafts, commenting on and revising the manuscript as the story slowly began to unfold. Her support through the painful extraction of the story has been invaluable (in fact it is hard to imagine the story's successful completion without her love and commitment to the project). With typical generous gusto, Ian Crosson read and commented on the book when his own life allowed him little peace. I have tried to follow Philip Murphy's and David Renton's insistence to include artifice and metaphor.

If there are fragments in the story that people near me recognise, I have always attempted to write them with great sensitivity. None of this work (or anything else) would have been possible if it was not for the solidarity and love of Gillian Zeilig, Hannah Zeilig and Maurice Caplan. As I have struggled over the last few years with the story (and much more), Benjamin Joseph has, as always, been my friend and champion *par excellence*. My daughter Zola may be bemused that I have written a story without pictures, but her presence, if not always physical, has always been with me.

The extraordinary editing and revisions by Sarah Grey of Grey Editing (www.greyediting.com) have helped to secure her complicity in the 'collective shortcomings' that Rodney celebrates. She has gone beyond the call of a professional editor and become an accomplice in the story. I have taken her advice, given during one of my regular bouts of self-doubt, to 'Let your freak flag fly.' Tariq Goddard's enthusiasm and comments helped the book immensely. It is my hope that *Eddie the Kid*, in a small way, will further Zer0 Books' endeavour for critical engagement with the world.

Leo Zeilig
London
June 2012

Contemporary culture has eliminated both the concept of the public and the figure of the intellectual. Former public spaces – both physical and cultural – are now either derelict or colonized by advertising. A cretinous anti-intellectualism presides, cheerled by expensively educated hacks in the pay of multinational corporations who reassure their bored readers that there is no need to rouse themselves from their interpassive stupor. The informal censorship internalized and propagated by the cultural workers of late capitalism generates a banal conformity that the propaganda chiefs of Stalinism could only ever have dreamt of imposing. Zer0 Books knows that another kind of discourse – intellectual without being academic, popular without being populist – is not only possible: it is already flourishing, in the regions beyond the striplit malls of so-called mass media and the neurotically bureaucratic halls of the academy. Zer0 is committed to the idea of publishing as a making public of the intellectual. It is convinced that in the unthinking, blandly consensual culture in which we live, critical and engaged theoretical reflection is more important than ever before.